*ALSO BY GLENVILLE LOVELL*

**SONG OF NIGHT**
**FIRE IN THE CANES**

# Too Beautiful to Die

## GLENVILLE LOVELL

BERKLEY BOOKS, NEW YORK

TOO BEAUTIFUL TO DIE

A Berkley Book / published by arrangement with
the author

PRINTING HISTORY
G. P. Putnam's Sons hardcover edition / July 2003
Berkley mass-market edition / July 2004

For information address: The Berkley Publishing Group,
a division of Penguin Group (USA) Inc.,
375 Hudson Street, New York, New York 10014.

ISBN: 0-425-19702-6

BERKLEY®
Berkley Books are published by The Berkley Publishing Group,
a division of Penguin Group (USA) Inc.,
375 Hudson Street, New York, New York 10014.
BERKLEY and the "B" design
are trademarks belonging to Penguin Group (USA) Inc.

PRINTED IN THE UNITED STATES OF AMERICA

10  9  8  7  6  5  4  3  2  1

*For my brother Elvis:*
*In our hearts you're too beautiful to die*

1

❧ MY WIFE, ANAIS, was one of those women who not only turned heads—she confused minds. With skin that always shone like a well-buffed car and a smile so bewitching it could easily strip a blind man of his dignity, the grandness of her beauty had been burnt into my mind since the day I laid eyes on her.

I first met Anais one soggy Sunday afternoon in Central Park, and thought then that she was the most beautiful woman I'd ever seen. I still think so, though I'm not sure she cares anymore what I think. You see, she split for California a year ago while I wallowed in a revenge-induced stupor. It's not always easy for a proud man, one as stubborn as I am, to admit his mistakes. A more humble man would've seen his error right away and gone after his wife. What fool would let a woman like Anais get away? A smarter man would've seen it coming and done something to prevent it. Unfortunately I wasn't nearly so humble or smart, and it took me a while—too long by Anais' standards—to realize or accept that life was not the same without her. And now I wasn't sure I could win her back.

Despite countless letters and emails, numerous calls, and dozens of presents, my efforts to draw her back from the West Coast failed, so I flew out there to woo her again, hoping to use the blueprint that got us married. And for a while it appeared that I was winning the battle. We drank wine and laughed over candlelit dinners in chic restaurants; we held hands and walked in the park; we went to museums. And we argued. But even when we argued I tried to remain open-minded, not letting my stubbornness obstruct my goal. By the time we made love I thought for sure I'd won my prize. But two weeks later I returned to New York without Anais or a promise of permanent reconciliation.

I flew back to New York with a fear deep in my soul that Anais was never coming back to me. But I did not give up. I kept calling and sending email with funny e-greeting cards of dancing bears and singing dogs. If only I could convince her to come east for a weekend. New York was my turf. I'd won her here once, and I fancied my chances of doing it again. What I got was even better. She promised me one week.

I'd spent the day sprucing up the apartment, hanging art I'd bought at a gallery in Harlem and strategically placing photos of the two of us in happier times. It was a steamy summer day, hotter inside the apartment, but I was able to ignore the heat as I worked, buoyed by thoughts that soon Anais and I would be sharing an intimate laugh over wine, or a scented bath in my oversized bathtub.

Late in the afternoon I lay on my bed lathered in sweat thinking up ways to convince her that no man could make her as happy as I could. Early in our courtship I'd made a big impression with my cooking, the benefit of having a

mother whose birthplace was New Orleans and a grandmother from the Caribbean. Born into a well-off Atlanta
family, Anais had rebelled against the notion that something in a Southern woman's genes left her predisposed to
developing culinary skills, and she made no attempt growing up to learn anything about the kitchen other than its ge-
ographical location in the house so she could avoid it.
When she left home to become a dancer in New York without her family's blessing, it all caught up with her. Cut off
from their money she had to find ways to survive, including learning how to cook for herself. She was thrilled that I
knew how and could do it well.

That morning I'd stopped in at Fish Tales and bought
three pounds of Chilean sea bass, a sweet oily fish from
South America. This was my secret weapon. Done well and
served with a crisp white wine, this dish could open up any
woman to romance. It always worked on Anais. She loved
this fish almost as much as she loved me to massage her
feet after a tough ballet class.

My thoughts flew back to Los Angeles a month ago and
our lovemaking there in her apartment overlooking a park.
Seeing her spread atop new blue sheets wearing white
panties and nothing else. To taste her was to eat a ripe, full-
bodied fig, the dark spread of her skin a mystery I told myself only I could unravel. When she touched me, her
nimble soft hands seemed to transmit her soul's meaning,
making me want to break out in song. Drawing those
panties down her brown legs with my eyes closed. And
when I opened them again to her naked body sprawled on
the bed, she was watching me so intently I wanted to cry.

Just as I saw myself falling to my knees to bury my face
in the cave of her thighs, my phone rang. I ran to pick it up,
thinking it was her. She'd promised to call to let me know
what time to pick her up tomorrow. It was a voice from my
past. A voice I wasn't at all happy to hear.

"Blades?"

I would know that whine anywhere.

The cracked voice spilled into my ear again. "I need to see you, man. Today."

THE GREEN-UNIFORMED LATINO doorman looked at me cockeyed before asking if he could help.

"Apartment C-Four," I said.

"And your name?"

"Blades."

He picked up the house phone and punched the keys with his index finger. "A Mr. Blaze to see you, Ma'am."

"That's Blades with a D," I corrected.

He turned to me and smiled. His teeth were short and shiny and pointy like a cat's. "Blaze?"

I shrugged. "Whatever."

"Third floor. Elevator right, Mr. Blaze."

I walked off muttering to myself.

COORS IN HAND, Jimmy was waiting for me when I ducked off the elevator. I hadn't seen him in six months; he'd improved his wardrobe, but other than that he looked much the same. He smiled as if he was happy to see me. I can't say the feeling was mutual. Perhaps some other time, but not today. For starters, at a time when all I had were dreams, he'd interrupted the daydream I was having with my wife as the centerpiece. But if that wasn't enough—and believe me, it was—when I tried to get rid of him by telling him I was waiting for a call from my wife, he invoked the *E*-word. Emergency. I had no answer for that word. Not from Jimmy. We had a history. I gave in to history.

The heat wave that had gripped New York by its throat was now in its third day with the mercury still hovering around 100. Not the kind of weather I like for my evening stroll. And were it not for the fact that he'd saved my life three years ago, I would've told Jimmy Lucas exactly where to bury his freaking head. I'd taken the train to Manhattan, walking as slowly as I could from the station, slimy sweat dripping off me as if I'd been slow dancing with the creature from *Alien*.

"Man, you don't know how happy I am to see your black ass," he said.

Other than my brother, Jimmy Lucas was the only white person who could speak to me this way without getting a bounty of their own enamel rammed down their throat. I gave Jimmy a lot of slack for saving my life. But one day, I told him, his honorary-black privilege would expire.

"I need a cold beer, kid," I said.

"You got it, baby."

He grinned and draped a scrawny arm around my shoulders. A loose silver watch dangled on his bony wrist as we walked awkwardly down the hospital-white hallway, which smelled of Pine-Sol. Jimmy was a tall dude, about an inch taller than me at six-two and skinny as a praying mantis. Sporting shoulder-length blond hair in a ponytail, he had a two-toned face with dark freckles around his nose and mouth.

A short distance later we paused opposite a green door with C-4 printed in gold lettering. Jimmy pushed the half-open door.

"I want you to meet somebody," he said, dragging me inside.

The apartment was large. And cool. We were standing in a wide room furnished minimalist-style, which emphasized the size. An imposing six-foot sculpture of a naked woman in polished black wood guarded one corner near a window. Posted against one wall was a cream leather sofa with a red wing chair a few feet away. The black marble-top table in the center of the room was no more than a foot off the floor. Several colorful paintings, tropical in tone, were evenly spaced on bone-white walls around the room.

It was a generous room that, despite its size and free space, felt warm and cozy. I imagined people dressed in black would retire to this room after a fancy four-course dinner to sip champagne and talk about art or the ballet. What was Jimmy doing in a place like this?

A woman with skin as smooth and brown as a crisp macadamia nut stood behind the sculpture almost mirroring its pose. She was dressed in white. Jimmy walked over and took her arm.

"Blades, meet Precious," he said.

"Nice to meet you, Precious," I said, extending my hand.

She captured my hand. "I'm so glad you could come." Her voice was dark rum being poured over ice on a very hot day.

"Sit down, man," Jimmy said. "What kind of beer you want?"

"I don't imagine you have Banks?" I said.

"Banks? Is that one of those European brews?" Jimmy said.

"It's from Barbados. I vacationed there earlier this summer. Very smooth lager. Didn't think you'd have it. Gimme a Coors."

Jimmy glanced at Precious, and silently a decision was made that she would get the beer. She quickly disappeared down the hallway.

"Sit down," Jimmy urged. "It's cool here, right?"

"It's cool."

"Sure it's cool. You didn't think it'd be this cool, did ya?"

"What's this all about, Jimmy? Who's this woman? Is this her place?"

"Sit down, man. What's the matter? You don't like the place? It ain't cool enough for ya?"

Someone must've been giving Jimmy fashion tips, because he was dressed more stylishly than I'd ever seen him, in a metallic blue shirt with a Donna Karan tag on the pocket and black flat-front pants. Donna Karan was a big step up from Buffalo Bills sweatshirts. I looked down at his feet to see if he was wearing sneakers. He was. Way to go, Jimmy. I settled into the cool leather of the sofa, and as I watched him milk the beer bottle, uneasiness crawled up my back.

"Nice, huh?" Jimmy chirped.

Precious returned with a tall bottle of Coors, half of which had been poured into a frosty glass on a black coaster. As she leaned toward me her whole body seemed to tremble. Her neatly manicured nails were painted a rich gold.

I chugged the beer as if I'd just staggered in from the Sahara, emptying the glass, allowing the cool frothy liquid to bubble noiselessly down my throat. The sensation was one of such incredible relief I couldn't hold back my smile. Jimmy sat cocked in the wing chair, his face stricken with the melancholy look of a sleepy dog. Precious had returned to the shadows behind the sculpture.

"I was asking Jimmy if this was your place," I said to her, after I'd slopped the other half of my beer from the bottle.

Jimmy rushed forward. "Let me get you another beer, man."

I indicated no with a wave of my hand. He took my glass and the empty bottle and flopped on the edge of the wing chair with them cupped in his lap.

Precious was smiling self-consciously. "I bought it five years ago."

"It's very nice."

"Thank you."

Damn, I liked her voice.

"Precious is an actress," Jimmy said.

"Really? Are you in anything I might've seen?" I said.

She smiled. "Do you watch *Dark Passions*? It's a day-time soap."

"Not lately," I said.

"I play a British physician, Dr. Antonia Parker."

"Is that right?"

Amused by my feeble attempt to hide my ignorance, she smiled. "It's a great part."

"I'm sure it is."

She was a tall woman, six or seven inches over five feet, with full, wide hips. Her white shorts showed off well-muscled legs and an apparent athleticism that made me think of Anais. A swanlike neck held her round head absolutely still, with cheeks that flared too faultlessly at its widest point. I wondered if she was the kind of woman who'd hand over her face to a cosmetic wizard.

"She needs your help," Jimmy said, standing up. "Tell him your story, Precious."

He went to draw her from the shadows. She waved him aside, gliding to the center of the room with balletic grace.

"Are you here to help me, Blades?"

"He'll help you," Jimmy said. "Ain't that right, Blades? Tell her how I saved your life."

"Tell me your story, Precious," I said, after a pointed stare in Jimmy's direction. He didn't have to bring that up.

"You promise to help me?" Precious said.

I hesitated. Looking into her impassioned hazel eyes, I wondered if anybody had ever said no to this woman.


"I FEEL SO ashamed talking about this." Her voice had the forced calmness of someone trying to hide her emotions.

She sat in the wing chair, long legs crossed, back erect. I kept my eyes focused on her face. When I was a cop I had honed to perfection the skill of reading the eyes of a witness or a suspect, but was my attention to her eyes, which could light a candle, force of habit or the fact that she was so damn beautiful?

"I don't know who my father is," she continued. "I don't

know his name or what he looks like. I never even saw a picture. I don't even know if he's alive. For years I've been trying without any luck to track him down. Last week, out of nowhere, I got a call from a man. He asked me how much was I willing to pay for information about my father. I asked him his name. He wouldn't tell me, so I hung up. He called back and told me that for fifty thousand dollars he would tell me who my father was and how to get in touch with him. He wouldn't give me any details about how he knew I'd been searching for my father, but the more he spoke the more I was taken in. There was something about his voice. He just seemed so sure. Like he knew things most people didn't know. In the end I agreed to pay him."

"That's a lot of money," I said.

She glanced at Jimmy and then back to me. "The money is nothing to me. I can afford it. I'd pay twice that to find my father."

"How many times have you spoken to this man?" I asked.

"Three or four."

"Did you get his name?"

"He called himself Antonio."

"It sounds like a hoax. A crazed fan," I said.

"That's why I need you."

Right there I should've gotten up, thanked her for the beer and the brief respite from the heat and made my way back to my Brooklyn sauna before I got so comfortable in her company and this *Town & Country* living room that I'd agree to slay a lion. Instead, I sat there looking like a schoolboy watching his first striptease.

Precious got up and went back to the sculpture, her gold-embroidered slippers smacking the floor. She bent down and picked up a black leather briefcase.

"I have the money. And I know where to take it. I want you to go with me."

At least she didn't say, *"I want you to take it."* Give her credit for that. She might be an actress, but she was no prima donna.

"I think you should call the police," I said.

"She don't want to do that," Jimmy said.

Precious stepped forward. "I don't want any publicity. I was ready to go myself, but Jimmy convinced me you would help."

"You have to help her, Blades," said Jimmy.

"You want my help, then take my advice," I said.

"Is it asking too much for you to go with her, man?" Jimmy's voice rose impatiently.

The actress completed her parade across the room and sat opposite me again, leaning forward. I could feel her sharp eyes scaling my face.

"Please, I'm willing to pay you," she said.

Jimmy stood guard near the hip of the couch, watching me warily.

I looked up at Jimmy. "Why don't you go with her?"

He snorted and then coughed, the wild rugged hack of someone with bronchial problems, his body shaking uncontrollably.

"You okay, man?" I stood up.

He clamped his hand over his mouth to try to control the coughing. After two or three more tremors, he stopped and looked at me, his eyes thin as glassine. "You used to be a cop. You would know what to do if things aren't on the up and up."

"I'm sorry, but I can't do it," I said and sat back down.

Precious looked at me, surprised, almost stunned. Jimmy had obviously convinced her that I was in his hip pocket.

"Leave us alone for a minute, Precious," Jimmy said.

Precious sighed softly and rubbed the back of her neck. She rose from the wing chair and left the room. Jimmy plunked himself down in front of me.

"You owe me, Blades," he said quietly.

"I don't want to do it, Jimmy."

Perhaps my thinking was self-serving, but no matter what he said I was determined to stay firm. What did I know about this woman or the man she was going to meet? How did I know she was telling the truth? Until I got my settlement from the City, I had planned to keep my nose clean.

Jimmy got up slowly and stood staring into my face, leaning his face closer to mine, baring his teeth, showing red, agitated gums. I don't know if this was an attempt at a smile or meant to intimidate me, but it was only getting me pissed off. His eyes were morning gray, and underneath the surface tiny green lines raced back and forth like baby worms. He was so close I could have counted the creases at the corner of his eyes and the freckles on his face if I'd wanted to, but right now I was more apt to punch him and leave. There was still time to pick up my daydream where he'd interrupted it.

"This ain't good, Blades."

"Well, fuck, Jimmy, it's all I got."

"What the hell do you want, man? She offered to pay you." He slammed his open hand onto the wall behind my head. He seemed ready to jump out of his skin. If I didn't know better I'd say Jimmy was jacked on drugs.

"Hey, you better slow your roll, cuz." I stood up, more to prepare myself should he take a swing at me than anything else. "And the fuck out my face like you wanna kiss me."

"Where's your fucking heart, man?" He stood there glowering over me, and just when I was about to push him away, he stepped back and took a pack of Marlboros and a Zippo lighter from his shirt pocket. He struggled to light the cigarette. The fuel was low and the flame never flickered for more than a second.

"Are you fucking her?"

"Watch your manners, dude."

I started to laugh.

"You see, that's your freaking problem." He finally lit the cigarette and sat down, taking a deep drag with caved-in jaws. "You don't respect nothing. You think only about yourself. How could you ask me a question like that? Why I gotta be fucking her 'cause I wanna help her?"

I didn't know what to say. I looked at my friend's face, all bone and sagging skin. His eyes were drawn tight. Somewhere in the mirror of his eyes there might've been a reflection of my soul, but I tried not to see it. But that didn't keep the dogs of guilt at bay: *How could you refuse this man who saved your life?*

"Have you settled your lawsuit against the City?" he said.

I hunched over and said nothing.

"I know you got money coming from the City," he continued. "Maybe you can buy a heart. Man, did I ask you for anything for saving your life?"

I straightened up and stared him dead in the eye. He flinched.

"What the hell you want from me, Jimmy? You want me to bleed for you because you saved my life?" I extended my hand. "Go ahead. Cut me. But don't ask me to get involved in shit I know nothing about."

He blew a wad of smoke in my face. "Let me tell you about her little girl."

I felt the urge to have a cigarette but decided to fight it.

"She's about three now," he continued. "She's in a home."

"What kinda home?" I asked.

"Don't ever let Precious know I told you this, understand."

I nodded.

"She needs around-the-clock care."

"What's this got to do with finding Precious' father?"

"I'm trying to show you that even though she's got money, she's got problems like anybody else. She's got her weaknesses. She's got her strengths. She needs love. She needs help. Right now she needs you. You can't begin to understand how good she has been to me. I need you to do this for me, dude."

"Where'd you two meet?"

"I was out of work, homeless, hanging around this soup kitchen trying to get a sandwich, and she came in one day. Said she was doing research for her show. She asked if she could talk to me. I was very honest with her. Next week she came back, told me about a friend of hers who needed a chauffeur."

"I was wondering what happened to you."

"She's a good woman, Blades. If you turn your back on her, you're turning your back on me. I mean it."

His face was fixed in an intense scowl. He blew a ring of smoke as Precious returned in a new outfit.

"Listen, Jimmy," she said. "If your friend doesn't want to help me, it's okay. I understand."

I turned to her. "Where do you have to deliver this money?"

"Brooklyn. Does this mean you'll help?" she asked.

# 2

**PRECIOUS HAD CHANGED** into an outfit befitting a daytime soap star: coral-washed knee-length linen dress, pink leather knot sandals and Gucci glasses. She wore no makeup except purple lipstick which gave her lips a fullness that made me think of Angela Bassett. With a body to flaunt, she did just that. It looked as though she wore no bra underneath her dress; her breasts sprang forward as if being called by the flute of a snake charmer, her outsized nipples like buttons on the front of her dress. She called ahead to have her car cooled, and we left the apartment on Fifth Avenue and Tenth Street half an hour later. When we reached the garage a block away, the red late-model BMW was ready to rock.

She asked me to drive. I declined. I wanted to think. As we merged into the stream of cars along Broadway heading to the Brooklyn Bridge, I leaned back in the cool leather seat brooding over my decision. It was too late to change my mind, but I wondered what had made me agree to be Precious' bodyguard. Was it Jimmy's whining or was it just an excuse to be in her company a bit longer?

Ever since Jimmy had saved my life I'd felt beholden. It was a reality that stuck in my craw like tainted fish. The memory of Jimmy lifting me from the street into the backseat of his cab had always left me raw, and though we'd become friends afterward, I always resented that he had this thing over me. I suppose I'm too proud to accept being indebted to anyone. Doing Jimmy this favor would win me some measure of dignity back, I concluded.

Traffic was light on the Brooklyn Bridge. Daylight was beginning to fade. The sky was a flat stretch of red clouds that seemed to be radiating high-energy gamma rays. From the bridge the low buildings of Brooklyn Heights looked to be encased in a ring of yellow fire.

I'd left home in shorts and tee, so our first stop in Brooklyn was my apartment, where I went upstairs to dress the part of bodyguard to a star. Precious stayed in the car. It took me ten minutes to outfit myself in black jeans, black polo shirt and black Rockport boots. I was counting on not having to wear this costume for too long in this heat.

When I returned, Precious was talking on her cell phone. She ended her conversation and looked at me with a discreet smile of approval. As we drove off she glanced at me again and her smile deepened to a wide grin. For some foolish reason I felt elated.

As Precious navigated the clogged Brooklyn streets, I stole glances at her, admiring the curve of her neck and shoulders. A light net of rain began to spread before us. Her pale perfume spiced the BMW's leathery essence, and again I thought of Anais and felt guilty for even being alone with this bewitchingly beautiful woman.

Fifteen minutes later she slowed down opposite

Caribbean Pride, a restaurant on the ground floor of a run-down building on St. Johns Place, and parked behind a tour bus being loaded with senior citizens wrapped in shimmering African garments, many of them bedecked in colorful, elaborate headdress.

I spent a good deal of time in this neighborhood when I was a kid. My grandmother lived five blocks away on Kingston Avenue, on the other side of Eastern Parkway. Steelpan music, no doubt a practice session for the upcoming West Indian Carnival Day Parade, filled the air. And I could hear reggae music bubbling from an apartment above me.

We got out, and Precious headed east on St. Johns Place. I followed a step behind. Walking along the street, the distinct accents of the Caribbean made a bouquet around me. Street vendors, selling anything from books to bananas, from coconut milk in the husks to chilled sugar-cane juice, hogged the sidewalk calling to passersby, enticing them with smiles and offers of bargains that could not be gotten in Manhattan. A bicyclist zipping along the sidewalk bore down on me and I skipped into the street. I turned to glare after the youngster, but having scored his victory in the game of chicken, he was already spinning around the corner and out of sight.

We came to a large apartment building with a deep courtyard that was surrounded by a high iron fence. Over time, broken bottles on the sidewalk had been trampled to a fine grid. A number of youths, backs glistening with sweat, shirts hanging from back pockets of baggy cutoff jeans, stood outside jawing good-naturedly. A noisier group played C-low or craps in the courtyard. Rap music from a boom box on a milk crate shrieked with false bravado the authenticity of a thug's life.

"This is it," Precious said. "Seven twenty-five St. Johns Place."

The heavy metal gate to the courtyard gaped open, kept

so by a large brown brick at its base. We crossed the court-yard littered with empty soda cans and plastic wrappers, past the dried-up fountain in the center, now home to summer weeds. We reached the apartments just as two pint-sized Rambo wannabes, balancing Super Squirters under their armpits bounded through the door, hopping over empty bottles as if they were electric bunnies. I held the door open for Precious, then followed her inside.

The dingy elevator reeked of stale Chinese food and cigarette smoke. Graffiti and grease stained the walls black and blue, and cigarette stubs were stacked in one corner like a clot of dead worms. It seemed as though someone had made a valiant effort to herd them together. I imagined the elevator once had a bright red color that was now indistinguishable from the dirt.

I felt a panic rise in my chest. When I was a cop I hated going after perps in large apartment buildings. Too many places to hide, too many chances for ambush. Instinctively, my hand brushed against my hip, searching for my gun. I took a deep breath and glanced at Precious. Her face was impenetrable as she hugged the briefcase to her bosom.

After a noisy bumpy ride, we emptied onto the tenth floor. The gloomy hallway had a moldy odor as if its stained walls were oozing something foreign. One fluorescent bulb above flickered haphazardly like a ship sending out a distress signal.

I kept pace with Precious as she marched determinedly down the narrow stretch. She turned left, coming to a crisp stop at the end of the hall in front of apartment 10-D. We stood outside the red door for about a minute doing nothing. Was she summoning the resolve to part with so much money? I was trying to keep my mind clear and calm, hoping nothing crazy happened. I still couldn't believe I'd agreed to do this. It felt like something out of the movies.

Precious knocked twice. No answer.

Stepping forward, I thumped the metal door powerfully. Once. Twice. Three times. Still no answer.

"Don't look like anybody's here," I said, happy that this melodrama had fizzled to a ho-hum ending.

"He's got to be here," Precious announced.

"Then he must be dead," I joked.

She reached out and twisted the doorknob. With a soft clack the lock released. Slowly easing the door open, she poked her head into the room.

"Hello," she called. "Anybody here?"

Then she surprised me by slithering softly inside. I remained outside, nervously looking around, straining against the anger I felt rising.

"What the hell you think you're doing?" I said.

She didn't answer. Not knowing whether to drag her back into the hallway or follow her blindly, I slipped into the room.

"Let's get out of here," I said.

"Anybody home?" Precious called again.

The place had been ransacked: boxes ripped open; clothes, papers, pictures, computer diskettes and CDs strewn about. The gray sofa had been turned upside down and carved up. Broken glass speckled the floor. A couple of ten-year-olds on a tantrum couldn't have done a better job.

I checked for my gun again and cursed. Heat and anxiety combined to bring sweat streaming to the surface of my skin. New York was a city where people triple-locked their doors before taking garbage downstairs. This shit was whack, and I wasn't sticking around for the remix. I grabbed Precious by the arm and opened the door.

"No!" she screamed, pulling away from me.

"You've been duped."

Her eyes flamed defiantly. Turning away, she stepped on a crushed plate of glass from a mirror and tripped. I rushed forward, catching her before she fell. She steadied herself and struggled to get free.

"Will you please take your hands off me?" she said.

"Are you always this stubborn?"

"Only when I'm dealing with wimps."

"Listen, I'm doing you a favor, you know."

She glanced to the floor, then back to me. Her eyes softened. "I'm sorry. You're right. And I appreciate it. But I can't leave until I'm sure."

"Okay," I said. "Let me take a quick look around before you do anything else."

In the kitchen, a few feet around the corner to the left, the garbage can had been overturned and New York's finest cockroach specimens were hurdling each other to get at the leftover chicken and fries, minced by a heavy boot into the linoleum floor.

I decided to back out before those fattened crawlers took to the friendly skies. It seemed unlikely that anyone was in the apartment. Still I advanced cautiously down the corridor, listening for movement ahead. The bathroom was on my right. It was empty and intact.

I reached the bedroom straight ahead. The drawn blinds made the room shadowy. Dense incense hovered in the air. I found the switch and with an upward flick of my wrist doused the room with light. There is much truth to the saying that some things are better left in the dark.

There was a dead body on the bed.

I scanned the room quickly. It was in a state of chaos similar to the kitchen and living room. Stepping over broken glass and other debris, I moved closer to the bed. The bare-chested stocky black man laying on his back in Loony Toons boxers was stiffer than my last boner.

My Caribbean grandmother loved looking at dead bodies. Especially after they had been prepared for burial. I, on the other hand, found the stillness of death bewildering.

He'd been shot at close range in the temple, a death that would've been mercifully quick. Blood and bits of skull had dried on the side of his face. A broad patch of crimson stained the bed next to his head. He lay framed by pictures, as if the killer had seized on the opportunity to display his decorative talents.

I heard footsteps behind me and spun around. I'd completely forgotten about Precious. She danced around me even as I tried to block her, posting herself by the shaded window to stare in silent shock at the body.

"Do you know him?" I asked.

She shook her head. "Is he really dead?"

"You can't fake that kind of stillness." I didn't bother shaving the annoyance I was feeling from my voice. I didn't want to be here. The last thing I needed was to be involved in a murder investigation.

I picked up one picture after another. The subject matter was all the same: a disgusting display of raw sex between adult men and young girls. I paused a few moments on one girl's face, thinking it was familiar. But I couldn't remember where I'd seen it. I looked at the man again and decided that if this was Antonio and taking these pictures had been his gig, then he deserved to die.

# 3

**AS PRECIOUS FRANTICALLY** rummaged through dresser drawers, emptying contents onto the floor, I used her mobile to call the police. When the dispatcher asked for my name, I hung up.

"Let's go," I said to Precious.

She didn't look around.

I grabbed her arm. "We're getting out of here."

Impassively she stared at me, her body limp, sweat streaming down her dark face.

"The police will be here any minute and I don't intend to be part of a welcoming party," I said.

I released her and walked away. She hustled after me, catching up with me in the living room where she grasped my elbow with sweaty palms.

"He said he had proof."

"I think it's a little late for that," I said.

"Maybe it's here somewhere."

"You don't even know if this is the man you talked to on the phone."

"It's him. It's gotta be."

I turned away. "Are you coming?"

"No."

"Just try to forget my name when the police get here, okay?"

Leaving her staring stiffly into space, her face shiny and severe, I walked to the door. On the wall, to the right of the door, was a picture in a gold frame of a man cradling a little girl on his right hip. It was the dead man. I studied the picture for a second. He was smiling, but looked unsettled; the girl, though, seemed happy. Then I opened the door and walked out. As I approached the elevator I heard Precious behind me and turned around. She walked brusquely past, almost tripping over my foot.


ON THE WAY back I drove. We didn't speak. I was angry. I'd had a bad feeling about this from the start, and I should've followed my instincts. I didn't need this situation. It could only complicate my chances of a quick settlement with the City. The Mayor hated my guts. Given any chance to screw me, he'd jump on it. In this mood I knew I wouldn't be able to express myself without blaming her for putting me in this mess. I just wanted to get home and out of her life.

To avoid looking at her when we stopped for the light at Grand Army Plaza, I focused my gaze out the window at the gray edifice of the Brooklyn Public Library. She spoke for the first time, words ushered out in the quietest of breaths.

"You have to help me find it."

I glanced at her sitting tightly drawn in the seat, staring straight ahead.

The lights changed, and I pumped gas to the powerful engine, circling the roundabout before veering right and shooting up Union Street.

"You can have the fifty thousand dollars." The remote calmness in her voice sent a chill through me.

"Save your money," I said, trying to match her self-control.

"One hundred thousand."

I exploded. "Listen, I don't care how much goddamn money you have, I want nothing more to do with this shit."

We didn't speak again until we reached Carroll Gardens where I said good-bye outside the Yemeni-owned newsstand at President and Smith. I watched her drive off before I went inside to get a pack of cigarettes. I hadn't had a cigarette in five months and cursed Precious and Jimmy for throwing me back onto a path from which I thought I'd escaped.

When I came out, Salvatore Carmine, the short white-headed Italian owner of Bagel on the Green, walked by with a few of his pals. Always with a smile on his face, Sal was one of the few people in the neighborhood who knew I'd been a cop before my shooting became the buzz of New York. His brother owned the building I lived in.

"How's it going, Blades?"

"You tell me, Sal. All I can see is smoke."

He winked. "Don't let the smoke get in your eyes."

Set in the middle of President Street, between Smith and Hoyt, the prewar brownstone I lived in was one of many landmark buildings in this old Italian neighborhood of South Brooklyn, now being forced to accommodate the influx of young professionals, students and artists fleeing Manhattan's exorbitant rents but still wanting to live close enough to the Village to take a cab home after midnight when the subways were deemed too dangerous for white people.

I CHECKED MY machine first thing. Anais still hadn't called. I called her but she wasn't in. I left a message for her to call me as soon as she got home. After a shower I heated some leftover chicken and Chinese cabbage. I tried to eat, but I couldn't find my appetite. I went to lie down. The obnoxious DJ on BLS seemed to be getting his freak on playing Third World's *96 Degrees in the Shade* over and over again.

"What fucking shade?" I screamed at the radio.

Air churning from the fan at the foot of my bed felt as if it were coming from an eighteen-wheeler's exhaust. I kicked the fan in disgust. It toppled to the floor with a heavy clank and droned to a stop.

I sat up. Fat beads of sweat wobbled down my naked chest. Righting the fan, I tried to start it again. It gurgled like a clogged sewer and died. I knew it was a piece of crap, but did it have to die in the middle of a goddamn heat wave? My air conditioner had croaked earlier, and now this. Inside my one-bedroom apartment, you could've sizzled a steak on my body. And I'm talking well-done.

The DJ laughed insidiously and decided to play *96 Degrees in the Shade* one more time. Not funny, brother. Not funny. I got up and switched the dial to WGBO, a jazz station.

The only cool place in my apartment was the fridge, and that's where I headed as sweat flowed down my armpits. Standing with the fridge door open, I welcomed the cold blast, hoping the capsules of water would permanently crystallize on my body.

I grabbed a jug of water and drank half with controlled carelessness, letting most of it escape the corners of my mouth to waterfall down my neck and chest before closing the fridge door reluctantly. My head pulsed from a tension-induced headache. Jug in hand, I treaded wearily across the blotchy wood floor to the bathroom. I took a leak, shook my Johnson, and waddled back to the bedroom, my Johnson swinging outside my shorts.

As I was about to lie down again the telephone rang. I snatched up the phone.

"Hello?"

"There must be something I can do to change your mind." It was Precious.

"I really can't help you," I said.

"You could've helped me search that apartment."

"Looked like somebody already did that."

"I don't often beg, Mr. Overstreet."

"This guy could've been selling you bubble gum."

"What would it take for you to find that out?"

There was a long silence.

"I'm sorry I troubled you," she said, and hung up.

I lit a cigarette and decided to try the old air conditioner again. Incredibly, I was greeted by the familiar hum of the engine. It hummed melodiously like an opera singer tuning her voice. Then cool air began to sift the heat. I sat back on the bed and smiled. If only Anais would call.

# 4

FOR AGES NEW York has been a Mecca for immigrants. The boom in Caribbean immigration to New
York began in the late 1950s, but long before that tide,
Caribbean people had been flowing through this city in a
steady stream since the early twentieth century. Many of
these early immigrants settled in Harlem. Some, like
Claude McKay, gained fame for their artistic talents in the
glory days of the Harlem Renaissance. Other sages like
Marcus Garvey propelled the Black Nationalist movement.
My grandmother was among those early immigrants. Ar-
riving from Panama, she lived first on Madison Avenue in
Harlem, before buying her only other home, in Brooklyn.

For some Manhattanites, Brooklyn Heights was the
only part of Brooklyn worth visiting, and then only under
the duress of calling on a sick friend. It was their only

point of reference when talking about the borough. Others might venture as far as Park Slope to attend a controversial exhibit at the Brooklyn Museum—which is technically in Crown Heights, but don't tell them that. To them, the areas east or south of Brooklyn Heights were vast expanses of empty spaces, where the flotsam of Third World ineptness came to hide from despots, lurching about dark streets with angry scowls and barking guns, a hysteria constantly fueled by the media. Those of us who've entered this ugly gray matter beyond Brooklyn Heights have discovered real people, attempting to live the American Dream in places like Crown Heights.

With its nineteenth-century mansions in the northern section, limestone row houses and apartment buildings in the southern section, Crown Heights—which serves as the backdrop for the annual West Indian Carnival Day Parade—remains the neighborhood of choice for most Caribbean immigrants who still flock to New York, but East Flatbush and Canarsie have gained in popularity over the years as whites continue their flight to the suburbs. Many of these immigrants now own businesses along Brooklyn's main thoroughfares.

Leroy James came to New York from Trinidad in 1968. Under the name of Mello-Creme he sang calypso in Trinidad, but his meager recordings reaped little success. In America, with a new alias, Milo-Tea, he suffered the indignity of being banned from performing on the Parkway one Labor Day for offensive lyrics. He retired from calypso after that.

When I joined the NYPD in 1988 he was a caretaker at the academy. I told him how much I loved calypso music since my grandmother played nothing but Roaring Lion and Mighty Sparrow in her house. He began feeding me tapes of himself, Sparrow, Lord Kitchener, Blakey and others.

Out of this camaraderie grew a business idea. Five years later, while I was still an undercover cop, we opened

Caribbean Music City on Nostrand Avenue across from the St. Francis of Assisi Roman Catholic Church. The next year I was off the force.

We lost money the first year and almost closed. The next few years we broke even thanks to Milo's charm, especially with women. Sometimes I'd come into the store to find him singing a cappella to customers. Our roles became clearly defined. In the business of selling, seduction was Milo's game. I took care of the books.

I got to the record store around ten the next day. My usual parking spot in front of the store was taken, so I circled the block twice before parking on Midwood, two blocks away.

I locked the car and walked north. It was another humid day in New York; by the time I reached Allan's Bakery, one block away, my blue polo shirt had stuck to my back. On a day like today, standing in Allan's Bakery would've been unbearable. The place had no air-conditioning, and with its standing in the community as one of the most popular bakeries, the line sometimes linked twenty people or more; luckily, there was no line today. I ordered codfish and spinach patties for breakfast and a few currant rolls for my partner and lit out of there in two minutes with my self-respect still intact having sweated no more than normal.

As I paused for the light opposite the opulent summer gardens of St. Francis of Assisi, I realized I was still suffering from last night's events. I hadn't slept well. There was a queasy feeling in the pit of my stomach and my head throbbed.

Milo was alone in the store. He was a small man, thin as a guitar string but as dependable as a priest. Generally a sharp dresser, he wore jeans and a blue cotton tee this morning. Recently he'd begun dyeing his hair. He didn't need to. His unmarked face and clear eyes would never betray his true age—sixty—even if he allowed his gray to show.

"What's the matter, Milo, your woman burned your good threads?"

"Hey Blades, I thought you weren't coming in today."

"Why not?"

"You said so yesterday. That you was picking up Anais at the airport today."

"Yeah, well, she's taking a late flight," I lied. "Kinda quiet today, huh?" I said to change the subject. I was very annoyed that Anais hadn't called.

"It's early, man. You know how it is. This ain't Manhattan. Poor folks gotta work. They don't shop till evening."

"Well, these poor folks better start spending some money in here soon or we gonna have to stand on the corner with a tin cup," I joked.

"Aw, c'mon. Things smooth."

I gave him the bag with the currant rolls. "You might be smooth, Milo, but not *things*. I do the books, remember."

Knowing its contents he placed the bag on the shelf beneath the register; he'd open it when he got hungry. "We need to do some more advertising."

"Milo, we have more traffic in here than a crack house. The problem is that most of the people who clog up the store are your friends and they don't buy shit. They just come to hear you talk, and to brag about how many women they boned. If I could get a dollar for every lie you guys tell on your dicks, I could retire."

He laughed cheerfully. "I tell you, Blades, you can't blame we, man. Trini woman sweet, but like money. Hard to get. Harder to keep. American woman now: easy as picking mangoes. So the fellas having a good time. If I was younger—"

"If you were younger you'd be dead. These young girls would drink your skinny Milo ass in one slurp."

He sucked his teeth and laughed out loud. "American girls might be easy, but if you think them can take more dick than Trini gal, man, is joke you making. When I was back in Port of Spain, I lived with this woman. Boy, she wanting the thing the minute I wake up and the minute I get home. I get to find out me next-door neighbor was coming by to work the ground when I was at work. Boy, I was never so happy to take a horn. But you know, I couldn't leave she out. She was just too sweet."

I laughed and went through the door behind the register into the office.

On the office walls, freshly painted a glossy white, were two life-size posters: a bright color print of Bob Marley smoking a spliff, a wave of thick blue smoke curling into the air; and one of Pam Grier in a low-cut red dress smiling seductively at me. Bob was my favorite musician. Pam had been the source of many wet dreams when I was growing up, ever since I saw *Foxy Brown*.

The phone rang before I could sit down. I let it ring, knowing that Milo would pick up outside. A few seconds later I heard his voice: "It's the preacher."

I'd hired three high-profile lawyers to handle my case against the City, which had been dragging its feet over a settlement. My case was too strong for the City to risk a trial, my lawyers kept telling me, but I was yet to smell a dime. One of my lawyers, Franklyn Rose, a black Harvard-educated Gucci-dressing Wall Street huckster, was on the line. Milo called him the preacher.

"What's up, Frankie?"

"Good morning, Blades." His voice boomed with the melodic riff of a preacher in mid sermon. "I think they're ready to talk some numbers."

"I've heard that before, Frankie. I ain't smiling."

"I got a call from their lead attorney. They want to talk. Over lunch."

"I don't trust them, Frankie. The Mayor will do anything to make me sweat."

"Jesus, you're kind of raw today, my brother."

"Just get it settled, Frankie. I'm tired of being dicked around."

I hung up the phone. Seconds later it rang again. This time I picked up. Anais' voice, like a smoky Cassandra Wilson solo, expanded in my ear.

"Blades, I'm sorry, but I won't be coming tonight after all."

"I guessed that. Why? What's the matter?" I tried not to sound annoyed.

"My agent has set up another screen test. Are you upset?"

"I'm not upset."

"Are you sure?"

"When're you coming?"

"I don't know. I'll have to get back to you."

"I was really looking forward to seeing you, Anais."

"You're upset, aren't you?"

"You could've called last night. Why didn't you call? I called you twice."

"Look, Blades, we've been apart over a year now. Don't let what happened last month go to your head, okay? It was nothing."

"What do you mean it was nothing?"

"That's what I mean."

"I don't believe you."

"Believe it."

"It meant nothing to you?"

"I didn't say that."

"Then what do you mean?"

"Look, Blades, I gotta go."

"We gotta talk this through, Anais."

"I need more than talk, Blades."

"What the fuck do you want me to do, Anais? I'm trying. But you're not working with me."

Her voice perked up. "You're trying? You never take my concerns seriously, Blades."

"You really think I would hurt you, Anais?"

"I don't know, Blades. And I need to be sure."

"Didn't I seem calmer in L.A.?"

Pause. I listened to her heavy breathing. I imagined she was next to me and I could smell her perfume.

"Well, answer me. You said so yourself. I'm over it, Anais. The NYPD is out of my system. I'm ready to move on. But I can't do that without you. What's gotten into you all of a sudden?"

"I gotta go, Blades. I'll call you later."

"No, Anais! Tell me what's going on out there!"

"What do you mean?"

"If you're seeing somebody, tell me. Tell me the truth."

"I don't have to tell you anything, Blades. Because I got weak and gave you some when you were out here don't mean I'm ready to come back to you. I didn't promise you anything. Don't act like you own me because I gave you a sniff."

"A sniff? Did you say a sniff?"

"I'm sorry. I didn't mean that."

"I can't believe you said that. A sniff?"

Her voice grew thin, defensive. "Okay, Blades, don't get into one of your passions. Let it go."

"Why'd you say that?"

"I didn't mean it the way it sounded. It slipped out."

"Jesus, Anais. I came to California because I loved you. Not to get a sniff."

"Okay now, you're trying to browbeat me, and I'm not having it. Good-bye."

"You're seeing somebody, aren't you?"

"No, I'm not."

"Then why can't you come?"

"I just told you. I've got to work."

"So, when're you coming?"

"I don't know. I'll keep you informed."

"Sure," I replied. "Keep me informed."

I slammed the phone down and sat as the *ching*ing reverberation burned through my skin.

**5**

❦ NEW YORK IS one of those cities that can turn a gloomy day grand by force of its energy. And vice versa. It is a city open for anything, including spirituality. I'd been up all night, naked, listening to Mingus. I like listening to Mingus when I'm troubled. And troubled I was. Not only by Anais' decision not to return to New York, but by the consequences should the police find out about my presence in that apartment where a murder had taken place. Mingus' music unfolds in a kaleidoscope of sounds and ideas, which lifts me out of my head and gets me pondering things beyond my trifling worries. At dawn a sunny spirit surged through me. Many people would call me a skeptic, but I have my moments.

As the morning sun fattened I sipped coffee at the kitchen table with Mingus' *Haitian Fight Song* playing in

the background. After my second cup, taken with a
smidgen of cream, I got up to get dressed.

A breeze drifted in through the bedroom window. The
white gauzy curtains peeled back like moth's wings opening. Across the street the leaves of the pine trees danced
with a vitality I hadn't seen in days. It was a welcome sight
after the flat heat of the past few days. The smell of spilled
oil wafted in to remind me that dreams of tropical beaches
and coconut trees were still premature.

THE MINUTE I saw them I knew the two men hovering
around my car were Feds. It was the way they seemed to
appropriate everything around them. The space. The air.
The trees. The way they smirked as I approached. The way
they balanced space between them, like Judge and Jury.

They were both big men. The sweaty one leaning on the
trunk of my Volvo wore a tan suit, his stomach protruding
over the pants. With a round marshmallow face, gray stubble and a thick bristly mustache, he looked like someone
who'd woken up, discovered that razors had been banned
and said hallelujah. The other, in a dark gray suit, stood
erect near the passenger door cleaning his teeth with a
plastic toothpick. His receding wispy hair pulled back behind large fluffy ears, bulbous nose and silver-dollar eyes
presented an image of a cast-off villain from a Batman car-
toon.

"Good morning, gentlemen," I opened.

My greeting was flawlessly condescending. I smiled
amiably, shifting my gaze back and forth between them.
The smirks on their faces dried up. Clearly, these guys
were not here to escort me to the White House. And I
hadn't made them feel very welcome with my contemptu-
ous salutation.

"Mr. Overstreet?" The tooth picker spoke.

"Who's asking?"

He walked toward me. "Slate. That's Bressler."

"Slate and Bressler? If you guys are from a law firm I already got a lawyer."

Slate coughed and his smirk returned, this time with a sinister edge. "That's Special Agent Slate and Special Agent Bressler to you. We want to talk to you."

"About?"

"Murder."

"I'm not for hire."

"Don't get cute, guy." Bressler spoke for the first time, his voice round and punchy like a circus announcer's.

"Not my fault if you think I'm cute," I said with a snicker. "Blame my genes."

Slate spat the toothpick to the ground. "Look, we know you got a hard-on for the City; we don't care about that. But if you try to clown with us you might end up with rocks in your jock. An FBI agent was killed over on St. Johns Place yesterday. His name was Ricardo Edwards. Did you kill him?"

It wasn't a particularly warm morning, but sweat was beginning to stream down my back. I could feel a twitch in my right leg, just above my knee, a sign that I was tensed. I could kiss my settlement with the City good-bye if the Mayor found out I had been within spitting distance of a dead FBI agent.

"I don't know what you guys are talking about," I said.

"Where were you last night?" Slate said.

"In my apartment."

"Alone?"

"No, I was fucking Jennifer Lopez. You want her number?"

Slate took a step toward me. I stiffened and glared at him.

"What?" I taunted. My teeth were set hard. I could feel the ache in my jaw.

They looked at each other and smiled.

"Let's go for a ride," Bressler said.

"Where to?" I said.

"Downtown," Slate said. He dug his pinkie into his right ear, took it out and looked at the scab with a smile of morose pleasure.

"Am I under arrest?" I said.

"Not at all. We're asking you politely," said Bressler.

I shrugged and followed them to a tan Buick parked halfway up the block on Hoyt. Slate got behind the wheel as Bressler squeezed his large frame into the backseat beside me. The car reeked of ketchup and stale coffee.

I wasn't alarmed when the dynamic duo turned down Bergen instead of continuing along Smith. My thinking was that they wanted to take the Manhattan Bridge. But when they ran the light and made a right on Nevins, I shot forward in my seat.

"Where the fuck we going?" I said.

"Relax, Blades," Slate said. "You know the deal."

"Let me out now."

Bressler grabbed my neck and pulled me backward. "Just sit back and relax. We just wanna talk."

Realizing there was nothing I could do short of jumping out of the moving vehicle, I leaned back against the seat. We rolled past a solid block of warehouses. The street was deserted. Stray dogs straggled about the sidewalk like they were drugged, scrimmaging with garbage that had escaped the overstuffed bins. A woman with barely enough fabric on to cover her butt leaned against a shuttered-up pink building, in conversation with an older man. Unlike vampires, prostitutes never seemed to know when the sun came up.

The street came to a dead end and the car stopped a few feet from a group of mangy dogs. The agents got out. I stayed in the car. Slate stuck his head through the open door.

"Ain't no bed in there, Blades. Get your ass out."

I slid out into a tiny settled pool of dark water. The sun hit the water sharply and the reflection dazzled my eyes. Slate was grinning.

"Am I supposed to be intimidated now?" I said.

Slate took a pack of gum and a fresh pack of cigarettes from his jacket. His grainy blue eyes were slanted toward me, squinting to avoid the red sun. He popped a stick of gum into his large mouth, then passed the pack over to his partner, who reprised the action.

"What were you doing in that apartment?" Slate asked.

"What apartment?"

Slate tapped the cigarette box twice in the palm of his left hand, then tore the top from the Winston box with one pull. He put the packet to his mouth and deftly removed one cigarette with his lips and teeth. He felt around in his trousers for a lighter, coming up with a green Bic. After lighting the cigarette, he hitched his right pants leg and rested his foot on the car bumper, puffing vigorously.

"We got a tip that you might've gone to that apartment," Bressler said.

"You should get your money back from that snitch."

"We could shut down your business in a heartbeat," Slate said.

"I don't care if you stopped the rain from falling."

"Don't lie to us, tough guy. If your prints turn up at that apartment, you ain't gonna be talking so tough," Slate growled.

I took a step back and spat. "Fuck ya'll. This conversation is over."

Slate grabbed me by the neck and slammed my face onto the hood of the Buick. "We're not your uncles from out of town, get what I'm saying?"

"My aunts never scared me either."

"If you whacked Agent Edwards, there won't be a sewer dark enough to hide your black ass."

He released me. I backed off slowly, anger roiling inside me.

"Hey, Blades," Bressler said, his jaws moving swiftly to pulverize the gum in his mouth. "I know your reputation.

You were a tough guy, but a good cop. The City is trying to screw you. I know that too. But don't let that cloud your judgment here. We're not your enemy. We don't work for the Mayor, so don't try to fuck us over. You don't know what you're dealing with here." He flipped a card in my direction. I snatched it out of the air.

"If you know anything about what went down in that apartment, call me," he said. "But make it soon. If shit starts falling on your head, you can't say we didn't give you a chance to buy a hard hat."

They got into the car. As the car rolled away, I kicked black water on the wheels.

## 6

❧ MUMBLING TO MYSELF, I began the walk back to
 Smith Street. Morning had quickly turned overcast. As
I crossed the bridge over the grimy, oil-slicked Gowanus
Canal, the gray clouds matched my mood.

Slate was right. My hard-on for the City was the size of
the Empire State Building, as much for my shooting as for
what happened afterward. I remember it like it happened
yesterday. The nine-millimeter slug, which passed through
my left shoulder, came from the gun of Troy Pagano, the
lone white officer in our crew. Had it struck lower, I might
be dead.

It was a bust-and-buy operation in Harlem. Burdened
with fog and steady drizzle, the night was cold and damp.
Cars moved like hearses through the wet streets. I'd been
working with this undercover team for about a month.

There were four of us: Nelson Rodriquez, a young tattooed Puerto Rican; Evan Miguel, a Dominican from the Bronx who swore he slept with Madonna; Troy Pagano, a leather-wearing gym rat who was using steroids to morph himself into Arnold Schwarzenegger; and myself. That night I was wearing the same long black leather coat I always wear in cold weather. After I made the buy from a skeleton-thin black youth in a gray Kangol hat and brown leather jacket, I called for my backup to move in, then I ran from the scene so as not to blow my cover.

I was about to turn down a dark alley when I heard shooting. Instinctively I ran faster, looking for cover.

I heard Troy's voice behind me: *Stop, nigger, or you're dead!*

I kept running, sure that he couldn't be talking to me. The next instant I felt a sharp burning in my left shoulder. I stumbled, but did not fall. Troy kept shooting. I ducked and zigzagged as I raced away. My back was ablaze. It felt like someone had stuck a firecracker in a nerve. I could feel the blood rushing down my side like an army of angry ants. I heard a car approach and with my badge in my hand I stepped into the street and collapsed.

The driver loaded me into his cab and took me to the hospital. His name was Jimmy Lucas.

Before I was out of surgery the news broke that a fellow officer had shot me. But the Mayor and the Commissioner, trying to head off a public-relations disaster, began to spin the shooting as a tragic accident.

Troy Pagano claimed he thought I was the perp. Never mind the suspect was six or seven inches shorter and was wearing a brown waist-length jacket.

I'd seen this rerun before and was not going to be played. My lawyer called on the Reverend Jerome Mc-Knight, a firebrand civil-rights activist, who organized daily protest marches downtown demanding a grand jury investigation. After two weeks of testimony the grand jury determined that the shooting was an accident. A week later Detective Pagano was back on the job.

The good reverend and my lawyer weren't done, however. Renewing their daily protests, they pressured the U.S. Attorney's Office to look at the case. Pagano was charged in Federal Court with violating my civil rights, convicted and sentenced to three years in jail and five years probation.

Leading up to the trial, the Mayor began leaking information to the press. First came the claim that I was mentally unstable, since I'd spent some time in therapy. That opened the floodgates to articles about my father's involvement with the Panthers, about my brother's drug addiction and my parents' arrest in the seventies for possession of pot and for taking part in demonstrations against the Vietnam War.

I wasn't surprised. The Mayor and the Police Benevolent Association were known for fighting dirty. But my family wasn't prepared for a guerrilla war. Reporters ambushed my mother. She didn't answer her phone for months. My brother laughed it off, when he wasn't high. My sister ran off to California. First I got pissed, then numbness took over.

There was a time when I got amped on rousting suspects and roughing them up. And because I made detective right out of the academy, I had an arrogance and swagger, which suspects hated. That swagger was gone. A civilian now, I was easy prey for over-eager FBI agents if I didn't find Agent Edwards' killer first.

By the time I reached Smith Street, clear drizzle spotted the leaves and windows along the block.

Unhooking my phone from my belt, I called Precious. Her voice came from the distance. I imagined she was on a speakerphone.

"I never thought I'd hear from you again," she said.

"Let's meet for coffee."

"There's a café on Sixth and Tenth. Matisse. I can meet you in half an hour."

* * *

LOOKING LIKE A Modigliani model, she leaned against the wall near the café's entrance in black leggings and a sleeveless white blouse. Around her neck hung a sterling silver chain; silver bangles jingled on her right wrist.

"Hello." She smiled and squeezed my arm when I reached her. Taking control, she guided me through the open glass door.

It was crowded inside, the clientele a mix of students from nearby universities and would-be bestselling novelists dressed in shiny downtown black hunched over laptop computers and sipping frothy drinks.

The walls were plastered with vintage ad signs in French. Below a large clock was an antique mirror. Dimmed chandeliers provided muted lighting. We sat in leather chairs facing the door. A waiter in dull black came over quickly.

"The almond cappuccino is great here," Precious said.

Before I could answer, she ordered two almond cappuccinos.

"Don't worry," she said, seeing hesitancy in my eyes. "If you don't like it I'll take you home and make you whatever you like."

Her voice reminded me of my grandmother's, that mesmerizing musical dance between phrases where the pauses and spaces said more about harmony than any symphony could. She was either English-born with some time spent in the Caribbean or vice versa. That musical accent was one of the things that attracted me to Anais. In her mouth speech was an erotic fantasy come alive.

"You look great," was all I could stammer.

"Thanks." She smiled, exposing perfectly shaped teeth.

"Where're you from, Precious?" I asked.

She laughed unpretentiously. "All over. I was born here. I spent my early years in London. Then Jamaica, before I moved back here. Does this line of questioning mean you're going to help me?

"Yes. I might need that money after all."

"Jimmy said you owned a business."

"A struggling concern."

"What kind of business?"

"A music store."

We lapsed into silence. She spread her arms out and leaned forward in a movement that reminded me of a dancer stretching. I studied her face for what must have been the hundredth time now since we met. Her skin was bright and healthy looking; the area under her eyes appeared tender as if she'd been crying. She had a strong chin, almost masculine, which was balanced against wide, egg-shaped eyes, giving her a confident appearance.

"Have you ever danced?" I asked.

She smiled. "Is it that obvious? I studied ballet in England until I was fourteen. That's when my mother died. I moved to Jamaica to live with my granny. I picked it up again when I moved back here."

Our waiter, a cheerfully chubby young woman wearing spectacles, brought our order. After she'd set the two cups down on the table, she stared at Precious.

"Excuse me. Aren't you Dr. Antonia Parker?" said the waitress. "I just love you."

Precious smiled graciously. "Thank you."

"Would you sign my book?"

From her pocket the waitress whipped out a red, artfully decorated notepad, which I suspected she kept handy for such chance meetings with stars. Precious signed her book, and the girl left with her face lit up.

"Do you have a last name, or are you like Madonna and Prince: one-name wonders?" I said.

She laughed. "You say that like it's a bad thing."

"Takes a lot of confidence to pull that off."

"How'm I doing?"

"Better than most." I tested the cappuccino. It was pretty good. "So why'd you become an actress?"

"Dance took too much time for too little financial reward. Plus, I couldn't keep my hips under control."

"That's what my wife said."

"You're married?"

"And holding."

"What does that mean?"

"I don't know myself."

"But you live alone."

"How could you tell?"

"We can tell."

"Humor me. What? My socks don't match?"

She giggled. "My secret."

"That's not fair," I said, pretending to sulk.

"Where is your wife?"

"In L.A. She's been trying out for the same movie for the last six months. I think the movie's been made and released; only my wife don't know it."

Leaning back in the seat she arched her thin eyebrows and chuckled. "So your wife's an actress too. I figured your wife would be a lawyer or something like that. Something stern."

It was my turn to chuckle. "She's stern enough without knowing the law."

We sipped casually while studying each other's faces.

"You're biracial, aren't you?" she asked, her eyes flushed with a buoyant smile.

"I'm me, Blades Overstreet," I said, my voice crusty with annoyance.

She grimaced. "I've offended you. I'm sorry."

I leaned back against the leather seat and tried to make my voice sound ordinary, untroubled. "I'm not offended."

She retaliated quickly. "Yes you are. And I apologize. I know race is a very sensitive issue in this country. Some people don't like being identified a certain way. People ask me all the time if I'm part Indian, or Brazilian. It hurts that I can't tell them exactly what I am."

"You're whoever you think you are."

"I wish it was that simple for me. We may both be of mixed race, but that's where the similarity ends."

I smiled weakly. "We may have more in common than you think."

She tried to veil her skepticism with a sweet lilt. "Really? I'd like to be able to celebrate all of my heritage. Do you feel the same way?"

"I'm a black man living in America. That says everything you need to know."

"Somehow I can't believe that."

"Why not?"

"For people like us, it can never be that simple."

"I didn't say it was simple, but because we're mixed doesn't mean we have to be confused."

"You think I'm confused?"

"I don't know."

"Were you ever confused?"

I paused for a moment. I didn't enjoy this probing. It reminded me of the sessions with the psychologist who tried to tell me that my dreams hid a deep resentment for my white siblings, perhaps even my mother. I told her she was talking crap. "Look, I don't want to talk about this anymore."

She leaned forward, her eyes luminous and shiny. "You've made a choice, it's clear. But at least you were given a choice."

"I didn't have a choice. That's the point. That choice was made for me long before I was born. Written into the American constitution, in fact, and into the minds of most Americans."

"So you don't really believe you're whatever you think you are. It's what society decides that you should be? I hate being patronized, Mr. Overstreet."

"Did you get a visit from the FBI?" I said, changing the subject. She was a little too clever for me, and I was in no mood to debate race and American society when the FBI was looking to pin a murder rap on me.

She set down her cup. "No. Why?"

"I need you to tell me the truth," I said.

She glanced away, staring off into space. "I've told you the truth."

"Did you ever meet this man?"

Her eyes darkened and she shook her head silently.

"Did you know he was an FBI agent?" I said.

"I didn't know anything about him."

"Is there anything at all you can tell me about your father?"

She sipped her cappuccino. "Nothing."

"Your mother, where was she from?"

"Jamaica."

"Why did she take you to live in England?"

"I don't know. She was a nurse. She might've been running from my father. But that's only a guess. She never explained anything to me."

"What was this proof the FBI agent had? Did he tell you?"

"He never said."

"Think. Did he give you any clue as to what it might be? A birth certificate maybe?"

"Nothing. I just remember how convincing his voice was. He just seemed to be sure of what he was saying. Maybe I just wanted to believe something." She pushed her glass to the middle of the table. "When I was ten, my ballet school had a recital. And I was given a little solo. I was very proud of myself. My best friend, Rebecca, was also in the recital. Both her parents came. After the recital we went out together to get a bite to eat: Rebecca and her family and my mother and me. At the restaurant Rebecca was sitting in her daddy's lap, and he was kissing and hugging her and telling her how good she was. I was a better dancer. And I know my mother was very proud of me, but I remember feeling jealous and hurt. When I got home I told my mother I would like to see my father. She beat me with a strap and forbade me to ever mention it again. I don't know how close I am to finding him, but the fact that this man was an FBI agent makes me feel even more hopeful that my father might one day be more than a phantom to me."

"You may not like what you find, you know."

"What do you mean?"

I hesitated, not wanting to burst her optimistic bubble. I knew intimately the hazards of digging through the rubble of the past. There was always the chance of unearthing something detrimental to your mental health. I'd found that out the hard way when I'd gone searching for my own father a few years before.

"There's probably a good reason why your father disappeared."

"I don't know that. I don't know that he disappeared. As far as I've been told he never existed. I want to make him exist. I don't care if he's some kind of criminal. I want to know."

"This could be like searching for a needle in a haystack."

"Unless you have a magnet. And maybe that's what you are. Just the right magnet." She glanced at her watch and stood up. "I'm sorry, but I have to go. I have an audition."

"You still audition for roles?"

"For certain directors. Spike Lee is casting a new movie. Soap stars don't register on certain radars in the movie business. It's a chance for me to move to the next level."

"Good luck."

She smiled and opened her bag, taking out a blue leather wallet. "Thank you."

"I've got it," I said, standing up and reaching into my back pocket.

"Nonsense," she said. "Besides, you're buying me dinner tomorrow night."

"Oh, am I?" I laughed.

"Yes. And I like very expensive restaurants, so you'd better save your money."

She put twenty dollars on the table and closed her wallet.

"Come, walk me back to my apartment so I can change."

She hooked her arm in the crook of my elbow as we walked along Tenth Street. I couldn't help but feel privileged. She was an incredibly beautiful woman, assured and warmly sensuous.

Outside her apartment building she kissed my cheek.

"Pick me up at eight," she said.

"What if I can't make it?"

"I hate being stood up, Mr. Overstreet."

"Blades. Call me Blades."

She smiled. "Eight sharp?"

I watched her disappear inside, her rampaging hips doing a silent rumba on the air.

# 7

AROUND SIX THAT evening I parked my '96 Volvo opposite a funeral home two blocks from the murder scene. With an easy gait, hoping not to look like the aggressive detective I used to be, I swung through the open gate. Festivity buzzed about the courtyard, which had been turned into a picnic ground.

Preteen girls jutting precocious breasts in the face of older boys, their wiry bodies snapping like elastic, daring the young pups to match their sauciness, jitterbugged to rap music rat-a-tat-ting from open windows like automatic gunfire. Tattered lounge chairs held up the meaty bodies of old men and women in the throes of storytelling. Barbecue grills of all sizes staked out family lots in the yard, spitting smoke and that sickening smell of burnt stale meat.

Squinting, I rolled through the yard with the appropriate

nonchalance, offering a stiff smile to a young toothless woman in red shorts who had the emaciated look of a drug addict.

As I entered the building I was struck by the manic urge to puke. There was something menacing and mysterious about large apartment buildings.

A dried-out old man, barely a fleck of flesh left on his bones, held the elevator door open for me. I thanked him and sidled to a corner as the warped graffiti-covered door closed. I took my car keys out of my pocket and spun them around on my finger. The old man, wearing shimmering disco-colored shorts and matching shirt, stared at me dolefully.

"Heard about the guy who got smoked in here yesterday," I muttered, sounding like a disgruntled insider.

The old man continued to stare as if I was speaking Greek. The elevator shook to a halt at the fourth floor. Before he got off, the old man shot me a weary smile. "Muthafuckers always getting killed in here," he said.

The entrance to Ricardo's apartment was sealed with yellow police tape. I tested the door. It was still unlocked. Ducking under the tape, I entered and stood on the rubber mat as the door creaked to a close behind me.

Tiptoeing through the debris, I wondered why the hell an FBI agent was living in this dump. Was he undercover? The air was thick with the sweet sickly odor of rot and death. Homicide had taken the garbage bucket from the kitchen, but scabs of decaying food spotted the floor, enough to keep the vermin partying. I left them to their carnival and headed for the bedroom.

What did I expect to find?

The bedroom was pretty much as I'd left it, except the mattress had been removed. Sunlight, smashing through trees and the clear glass window, pasted a pattern of leaves to the wall. Aimlessly I opened the same drawers Precious had searched, knowing I would find them empty.

There was nothing here. I was about to leave when I heard voices at the door. The door creaked open. For a second I froze, looking around for the fire escape. My eyes caught the open walk-in closet and I scuttled inside, pulling the door tightly behind me as the voices got closer.

I recognized the voices as belonging to Bressler and Slate as they entered the bedroom.

"You'd think he could find a better place to live," Slate was saying.

"If your wife kicked you out and the Bureau was getting ready to tie your ass to the back of a moving train, where would you hide?" Bressler said.

"He brought it all on himself, the fucking traitor."

The window opened and closed. Someone hawked and spat on the floor.

"You're a dirty son-of-a-bitch," Bressler said.

Slate laughed. "What? Who the fuck cares? This whole neighborhood is a pigsty."

"What do you think about this Blades?" Bressler said.

"We should arrest him."

"You're new to New York. But I've been here awhile. This guy was one of the best undercover cops around."

"So what? Edwards was one of our best agents. Look what he done. I did some checking on Blades. Do you know about his father?"

"Yes, I know all about his father."

Slate growled. "And you're convinced Blades is a good guy?"

"I'm telling you the guy was a good cop."

"People change. Do you know about Miami?"

"What're you talking about?"

"He was down in Miami with his father a few years ago."

"So what?"

"An ex-Panther turned up dead around the same time in Miami. Word was he went gunning for Blades' father. What if Blades popped him to protect his old man?"

"Wouldn't you do the same thing?"

"Why're you so protective of this guy, anyway?"

"I know someone in undercover. Told me a story about how Blades pulled him out of a tight spot in Brighton Beach where he was investigating some Russians involved in a money-laundering scheme. Saved his life."

"So are we supposed to kiss his ass now?"

"This someone is my brother."

"I don't care if it was your mama. I don't like him. He's arrogant. Nothing like a nigger with a little white blood. I bet when he was a kid his mother convinced him he was better than other niggers cause he's mixed."

"Shut up!"

"Don't tell me to shut up. You shut up!"

"I'm getting outta here," Bressler said.

I listened to their heavy retreating footsteps and waited for the friendly creak of the door before leaving my hiding place. As I stepped out, the floor beneath me buckled. I hesitated. Bouncing my full weight on it confirmed my suspicion. There was a hollow underneath. I got down on my knees to inspect the joints. A small section of the floor had been taken up and replaced.

I found a hammer in the kitchen and returned to the bedroom, where I used the claw to pry the boards from their flimsy moorings. Reaching into the tiny hollow chamber, I felt around. There was something tucked away in the tight cavern, which I grasped and pulled out into the light. It was a laptop computer.

With the computer tucked under my arm I stepped out into the hallway, drawing deep breaths. The hallway was musty and dank, but much better than the acrid smell of decay I'd left behind. Across the hall, a few feet to my left, the door to apartment 10-C was slightly ajar. I took a step toward it. The door closed quickly.

I went ahead and knocked on the door.

"What the fuck you want?" a throaty, phlegm-crusted voice barked from behind the door.

"Just wanna ask you a few questions," I said.

"I already talk to you muthafuckers."

"This won't take long."

A moment later I heard the shuffle of slippers and the door cracked slightly. I flashed my friendliest smile. The door swung open and a fleshy woman, her head tied with a yellow bandana, stood scowling.

"Can I come in?" I said.

"You think this is a muthafucking hotel?"

She looked like she'd not long ago gotten out of bed. The black robe draped around her was tattered and tied carelessly at the waist. She wore absolutely nothing underneath. I could understand that. It was a hot evening by any standard.

"I promise it'll only take a few minutes," I pleaded.

Leaving the door ajar, she turned and walked into the apartment. By the time I stepped in she was already sitting on a green sofa with zebra stripes, lighting a cigarette. The floor was strewn with magazines and newspapers; I surmised she'd just moved in. Several large unpacked boxes filled the room. Above a shiny grand piano set against the far wall was a framed picture of Harriet Tubman.

I must've been staring at the grand piano.

"It's my daughter's," she said, puffing a bar of smoke in my direction. "The piano. She just got into Juilliard. Will be starting in September. She so good they gave her a scholarship and accepted her a year early. She's going to be a concert pianist. If she don't, I'ma kill her for making me fuck these nasty-ass men who ain't wash their balls in months."

"I hope for her sake she does," I joked.

"Ain't no muthafucking joke."

"Well, she must be good for you to go to all this trouble for her."

She smiled. "Yeah, she good. She be having that fucking piano talking in tongues and shit 'cause I don't understand anything she be playing. But I go to all her concerts. She the best thing going in this fucked-up city. Now what the fuck you want with me?"

"What's your name?"

"Why you gotta know my name? You planning to propose?"

Her eyes dimmed insolently, and through the gray maze of smoke she looked like a Buddha in rags. Blowing a cloud straight up in the air, she then snuffed the cigarette in an ashtray.

"T-J's the name," she said, tilting her chin. "What's your?"

"Blades Overstreet."

She smiled. "Are you a sharp or dull blade?"

"Neither. I bet you knew the guy across the hall who was killed."

Her eyes grew keen. "What makes you think that?"

"Well, you see, I heard he was a ladies' man. And I'm thinking, if I were him, and a woman as beautiful as you lived across from me, I'd make it my business to get to know you."

She smiled, showing evenly spaced teeth. "Why don't you sid-down?"

"It's okay."

"Not to me. I don't like you standing up over me like you some fucking foreman. I used to work in a factory one time. That's all the foreman be doing. Standing up over people. I wanted to kill him."

I sat on the sofa next to her.

"Ain't that better?" she said. "Are you a ladies' man?"

"I know good work when I see it."

Her body quivered as though she'd just felt a draft. She rubbed her chest vigorously. "You think you slick, muthafucker. Where'd you hear he was a ladies' man?"

"What kind of person was he?" I said with a smile.

"Big spender. Big drinker. Big feet, if you know what I mean. One night he took me to Atlantic City and blew ten grand on blackjack."

"Did you know he was FBI?"

"You kidding? I didn't even know the muthafucker's real name. Didn't talk much, that one. Very quiet."

"When's the last time you saw him?"

"Three nights ago."

"Where?"

"In his apartment."

"Did he seem normal?"

"What's normal? He gave me a hundred bucks for some pussy. His dick got hard after some effort. That's normal for me."

"And you didn't see him after that?"

"No."

"Did you see anyone go into his apartment the day he was killed?"

"I already told the other detectives. No. Don't you guys talk to each other?"

"Thanks for your time," I said, getting up.

"You leaving already?" She got up and drew the robe around her. Her breasts threatened to jump out of the terry-cloth garment. I could see a scar just above her left breast. She inched over to me, her round brown eyes focused on my face. "Thanks? That's all I get?" she said. "You ain't even giving me a card? Them other two muthafuckers gave me a card. Where's your card? Suppose I remember something and want to call you?"

I hesitated.

"You ain't no muthafucking detective, are you?" she said.

"I used to be a cop."

"What're you now? A private dick?" She laughed. "That's what they call them in the detective novels. I always wanted to get my own private dick. Why you in such a hurry, Mr. Private Dick? Ain't you supposed to come gimme some of that private dick now? That's how it be in the novels and movies. The detective goes to question the whore, she be wearing nothing underneath her robe and he can't resist her."

She broke into raucous laughter.

"Perhaps another time," I said.

"Yeah. Whatever. Don't trip on the way out, Mr. Dull Blade."

She opened the door and I stepped outside. I could feel her eyes on me as I strolled down the hallway. I was getting hungry.

# 8

MY MOTHER CALLED as soon as I walked into my apartment, to remind me of my brother's birthday party the next day, which I'd completely forgotten about. After our conversation, I dumped the roti I'd bought onto a plate and sat at my desk, where I flipped the cover and powered up the laptop. It was a powerful machine, an IBM Thinkpad with a Pentium III processor. That's as far as I got. Anything beyond that needed a password.

I ate my roti and drank a beer. Then I rang Trevor Lester, a young man I'd met roughly seven years before. He was nineteen then. Had been in and out of the system from the time he was fourteen. At the time he lived with his old man, a sanitation worker. His mother split when he was nine. Trevor's story was that of many young black kids in New York City. It started with harassment by the police, who would stop and frisk him anytime they wanted. Then they'd release him without so much as an apology. It was sport to them. One day, after one of these stops, Trevor threw the apple he was eating at the squad car. The cops came back and kicked him around. After that the cops would pick him up anytime they saw him on the street. Day or night.

One day the cops charged him with possession of marijuana. That charge was dropped. From then the number of arrests escalated for offenses ranging from drug possession to arms possession to second-degree attempted murder. He was never convicted on any of these charges, but spent a lot of time in jail, being ground to dust by the system.

When he was charged with the attempted murder of an off-duty narcotics officer, he fled to Fayetteville, North Carolina, where he worked as a hotel clerk for three years. In his spare time he studied computers and became an expert hacker. He was arrested for breaking into the computer network of Citibank, which blew his cover. I was sent to bring him back to New York.

I took a liking to the brother. It's not usual that this happens to me. But he was a smart kid. He said he didn't shoot the officer, and I believed him. I helped him get a good attorney and he beat the rap. Four years later, armed with a degree in computer technology from New York University, he started his own Internet security company.

"Trevor, it's Blades," I said when I heard his Barry White voice at the other end.

"Blades, whaddup, cuz?"

"Trying to monopolize, you know."

"No doubt." He laughed.

"What about you?"

"Same. Still trying to get mine, you know."

"Listen, Trevor . . ."

"Yeah . . . ?"

"I need a favor. Can I come see you?"

"Anytime, cuz. I'll be here."

TREVOR WORKED OUT of his duplex in Fort Greene. I parked outside his building on South Portland Avenue and climbed the ten steps to the front door of the refurbished brownstone to ring the buzzer. The heavy oak door opened and a dark chunky man wearing khaki shorts and an unbuttoned Hawaiian-style shirt stood in front of me, smiling.

He clasped my hand and we hugged.

"Good to see you, cuz," he said.

I laughed.

"What's so funny?" he said.

"Man, I never get over how deep your damn voice is."

"Just don't ever tell me my voice is sexy, okay?"

We laughed and I followed him inside.

Coming down the stairs of the duplex was a slender light-skinned young woman with dreadlocks pulled back into a ponytail, a large black Labrador trailing her. There was an air of mischief about her smile. She came up to Trevor and slipped comfortably into his arms. Like she knew exactly where the sweet spots were. Then she turned to me.

"Good to see you again, Blades."

"It's always a pleasure to see you, Patricia."

"I'm going to take Jordan for his walk, baby," she said to Trevor. "Be back in an hour."

"Pick up a movie on your way back."

"Anything special?"

"Something funny. I don't care."

She slipped a leash on the dog and opened the door and went out.

"Man, that woman still looks at you like she's seeing you for the first time. How the fuck do you do that?"

"That's why I married her, man. After we'd been going out for a year, she said to me one day: *Trevor, every time I look at you I feel like I'm looking at you for the first time.*" He started to laugh.

I didn't know whether to believe him. "You dogging me, aren't you?"

"You so corny."

"I'm jealous, that's all. I'm man enough to admit it."

"Let's go into my office."

His large office took up all of the space behind the stairs. Along with computers and electronic equipment, there were bookshelves filled with technical books and magazines. A photo of Trevor's father, who died the year he graduated from NYU, hung on the wall behind his desk next to a photo of his wife.

I sat on the wheat-colored sofa. He got behind his desk.

"What can I do for you, my brother?"

I put the laptop on his desk. "I need to get into this computer."

"You forgot the password?"

"I never memorized it."

"This ain't your computer, is it?"

"Technically it is. I found it."

"A case of finders keepers?"

"Can you do it?"

"Any reason why you want to access the files? We could reformat the hard drive and start fresh."

"I'm trying to impress a woman, you know what I mean. There's some information on here which might help her out."

"Cuz, I told you to let Pat hook you up. She got some friends who're mad fly. And they go crazy for your type. Would eat you for breakfast, lunch and dinner."

"I think I could get my own women, thank you."

"No need to front, cuz. I know you got that light-skin,

curly hair shit going on, but you might not know how to use it."

"Can you break the password?"

"Most passwords are a hundred sixty bits. That shit's impossible to break."

"You saying I can't get into this computer?"

"That ain't what I'm saying. There're ways. What's the operating system?"

"I don't know."

"You want a joint while I check it out?" ~

"I'm trying not to smoke. But I'll take a beer."

"Help yourself. You know where everything is. Bring me a Heineken."

I went through the door to my right, past shelves of books and discarded computer parts, and into a tiny kitchenette. Trevor kept beer and snacks in this area for when he worked late. I grabbed two Heinekens from the cooler and made my way back.

Trevor had already powered up the computer. He had a tensed look on his face.

"Problem?" I said.

"It's running UNIX. The network version. This is high-profile shit. More difficult to bypass than Windows or NT. You telling me the truth about this computer, cuz?"

"I'm telling you what I know."

"Alright, baby. I'ma hit it for you."

"Appreciate it, cuz." I sat down on the couch. "So how long you and Patricia been married now?"

"Five years."

"And you're as much in love today as when you first met?"

"More. I'm crazy about that woman. I would kill myself if she left me."

"No woman can be worth your life."

"Patricia is. You know what it is, man? It's about faith.

That's the difference. I believe in this woman. Like I believe in God."

"You saying that your wife is God?"

"That's exactly what I'm saying. My wife is God. I know you think I'm crazy. But I don't know what God looks like. And I believe God exists. I would give my life for this woman, so why can't I believe in her like I believe in God? See what I mean? It's a faith thing. Without faith, there can be no lasting love. I mean, there's the possibility that she might fuck somebody, or leave me. But I can't fear that. Because for me, to love her the way I do is the only way to love."

"You're a brave man."

"And you're a cynical fuck. That's why Anais left you."

"Now why you have to dog me out like that?"

"Am I lying?"

"I love my wife."

"You love Blades Overstreet. Or should I say God Overstreet. Your mother spoiled you, Blades, that's your problem. And you expect every woman to spoil you."

"I've been trying to get Anais to come back for months."

"Should never have let her get away."

"Yeah, yeah, skip that verse."

He chuckled. "The chorus is worse. You shoulda parked your black ass in L.A. and got on your knees and kissed her ass until Anais agreed to get on a plane with you."

"You don't know Anais."

"This ain't about Anais. It's about you. You think you're too good to beg. Yeah, you went out to L.A. But you still expected Anais to come to you. It's that arrogant white blood in you."

"Anybody ever tell you that you're racist, man?"

"Yeah, all the time. So tell me, cuz, who owned this computer?"

I was tempted to tell him the truth, but decided against

it. "Let's just say the person will never need it again. How long will it take?"

"I don't know. About two days."

"No sooner?"

"I gotta hook up two UNIX workstations to your computer and switch the hard drives. Then I gotta copy some files and run a utility to do a recovery from your computer. Then I have to do a reinstall. Then hope that I can use the network password from one of the workstations to bypass the one on your computer. It don't always work the first time."

"I need it as soon as possible, Trevor." I scribbled my cell-phone number on a pad on his desk. "Call me the minute you get in."

I took another long sip of beer. We pounded, hugged, and I left.

# 9

NEXT DAY I walked into the record store after lunch to the sweet sound of soca music. The euphoric cadence of the catchy tune and its sexually charged chants filled our tiny store. Face lit up like a Caribbean sunset, Milo was grinding his arthritic hips, such as he had, to the delight of three buxom women-in-waiting. He greeted me with a wave of his hand, beckoning me over.

"Blades," he sang. "The new Allison Hinds just come in. It hot, boy. Hot."

"Too hot for you, I see. You look like you about to have a stroke, old man."

The young girls laughed out loud, covering their mouths in modesty.

"Boy, is joke you making. Me back still strong. Me wining days ain't done."

"I ain't worried about your back. I just don't want you peeing yourself inside the store."

"You just jealous 'cause you can't dance to we music."

"You call that dancing? Well, when you recover from your epileptic attack, attend to the customer who just came in."

The tall man who'd just walked in looked to be in his early forties. Standing well over six feet, perhaps six-five, he wore tan slacks and a white polo shirt. Box-shaped designer wire-rim glasses gave him a professorial air, and he carried himself in the haughty manner I'd grown accustomed to seeing in many people of Caribbean descent.

"Somebody named Walter Lahore called," Milo said as he broke off his manic gyrations and hip thrusts.

"What'd he say?"

"He'll call back."

I went into the office and closed the door. Walter Lahore was an addict who used to be one of my informants when I worked undercover. Why was he calling me now? Old habits died hard, I suppose. I picked up the phone to call Precious. She wasn't home. I left her a message canceling our date that evening. The door opened and Milo's head bobbed into view.

"The *customer* is here to see you." He made a comical face. "Said he's a friend of Congresswoman Richardson."

"What does he want? A donation?"

"He didn't say."

"Tell him I'm busy."

"Come on, Blades. Congresswoman Richardson is a very important woman. It wouldn't hurt to contribute to her campaign."

"Out of your salary?"

"Ha, ha," he jeered.

"Send him in."

Congresswoman Richardson was a powerful Brooklyn politician originally from the island of Jamaica. Four years ago, after two terms in the City Council, she was elected to represent the tenth Brooklyn district in Congress, becoming the first person born in the English-speaking Caribbean to enter the House.

Seeking a second term in Congress, she was facing an old opponent in the upcoming primary. Malcolm Colon, an African-American, had held the seat for more than a decade until Congresswoman Richardson defeated him. Their contest had been a nasty brawl from the start, bringing to the surface age-old animosities between Caribbean-Americans and African-Americans. One host at the local black-owned talk-radio station, WBLI, stopped taking calls from listeners because of the anger with which supporters of both camps, sharply divided along national lines, attacked each other on her show.

The tall stranger entered my office with a painted-on smile and offered his hand.

"So sorry to drop in on you like this, Mr. Overstreet. Normally I would call first, but my business here is rather urgent."

"Good afternoon." I shook his hand. His palm was cold and soggy. "What can I do for you, Mr. . . . ?"

"I'm so sorry." He laughed apologetically. "Aquia. But you can call me Gabriel. May I sit down?"

"Please."

With unusual grace for such a large man, he sat in the only other chair in the room, a black tubular with a wicker bottom. He crossed his legs, and leaning his head on a side, he quickly scoped the room with a trained eye. This guy had spent some time in law enforcement or the armed forces. I could tell by his manner, by the way he took in everything in the room in one skillful sweep of his eyes.

He rested his hands on the edge of my desk. His shiny fingernails looked recently manicured. Freshly shaven, with a gleaming diamond stud in his right ear, he exuded an air of arrogance, and the expensive cologne with which he polluted my office made his presence slightly less obnoxious than sharing the same room with a camel.

"You're something of a hero in our community, Mr. Overstreet. Breaking the blue wall to take on your former employers for their racist attitudes toward black people in this city."

"Excuse me?"

"It's not every day I get to sit down with a man of your courage and integrity."

"Are you a reporter?" I wasn't feeling this guy.

He grounded his eyes sheepishly. "I'll get right to the point," he said, as if he'd read my mind. His even teeth glistened, and he reminded me of a taller Denzel Washington. He had a deep voice, which reverberated with a husky dissonance like a dog barking into a metal bucket. "I'm a very close associate of Congresswoman Richardson, who, as you may know, has rewritten the history books. I understand you've been hired by her niece."

"And who would that be?"

"Precious. The soap star."

"And who did you hear this from?"

"Come, Mr. Overstreet. Let's not play games."

"One man's game is another man's war," I said.

He cleared his throat. "Can you tell me why she hired you?"

"My business is selling music, Mr. Aquia. Now, if you're not here to talk about that, you're wasting my time."

He paused with a bewildered look before responding. "The congresswoman doesn't want any campaign surprises."

"You're burrowing into the wrong hole."

He took a deep breath, and I got the impression he was calculating his next move. As he twirled the stud in his ear between his thumb and index finger, his mouth curled into a presumptuous smirk. I looked at his pink lips and wondered if he wore lipstick.

"What else do you do besides run errands for the congresswoman?" I said.

He winced. I could tell that I'd slighted him. This was a proud man.

"I'm a businessman, like you. I'm also involved in charities. Trying to make sure our people get the services they need and deserve."

"And by *our people* you mean?"

He smiled. "Black people."

"Where're you from, Mr. Aquia?"

"Don't let the name fool you, Mr. Overstreet. I'm as American as you are. I'm prepared to offer you twenty-five thousand dollars for any information you might find which could affect Congresswoman Richardson's campaign."

"Don't insult me, Mr. Aquia."

"Fifty thousand?"

"Do I look like I got a hard-on?" I said. His prickly cologne was getting to me.

He stiffened and pulled his square chin into his fire-hydrant neck. His face sprung that smart-alecky smirk again, and he stood up. He took a business card from his wallet and placed it on my desk, then he opened the door. A happy blast of reggae music bounced past his huge frame.

"If you change your mind, you can reach me at Mosaic Gallery."

He made a starchy retreat. Presuming I'd be impressed by his political connections, he'd come here expecting me to do a jig to his mumbo jumbo like some nincompoop. Could I use a woman of Congresswoman Richardson's influence in my corner, especially with the legal battle looming between the City and myself? You bet. But when she was in the City Council, she had been one of the Mayor's lackeys anyway, and I don't like people taking me for granted. Before he waltzed into my office groomed like a *GQ* poster boy with his arrogant fuck-you smirk that to some unwitting bozo might indicate the presence of a personality, Gabriel Aquia should've done some research on me. I'm not easily bought.

I picked up the card and looked at it. It had his name in gold embossed lettering. Beneath it the word: *President*. Beneath that: *Mosaic Art Enterprises*.

How could my search for Precious' father affect the congresswoman's campaign? Why would they offer me money? Was he dead? Was there some dark family secret behind his disappearance? I remembered reading somewhere that the congresswoman was hosting a pre–Labor Day luncheon in Prospect Park the next day. I resolved to crash the party.

AROUND SIX THAT evening I stopped at my apartment to change, get Jason's present and check my messages. There was a message from Walter Lahore. He said it was urgent and mentioned something about Stubby Clapp planning to do me dirty. His speech slurred; he may've been jacked. But Walter has never given me bad information. And anytime I heard Stubby Clapp's name I paid attention. I called the number Walter had left. No one answered. I jotted the number down on a piece of paper and made a mental note to call him later.

# 10

I WAS NAMED for my grandmother, Carmen Blades, a chunky, fast-talking woman who died when I was twelve. All I can remember of her now is the way she out-talked and out-shouted everyone on her block. And her accent: a strange calypso blues dance with the English language, with the few Spanish words she'd picked up in Panama thrown in for counterpoint.

She had arrived in New York from Panama in 1921, at age fifteen, with her parents, who'd gone there from Barbados to work on the Canal. She married a Jamaican and bore three children. I was born in Park Slope on September 22, 1968, to Madison Blades, the first of the three sons.

"You were so beautiful. So lovely," my mother said when I complained about my name. "Besides, your father promised your grandmother he would name his firstborn after her."

"But, Ma," I'd say, "Carmen is a girl's name."

"No, it's not. What difference does it make, anyway? It's a lovely name. It's your grandmother's name. Don't you like your grandmother?"

This is the first time I'm saying this to anybody, but I prayed every day for my grandmother to die; maybe then my mother would change my name.

My grandmother died and everyone still called me Carmen. After countless fights at school with boys who teased me, and after being sent home from school more times than I could remember for threatening to cut somebody, I decided to run away.

One crisp October morning, dressed in blue jeans and a neatly pressed blue cotton shirt, I set off, ostensibly to visit my uncle on Clarendon Road. Instead, I boarded the Number 2 train to Manhattan, where I got off at Forty-second Street and fought my way through pimps and hustlers to the Port Authority Bus Terminal.

Tall for my age, about five-eight, with a smile that everybody said was cute, I ambled up to the Greyhound ticket window. Here was a chance to find if my smile possessed any mojo.

The attendant, a white woman with crinkled eyes and a branch of purple veins knotted in her forehead, asked me where I wanted to go.

I smiled.

She frowned and repeated her question in a voice that stung like my grandmother's lashes. I smiled again. I didn't know where I wanted to go. I hadn't worked out my flight plan that far ahead. She saw my dilemma.

"What's your name?"

I panicked. If I was running away I couldn't use my real name. Her name tag read *Brenda Overstreet*. Quickly I blurted out, "Blades Overstreet."

She laughed and signaled to a policeman strolling by.

"Well, Blades Overstreet, why don't you tell the officer where you live. I'm sure he'd be glad to see you get home safe."

I lived with Carmen until I was ready to sign up with the Marines. That's when I became Blades Overstreet.

MY MOTHER WAS barely five-two. She wore heels all the time to compensate, especially when she went anywhere with my dad, who was six-four. Unfortunately, in America's eyes, that was not the biggest difference between them. She was white; he was black.

Twice my mother married. Both men deserted her. Her first husband, Jason and Melanie's father, who was white, left when he discovered she was having an affair with my father, who she met at an artist colony in Boston in the sixties. My father left when I was fourteen. One night I woke up to screaming. He and my mother were having a terrible fight. I don't know what about. He left that night and never returned.

After it became clear that he was not coming home, I drifted from resentment to resignation about his absence. In the intervening years, needing an easy answer for his desertion, I imagined that he left because my sister constantly compared him to her father. Or that the militancy that had once captured his spirit as a member, for a brief time, of the Black Panther party, had returned, making him uncomfortable with the world he'd acquired because of love: the white world of my mother and her children. And in my many fights with my sister, I used these deductions like pylons against my sister's angry taunts that if my mother hadn't married my father, he would've ended up dead like the rest of the Panthers.

I don't know what set off my desire to find him, but when I came out of the hospital I resigned from the Department and went searching for him. I canvassed all my known relatives in New York and his old friends from the Panther days, and after a month of dead ends I got a good lead, which took me to Panama. There I spoke to one of my grandmother's brothers. My father had visited him about four months before I arrived. He gave me a number back in the States to call.

A week later I met my father in a Miami motel. Almost twenty years had passed. He looked nothing like the man I remembered. There was a dankness about his wrinkled eyes, as if he'd been submerged underwater for a long time. He was now slightly stooped, from a back injury, he told me. The only thing that remained of the man who taught me how to hit a baseball was his deep voice, which could still snap you to attention in an instant. His eyes were now empty of the presumptuousness that once stamped him as one of the most outspoken men in the community.

He'd changed his name to Paul Reese and apparently made a living selling prints of his paintings on the Internet. After the usual tango between estranged father and son, I asked him why he left. I rue the day I was so curious.

The story he told me was a rambling account of his short-lived involvement with the Panthers and its aftermath. He didn't leave the party because of his marriage to my mother as I'd presumed, but because of disillusionment with the ineffective leadership. Years after he'd left the party, indeed years after the Panthers had been silenced by COINTELPRO and had ceased to be a force in the national debate on race, my father, in a rash moment of guilt, informed on two past leaders of the party. Both were arrested, tried and sentenced to life in prison for the murder of a police officer. One escaped from jail, and after a shootout with police that left his wife dead, he disappeared. Soon afterward, death threats began to rain on my father. He decided to leave New York.

Why didn't you take us with you? I asked him.

He didn't have an answer.

I could not bring myself to accept that my father would run from anyone. Moreover, that he would leave his family behind. And I would never have believed his story had someone not tried to kill him while I was staying with him in Miami. The ghosts of the past had finally caught up with him. Luckily, I was there. After the Miami episode, my father moved to the island of Barbados.

My mother grew up in New Orleans. Of the two children by her first marriage, Melanie was the older. She was now a successful lawyer in California. Jason, the birthday boy, was three years my senior. For most of his life Jason has suffered with depression. He became addicted to drugs in college and has been unemployed since he was twenty-five.

When I was young I was very confused about my identity. It did not help that my parents couldn't agree either. My father saw the world in black and white. To him, I was black. My mother, kindled by optimism, refused to accept my father's declaration, insisting that I was neither black nor white but better because I was mixed. I had the best of both worlds, she told me. For a long time I actually believed I was better off for not being white or black. I had both black and white friends and was equally comfortable around them. All that changed at the age of thirteen.

I was the best swimmer in the Park Slope prep school I attended. I was also the only kid on the swim team who wasn't white. My black friends made fun of me; my white friends thought it was cool. There was a tradition at the school that the best swimmer was chosen as captain of the swim team. I was not chosen. The captaincy was given to another swimmer. When I asked the coach why I wasn't chosen captain as was the tradition, his eyes sank deep into his head and he hunched his shoulders, mumbling something to the effect that the school decided to use different criteria that year. I sensed that he was lying.

I withdrew from the swim team and joined the basketball team without telling my mother. I had been a better swimmer than anyone else, but I wasn't good enough to captain the swim team. My mother was wrong. At my school, it was better to be white than mixed.

I spent many afternoons staring at myself in the mirror. My face was seasoned with my father's genes. I had his chunky lips and my complexion was a tawny brown rather than light. My hair was thick with curls. There was no way I could pass for white. And being mixed was the same as being black in America.


I ARRIVED AT my mother's town house in Bloomfield, New Jersey, at seven-fifteen. I had keys and let myself in. Melanie was already there. When I entered she was sitting in a blue cotton dress, her legs crossed, on the red sofa. As always she looked stunning. She uncrossed her legs and got up to greet me.

I'd seen her briefly on the West Coast when I visited Anais earlier in the summer. Melanie and I have always had a volatile relationship, but the smile on her face when she saw me made me forget all the awkward moments and fights we'd had over the years.

"How're you doing, Blades?"

Melanie was frail and brittle in my arms. She'd lost some weight.

"I'm doing alright, sis. How're you?"

She stepped back, holding me at arm's length. "Fine."

"Lost weight?"

"Some."

"Everything okay?"

"Everything's fine. How's the business going?"

"Terrible."

We laughed and embraced again. It was good to see her in such high spirits.

My mother swept out of the kitchen looking handsome

in a long yellow tight-fitting dress. Holding onto her youthful figure with a combination of yoga, ballet and a daily regimen of two bottles of Avian water and little else, my mother was the quintessential New Age woman. She taught French literature at Bloomfield College and was an insatiable traveler who spent a part of every summer in Europe.

"Carmen!" She greeted me with her usual flourish, arms outstretched, a tent smile on her face.

We hugged for a long time. Her hair smelled of roast fish.

"Something smells good," I said.

"Wait until you see what I made you."

"What? Not seafood gumbo?"

"I'm not saying." Giggling, she pushed me back as I tried to go into the kitchen. "You have to wait."

"Making me wait for gumbo is torture, you know that."

"Who said anything about gumbo?"

"It's gumbo. It's got to be gumbo."

"You'll have to wait. Go make yourself a drink."

"Where's Jason?" I said.

From the painful silence that followed I knew that Jason had gotten into one of his moods. A wave of guilt washed over me. I'd been so consumed with my own personal troubles that I hadn't kept in touch with my brother.

Melanie took my arm. "Go talk to him. You're the only person who can talk to him when he gets like this."

That was not exactly true. Growing up I'd idolized my brother, but we had never been really close. He'd been a star athlete at St. Francis Academy in Park Slope, winning a scholarship to North Carolina University. It was there that he started experimenting with drugs. After he was expelled from school, he came back to New York, where, a week later, he almost died from a heroin overdose. One day I saw Jason buying drugs on Flatbush Avenue and I decided my mission in life would be to get rid of every drug dealer in the world.

In and out of rehab since he was twenty, Jason was later diagnosed with severe bipolar disorder and put on medication, which he refused to take, preferring to binge on alcohol, or cocaine, disappearing for days, sometimes weeks at a time.

My mother was very upset when I opted to go to Lincoln University instead of Villanova, which had offered me a baseball scholarship. I was good at it but didn't care that much about baseball and wasn't good enough to play basketball. When I dropped out of Lincoln at the end of my sophomore year to join the Marines, she protested that she had not demonstrated against the Vietnam War for one of her sons to become a trained killer. But my mind was made up. I knew what I wanted, and a college education wasn't necessary for catching bad guys. After four years of seasoning in the service, and two after that working on an oil rig in the Virgin Islands and security for rock bands, I was ready to join the NYPD.

The door to Jason's room was open. I knocked and walked in. It was dark inside. He was lying in bed, arms folded across his chest in the manner of a corpse. U2 sermonized from the boom box on the headboard. I started to speak but he held up his hand to silence me. While I leaned against the door waiting for his meditation to peak, I remembered how I used to love sneaking into his room to read his comics or look at pictures of naked women.

After the song finished, he turned the music off and sat up. His long blond hair was straggly about his face.

"Can I turn on the light?" I said.

His shoulders hunched violently, and I moved toward him, thinking he was going to topple over. Before I could reach him, he stood and walked to the light switch.

The light unfolded to my eyes the misery of my brother's life. He wore nothing. His crumpled-up face looked ready to be thrown away. It was a mass of stubble and scrapes as if he'd fallen on barbed wire or been in a fight with a cat. Empty Three Musketeers wrappers dotted the floor. In one corner rock magazines were piled a pillar high. Newspapers covered the bed. Clothes dangled from every protrusion in the room, and the walls were covered with pictures of naked black women. The room was hot and drenched with the sour smell of stale pizza.

"What's happening, man?" I said.

He rummaged around in a pile of clothes on the floor for a pair of shorts. Usually distant and cold when I came to see him, he surprised me with a deep embrace after he'd pulled on his shorts. It'd been two months since I last saw him. He was in rehab in Vermont when I left for the West Coast.

"I brought you something," I said.

The bag I handed him contained a vintage Dodgers baseball shirt with the name of his favorite player, Sandy Koufax, printed on the back.

His face exploded into a grin when he turned the shirt around and saw the name. He looked at me and he was shaking. I couldn't tell if it was from happiness or from exhaustion, for he truly looked bedraggled.

"It's signed," I said.

"Awesome. How'd you get it?"

"I was on the West Coast a few weeks ago. Anais knows some very important people. You like it?"

"It's great."

"I thought you would like it."

"It's very nice. Thank you."

"Hey, is everything alright?"

"Sure. Everything's cool." He laughed.

"Put it on, man. Put it on."

"Now?"

"It's your birthday, man. Put on!"

He slipped the shirt over his head and stood beaming like a twelve-year-old. "How's it look?"

I clapped my hands together, as I used to do when I

watched my brother strike out batters in little league. "You look great."

The smile in his eyes quietly died. He sat on the edge of the bed. "I fucked up, didn't I?"

"What do you mean?"

"I could've been good. I could've been as good as Sandy Koufax."

"You're still the best I ever seen."

"Yeah?"

"Always."

"I'm tired, man. Always so tired."

"Melanie is here. Flew all the way from California to be with you. Left her rich husband out there to be with her brother. Now what do you think about that? You can't disappoint her."

"What the fuck have I got to celebrate? I'm a loser."

"Hey, we're family."

He snickered. "That's a joke, and you know it."

"That's all in the past."

"Nothing is ever in the past, man. Nothing. It's all here." He tapped his head. "It never goes away. It just sits there and churns and churns like it's making butter. Turning your brain into fucking butter. Fuck it, man. I don't want to celebrate. I don't want a party. I just want you all to leave me the fuck alone."

He was becoming agitated. Once he became like that there was no way to talk to him until he'd calmed down.

I left him and went outside to explain Jason's logic, but my sister had dumped her compassion somewhere over the Grand Canyon.

"Does he understand that I'm a busy woman? That I canceled a number of engagements to fly across America to be here?" she snorted.

"He's just not up to it," I said. "He can't do it."

"That's not acceptable."

"Look, you'll be here tomorrow. Take him out to lunch."

"I won't be here tomorrow. I'm taking an early flight in the morning."

"When'd you get here?"

"It doesn't matter when I got here."

I turned to Mom. "When'd she get here?"

Before my mother could speak, Melanie screamed, "What're you? My fucking jailor! The issue is not when I got here; it's that Jason is acting like a jerk."

I caught my mother's weary eyes and was crushed by the weight of her pain. She sat silently on the sofa sipping coffee, her arthritic right wrist misshapen by years of wiping tears from her eyes. My mind flew back to waking up in the hospital flanked by my mother and my wife both crying. Now, as I watched my mother struggle to contain her anger at having to watch her two children continue the brawls that had marked their youth, a chill ran up my back. Her eyes were wet, and she kept blinking as though her vision was blurred. I felt myself lose steam for the battle with Melanie.

Melanie never forgave Mom for marrying a black man, and since that black man happened to be my father, I imagined that her fury was also directed at me. Perhaps trying to compensate for America's shortcoming, my mother made the mistake of trying to make me feel that I was somehow more special than special because I was mixed. That never sat well with Melanie.

I touched my mother's face. Her delicate skin seemed ready to crack. I could see the veins in her eyes.

"I'm leaving, Mom."

She clutched my arm. "No, Carmen. Stay and eat."

"I got some business to take care of back in New York."

"How can you leave now?" screamed Melanie, her eyes wide as saucers.

"Will you two stop it?" Mom said. "Carmen, I thought you would stay the night."

"I can't, Mom. You know I would if I could."

"What could you possibly have to do that can't wait until tomorrow? Anais isn't even in New York. How're things with her, by the way?"

"Not too good. I know you love her, Mom, but I really don't think Anais is coming back."

"Give her time."

"I'm running out of time."

"Why do you have to rush back to New York?"

"I promised to help a friend."

"You're choosing a friend over your family?" Melanie said.

"Just butt out, okay?" I said.

Mom got up. "Take some food with you if you have to go." She walked off toward the kitchen leaving me and Melanie to stare at each other.

"You're just like your father," Melanie whispered.

"What was that?"

"We were a very happy family until he came along. Nothing has been the same since."

"How happy could Mom have been with your father? She chose to have an affair. With my dad."

"He stole her with lies. And then ran away."

"You don't know why he left."

"He didn't leave," she taunted. "He ran. Just like you're doing now."

"Give it a rest, will you?"

"Your father deserted her and Mom still thinks of him as the love of her life. I told her she can have him declared dead since she hasn't heard from him in twenty years. She refused."

"My father isn't dead."

"How do you know? Have you heard from him?"

"My father isn't dead," I repeated.

"Why does she think he was so special?"

"That's her business."

"Well, let me let you in on a little secret. I don't care

what Mom thinks. He was nothing special. Neither are you."

"I didn't ask for special treatment, Melanie."

"You didn't have to ask. Mom made sure of that."

"If it's any consolation to you, Melanie, the rest of the world doesn't care what Mom thinks either. I didn't ask to be a walking label for integration. I didn't ask to be your brother, but that's our lot."

"And you couldn't help the way Mom treated you. If you don't think that had an effect on Jason, you're a fool."

"Look, Melanie, I came here to wish Jason a happy birthday, not to fight with you."

I walked over to her and hugged her. She stood stiff as a mule in harness. I held her for a while hoping she'd yield, hug me back. But she didn't. She smelled clean, like fresh snow. I wanted to tell her how much I missed her and wished that we, in our youth, had not bowed to the vulgarity of history in trying to destroy each other's self-esteem. There was no doubt that Melanie hated my father. Whether she would've felt the same way about him if he were white I'd never know. And because I still wanted to believe there was hope for Melanie and myself, I was too afraid of what the answer might be to ask.

Mom returned with a brown bag. Inside was a plastic Tupperware bowl.

"Don't open it until you get home," she said.

"Suppose I get hungry on the way?"

"Well, then you pull over and eat. I don't want you getting into any accidents."

"I love you, Mom."

She reached out and patted my arm as if to say *I know*, then turned and walked back to the kitchen.

# 11

❧ HEADING INTO NEW York through raggedy puke-colored smog, I found the Lincoln Tunnel backed up for miles. Killing time in traffic, I dialed Walter Lahore's number again. It continued to ring without an answer. I popped out the Nina Simone tape I was listening to and flipped the radio to WINS, a news station. The weather was on. A fire in Montreal had dumped acres of smoke over New York State, producing the hazy conditions. Then the newsman told me why it was impossible to get through the tunnel.

There'd been a shootout at the entrance of the Lincoln when Port Authority police investigating a minor traffic accident stumbled onto Gene Kurtz, an escaped convict who'd been serving a life sentence for bombing a church in Atlanta sometime back in the late sixties. I remember read-

ing about the case in the eighties because it took the FBI
some twenty years to bring him to justice. Gene Kurtz was
a former Green Beret commando and a leader of a far-right
militia who'd published a book calling for Aryan resur-
gence and the repatriation or voluntary homelands for mi-
norities. The case had garnered lots of media attention
because it was discovered that for years the FBI had had
enough evidence to arrest Mr. Kurtz and had sat on it for
reasons nobody could fathom until a reporter from *The
New Yorker* began digging into the case and discovered that
Kurtz was once an FBI informant. Kurtz had escaped from
a federal jail in Missouri a few months ago. In the shootout
at the tunnel, one police officer was killed; Kurtz escaped.

Realizing it would take forever to get into the Lincoln, I
got off the turnpike at the first exit and headed south to the
Holland. At least there traffic was moving, though at a
snail's pace. It took me an hour and a half to get into the
city. As soon as I exited the Holland Tunnel, I called Detective Tim Samuel, an old friend in the 77th. About a
month after Detective Pagano was sentenced, it was ru-
mored that he'd paid somebody to whack me. Tim got
wind of it and alerted me, offering to be my bodyguard.
The rumor turned out to be a dud, but it was good to know
I still had friends in the department.

Tim worked days and was finishing up paperwork when
I called. He had a thing for Caribbean women, and we became tight after I hooked him up with a young postal
worker from Jamaica.

"Yo, Tim! It's Blades. Whaddup!"

"I can't talk to you now, Blades."

"Give me a hearing, cuz."

"I'm busy, yo."

"Won't take but a minute of your precious time."

"Sarcasm is really gonna get me to listen to you,
Blades."

"One minute. You can't spare a minute?"

"I ain't got a minute to spare."

"I need a favor, Timmy. Just a little one."

"You got some nerve calling me asking for a favor, Blades. Heard you and Big Ron were partying in Le Bar with some Trinidadian honeys the other night. You didn't call me then? What's up with that?"

"Yo, you got the script flipped, cuz."

"Shit, I'll tell you who's flipped. Go ask Big Ron for a favor."

"Don't believe a word Big Ron tells you, man. You know that guy's a freak. He wants to keep all the women his way. I was just blocking for him. I swear."

"I know your ass is lying, man."

"Word up. Wasn't my show, babe."

"Big Ron says you were handling the joints."

"Man, you know I'm married."

"Fuck, that woman is ready to divorce your ass. And you know it. She probably got herself some hotshot Hollywood producer because that's the only way she's gonna get into a movie. We know she can't act her way out of a kitchen."

"You're cracking me up, man."

"Yeah, you must be on crack. Thinking I'd do anything for you after you gave Big Ron all the suction."

"I really need your help, kid."

"It's gonna cost you, man."

"You got it, babe. Anything. Anytime."

"Make it quick. I got me some Jamaican punany to stir up tonight, and I don't want to be late."

"Whatever you do, don't try to eat that pussy."

"What's that?"

"Jamaican women don't like that stuff." I was having trouble holding back my laughter.

"I ain't even trying to hear that."

"Word, man. Trust me. I'm married to a Jamaican woman."

"I've met your wife, remember? She ain't got no Jamaican accent. She from down south. Besides, all women like that shit. Not that I would ever do it, but I seen that on Oprah. Women go crazy for that shit. All women. Jamaican or not."

"Not Jamaican women. They prefer to ride the dick all night, so you better pop a V-pill before you bounce."

"Man, what the hell you want?"

"I want you to pull the jacket on Walter Lahore. I need his address."

He hesitated. "Why the hell you looking for that loser?"

"Just do it, Tim."

"You don't need no address for Walter. You need a . . . what do you call those people? A medium."

"A medium?"

"Walter has taken up residence in the morgue."

"When'd that happen?"

"He checked in this afternoon around six. Paid in full with a thirty-eight through his temple."

"Do you know who did it?"

"Could be anybody. That piece of dog meat was always hustling somebody."

"Who's working the case?"

"Jerry Potts and Jack Forrest."

"Are they still there?"

"Try Houlihan's. I don't think you'll get far with those two, though. Tell me something, why you looking for that guy?"

"He left a message on my machine."

"Saying what?"

"Nothing important. Thanks, Tim. Enjoy your Jamaican punany. And don't say I didn't warn you if you try to eat the pussy and get hurt."

"Fuck you, man."

I heard the click and released the cloud of laughter I'd been riding ever since I started messing with his head.

* * *

LIKE EXTRAS IN a Wes Craven movie, the crackheads be-bopped and shimmied outside the methadone clinic on Flatbush Avenue, which stayed open until midnight. The ghoulish silhouettes of their animated bodies prancing as if delighted by some rhythm far removed from the real world made me think of puppets in one of those Malaysian the-atrical shows that play in New York from time to time. It also made me think of Jason.

As I got close enough to make out some of their pain-locked faces under the pink glow of the streetlight, I felt a sudden desire to know their lives. What brought them here? Did they think they would ever escape the grip of addiction?

I cruised past them thinking of the many times we shut-tled my brother off to rehab, each time farther away from home. Until he was so far we had to take a plane to visit him, only to have him get high the moment he got close enough to sniff New York.

And I thought of the drug dealers I'd chased and ar-rested, especially those who'd accepted the cuffs with dis-dainful glee, fully aware that in a day or so they'd be through the system and back on a corner in Harlem or Washington Heights in time to catch the next wave of bored, middle-class thrill seekers crossing the George Washington Bridge in their BMWs and Mercedeses.

I thought also of the many times I'd had my gun cocked, finger trembling on the trigger, itching to blow some repeat offender away, one less person on the street to entice my brother to get high.

Once I chased a dealer down 131st Street in Harlem. As I got close he dropped to the ground and reached into his waistband. In a split second I determined he was going for a gun and emptied my Glock. One bullet struck him in the neck, one in the chest. The others missed. He died. The suspect did not have a gun, but I was never sorry about shooting him until I, myself, lay in the hospital fighting for my life, the victim of an out-of-control cop's bullet. I don't remember ever feeling so alone and insignificant. My hospital room was crammed with flowers and cards, obstacles to feeling the real weight of my dying heart, but not enough to keep the face of the man I'd killed on that dark street in Harlem from appearing to me. Back then, in my arrogance, I didn't even want to accept that I could've been wrong. But alone in the hospital bed, I remembered his eyes, wide as day, angry and scared. If only I'd waited a split second longer. If only.

I GOT TO Houlihan's at the corner of Flatbush and Park Place around ten. Several groups of men were already engaged in an orgy of booze, and their noisy carnival threatened to spill into the street. Their alcohol-flushed faces were bright as red tomatoes ready to be peeled, empty beer bottles were stacked in the centers of tables like medals.

I found Jerry Potts hunched over a large whisky, which, from the glaze pulled tight across his pink face like Saran Wrap holding shredded leftover roast beef together, had been refreshed a number of times.

"How you doing, Jerry?" I said.

He turned and stared at me for a long time. I wasn't sure if he was attempting to smile and the muscles of his face had ceased to respond, but his mouth was an abrupt line. His gray eyes had a stealthlike steadiness and an edge sharpened by too many drinks alone in darkened bars like Houlihan's.

"You got some nerve showing your face in here, Blaze," he slurred.

I started to correct his pronunciation but stopped myself. People mispronounced my name all the time. In his state I doubt if he would understand. The stool next to him was empty.

"Mind if I sit down?"

"Would I be able to stand the stench?" he sneered.

I fought the urge to push him off his stool. As loaded as
he was, it would've taken but a touch. The bartender, a
large ruddy-faced man with a goatee, came over.

"What you having, partner?"

"Bourbon. On the rocks." I sat down.

The bartender swiped a wet spot on the bar top before
he walked away.

"Where's your running mate?" I said.

"Where's your wife?" Potts replied, his eyes focused on
the Yankee game on the large ceiling-mounted TV.

For a while I sat in silence, trying to organize what tack
I should take. I didn't know Potts very well, and it was
clear he was in a foul mood. Trying to be friendly wasn't
working. I looked around the bar, noticing a few familiar
faces, watching men who strut the street with such com-
mand and arrogance now stagger about the shabby bar like
toddlers.

The bartender returned with my drink. I swirled it
around slowly, watching the ice carousel smoothly in the
wide glass.

"I hear you're working the Walter Lahore case," I said.

He turned to look at me with a lazy insolent eye.

"Do you know who killed him?" I asked.

He smiled. His teeth were like a rat's, tiny and sharp, his
lips thin as sliced American cheese. "Where you from,
Blaze?"

"Brooklyn."

"No, I mean your family. You Puerto Rican or Dominican?"

"I'm American."

"You're American?"

"Yes."

"You look Puerto Rican. Or Dominican."

"I'm American."

He gulped his whisky, draining the glass. "You speak Spanish?"

"Look, Potts. I just..."

He cut me off. "You know Blaze, most of the men in here never even met you, but they don't like you. If I were to tell them that you came in here bothering me, they'd fuck you up. I know a lot of cops who'd like to get a piece of you."

He stared at me for a long time, his face hard and impatient.

"I ain't scared, Potts."

"People like you should be more grateful."

"That's supposed to be funny?"

"There was a time when people like you couldn't get on the force, you know."

"People like me?"

"Yeah, people like you. You know what the fuck I'm getting at."

He signaled for another drink, resting his hand casually at his side.

The bartender brought his drink quickly. Potts guzzled half in one swill, then looked at me with a bored, distracted smile, breathing with his mouth wide like a fish.

"What you did was despicable," he said. "The NYPD's got the finest officers in the country. We don't see race. We're all brothers. For ten years I had a partner who was black. We ate together. Attended each other's children's high school graduations. What happened to you was an accident. Plain and simple. Accidents happen."

"It's all over, Potts. Move on."

"You ruined a man's life. Tell that to his kids."

"You weren't there. He would've killed me. I wasn't a cop. I was just another nigger to him."

"How much money those hotshot lawyers getting you?"

"You know, Potts, if he'd come to me in the hospital and told me he was sorry it might've gone down different."

"You hit the Lotto, that what it's all about. What do you think all that money's gonna get you?"

"Fuck you." I took ten dollars from my wallet and placed it on the bar.

He continued. "I gotta push another fifteen before I can retire. Who knows if I'm gonna make it. Some crackhead might finish me off with a lucky shot. You don't think I'd like to hit the Lotto too? I buy twenty-five dollars in tickets every week. A hundred dollars a month. The stock market belongs to the rich, and the rest of us slobs play Lotto. You hit the Lotto, Blaze. I envy you."

I wanted to hit him. Instead I turned and began to walk away. He grabbed my arm. His eyes were hollow and pitiful.

"Where you gonna go with all that money? Back to Puerto Rico? No point staying in New York. It's all fucked up here. I used to love New York. It used to be a great place to live. Until they started letting all the foreigners in. They're destroying America, these foreigners. They're destroying this city. New York ain't what it used to be. New York ain't New York no more. And it's going to get worse. You know why? Because they hate us. Hate our way of life. Why the fuck they wanna come here if they hate us? I'll tell you why. They wanna destroy us. They're like locusts. Coming in waves. You know why? The rest of the world is going to hell. The Third World will soon be the Dead World. More disease and famine is going to hit Africa than you read about in the Bible. AIDS will destroy all those countries in the Third World. If I was a religious man, I'd say these were the last days. The only country that will be spared is America. It's the only place that will be able to feed its people. That's why they wanna destroy us. So where should I go when I retire, Blaze? Do you think I'll be safe in Puerto Rico?"

I left him at the bar choking on his own words.

# 12

THE LAST TIME I ran into Walter Lahore he told me he worked for Iron "Stubby" Clapp, a known pimp. That was six months ago. Walter had called to warn me about Stubby Clapp. Now he was dead. Stubby and I had a history. It was going to be a bad night for one of us.

Stubby Clapp was a successful pimp largely because he was an ex-cop. His girls worked Linden Boulevard and the adjoining side streets. He also owned a greasy spoon on Hegeman as well as a number of run-down apartment buildings in East New York, where most of his girls lived. Cops looked the other way to Stubby's criminal activities because whenever one of them got horny they knew they could pick up one of his girls for a blow job.

Stubby Clapp had come to the NYPD by way of the Army. He'd been a drill sergeant for ten years before he resigned after being passed over for a promotion. When I was assigned to the Thirty-first Precinct in Harlem, he was the top undercover narcotics officer, bagging more collars than anyone else. We got on well. I was lucky to cut my narcotics teeth under him; it got me instant prestige.

Once, in the middle of an undercover operation where we were about to score five kilos from a group of Dominicans on 145th Street, someone who I'd busted about a month before and who was supposed to be in jail walked into the room. Stubby saw that my cover was about to be blown and flew into action.

"Yo, what the fuck this nigga doing here?" Stubby screamed, and tackled the guy who'd just entered the room.

Before the guy could speak, Stubby pulled out his gun and turned to the others in the room: "I just saw this muthafucker talking to Five-O down the block. I ain't waiting for them to pounce on my ass. I'm outta here."

Grabbing the money bag, I scooted out the door behind Stubby before they could collect themselves.

A year later Stubby was caught by the Feds taking bribes from Ice "Cash Money" Brixton, the biggest drug lord in Harlem.

Several times, through my network of informants, I was poised to bring Brixton down, only to have him slip through my fingers because, I discovered later, Stubby had been tipping him off. I had a personal dislike for Ice Brixton because one of his crew had passed my brother a batch of tainted cocaine that had left him in a coma for nine days.

Stubby Clapp cut a deal with the Feds and got off with probation. It didn't sit well with me, especially after Cash Money skipped bail and was never seen again. One night I stopped two New Orleans Bloods with two kilos of heroin and a bunch of choppers in the back of their Bronco. I took the guns and the heroin and put the gangsters on a bus to New Orleans. That night I broke into Stubby's car and planted the weapons and the drugs. Then I dropped a coin on his ass. The cops waited until he got into the car and arrested him.

The next day I bumped into Stubby as he was being transferred to Rikers. He was in handcuffs and spat at me. I slapped his face with the butt of my gun, breaking all of his front teeth.

Stubby got five years for the drugs; the weapons charge was thrown out. After serving three years he got probation.

It took me fifteen minutes to reach my destination on Hegeman Street in East New York, a neighborhood as different from the one I'd left in New Jersey as you could imagine.

I spotted Stubby's burgundy Caddy outside the diner and parked a block away, opposite a Dominican One-Stop grocery. Lotto was $118 million, and the store was doing brisk business, with a line that snaked around the block.

You can tell a lot about the affluence of a neighborhood by the number of trees or parks it contains. Hegeman was a shoddy street in a shoddy neighborhood, a neighborhood with no parks and treeless streets. A pair of women's undergarments lay on the sidewalk. I saw used condoms, used Pampers and hypodermic needles. The closest thing to an outdoor café in this neighborhood was eating fries in your car in the Burger King parking lot, and if you were looking for a bookstore you'd have to wait for the weekend sale at the East New York branch of the Brooklyn Public Library. It was a neighborhood of bars, liquor stores with bullet-proof shields, mom-and-pop stores manned by armed Dominicans, storefront churches sealed tight except for Sundays, and funeral parlors. A neighborhood of children, women and old men because most of the young men were in the armed forces or on lockdown.

The restaurant stood out against the grimy background. It had a shiny silver exterior, with a multitude of neon lights proclaiming its royal nature: Clapp's Palace.

I waited for two elderly gentlemen to exit the restaurant before entering. Inside, I stood scanning the room quickly. The low-intensity blue fluorescent lights gave the place a cloudy haze, like the opening shot of a noir movie. The sharp smell of hot grease and burnt meat pricked my nose, and I was glad I hadn't eaten my gumbo yet.

There were half a dozen customers in the place, each one sitting in a separate booth. I sat at the counter and ordered coffee. A plain-looking young girl with a face full of blackheads took my order with the indolence of someone who'd been on her feet all day and was beginning to cramp in the ankles. Her reserved smile showed off gold caps on her front teeth. She seemed to fit with the place: not too pretty, a little gaudy and overdone in some areas. I asked her if Stubby was around, and she pointed to his office in the back. Each finger on the hand she pointed was wrapped in gold. Just goes to show, you don't have to work at Goldman Sachs to know how to invest. I got up and walked back in the direction she pointed.

Struggling with his zipper, a middle-aged man came out of the bathroom opposite the office, letting out a dank urine-laced smell. I waited until he'd closed the door to the john and passed me along the narrow corridor before I knocked on the door to Stubby's office.

"Who the fuck is it?" Stubby's voice bellowed from behind the door.

That was all I needed to hear. Taking a step back for leverage, I executed a quick, powerful kick with the heel of my boot, busting the flimsy plywood door open.

Out of the corner of my eye I saw a squat man coming toward me moving crablike, low and sideways. I couldn't tell what it was, but he had something dark in his hand, raised to attack. I blocked his thrust partially, the blow glancing off the side of my head, and snapped the sword of my elbow as hard as I could into his windpipe. Like a shot bird, he fell without a sound, crashing into the side of

Stubby's desk. When I looked up, Stubby was reaching for
something inside his desk drawer.

I flew across the desk and drove my head into his stomach, piling him into the wall. I grabbed one of his trophies
off the wall and blasted it over his head. The trophy
snapped. He buckled and I brought my knee up as savagely
as I could, connecting with his chin. Blood splattered as I
felt his false teeth dislodge. He fell over onto his side, a
gun and his teeth clattering to the floor. I picked up the gun
and pressed cold steel to his face. Blood spewed from his
lips as if it were a broken pipe. He was in such pain, his
head kept rolling from side to side.

"Who killed Walter Lahore?"

"Fuck you, you half-white muthafucker!"

"Walter drops your name on my machine. Hours later
he's executed. Don't you think that's a little odd?"

He tilted his face, his eyes trying to focus on my face,
but said nothing.

I dragged him by his lapels to a brown love seat against
the wall. He wasn't a tall man, about five-six, round as a
rhino with a face to match. His head seemed too big for his
body, sitting square on broad shoulders with barely enough
neck to pivot. Doorknob eyes protruded from thick, meaty
eyelids below his high, beveled forehead.

The room was quite small, a huge desk and a black
leather chair taking up most of the space. The walls were
filled with pictures of Stubby in Army battle gear.

The air was damp. The room was sweating the odor of
stale fried egg. One shaded bulb in the ceiling offered a
dull light.

Stubby struggled to get to a sitting position and mumbled through the blood, sending a geyser of spittle into the
air. "I taught you everything you know, pussy."

I stepped away from him. Snapping the clip out of the
Glock, I tossed the gun onto his chest. "Not everything,

partner. If I find out you had anything to do with Walter's death, I'ma come back and make you eat those false teeth."

The short man who'd attacked me was out cold. His flat face and pointy ears gave him the appearance of a gargoyle. I stepped over him and went through the door.

The restaurant was empty. The rumble in Stubby's office had caused the patrons to leave their meatloaf and pork ribs on greasy plates and head for cover. The waitresses were bunched together on the sidewalk, I surmised waiting for the cops.

Mangy dogs prowled the debris in a lot across the street. As I walked to my car, the bark of sixteen-wheelers thundering along Linden Boulevard filled the night, and the smell of gasoline in the humid air made me think of exploding bombs.

# 13

THERE WAS PLENTY of parking on my block, and I found a spot opposite my building. As I squeezed out of my car I caught a shadow over my left shoulder. Instinctively, I swiveled on my heel, ready to strike.

"Blades, it's me!"

"Precious! Shit, I almost clocked you."

"I've been waiting for you."

I leaned against the car. A numbing ache blighted the side of my face. My heart thumped heavily against my chest.

Precious stood in front of me, her face wrapped in a smile of such innocence, it made my paranoia laughable. Dressed in a loose-fitting blue dress, she seemed to be waiting for me to say something.

"What're you doing here?"

"You left me at the altar," she said. "I came to give you a second chance."

"I'm sorry. I left you a voice message."

She touched the side of my head. "You're bleeding."

"It's a scratch."

She held my arm. "Come on, let me take a look at that."

Like a dutiful son I let her lead me across the street. The night air, full of sweet flowery scents, rustled the leaves of the giant oak tree in front of my building. A ghetto bird circled overhead, shining bright light down on the projects not far away.

Upstairs, she set me down at the kitchen table. "Do you have any antibiotic ointment?"

"There's something in the bathroom," I mumbled.

"Where?"

"Straight down, to your right."

She left and quickly returned with bacitracin, alcohol and cotton swabs.

"Take off your shirt."

"It's only a scratch, really. No need for all this fuss."

"Take off the shirt, big baby."

"I don't let anybody call me baby unless they're naked," I said.

"Are you propositioning me, Mr. Overstreet?" she said, her voice layered with mock surprise.

"Yes," I said, surprising myself.

She leaned forward to peer into my face. She looked tired. Yet, there was something in her eyes that held me transfixed, a remarkable steadiness like a deep flame.

She smiled. "Let's take a look at that cut, bad boy."

"A scratch is not a cut."

"Come on. Off with it."

I grabbed the tail of my polo shirt and yanked it over my head. Blood had trickled down my neck and chest.

She cleaned the blood, then applied ointment to the cut on my cheek. After depositing the soiled cotton in the garbage, she stood near the fridge, toying with the magnets, which kept an assortment of photographs, recipes and missed appointments in place on the fridge door.

"You have any coffee?" she said.

"Blue Mountain and some Brazilian."

"What's your favorite?"

I thought carefully. "Blue Mountain."

"Good choice. I'll make a pot."

My kitchen was small, but cozy. It had been freshly painted just months before, and was bright and clean. Fresh thyme and rosemary lay in baskets hung from the ceiling. Curry, cayenne pepper, peppermint and other spices were lined off on the shelves. It had an aroma of tropical spices, which was what I used to love about my grandmother's kitchen.

I sat watching her turn around in my kitchen with ease and precision, reminding me of my grandmother, who cooked these elaborate meals of spicy pork and chicken with rice and beans, and lots of pungent homemade drinks for her big family in Crown Heights. Even in the loose dress I could see the outline of Precious' potent hips.

I drank my coffee in silence. She methodically added sugar to hers and stirred it over and over before taking a tentative sip. Slowly she licked her upper lip, precipitating a smile.

"Good coffee," she said.

I smiled, feeling myself being drawn deeper into the dream of her presence.

"How was the audition?" I said.

"Oh, that. It got postponed."

"Why? What happened?"

"The person I was supposed to read with got sick."

"But you're still gonna read?"

"Eventually."

Her answers were snapped rather than spoken, and she seemed uneasy about answering questions about the audition. Perhaps, like some actors, she was superstitious about discussing roles she was interested in. Anais got like that sometimes.

"How'd you get that cut?" she said.

"Scratch."

"Whatever."

She was sitting across from me. A hushed sadness descended on her face. It was a rich face, finely tuned to the beat of her own inner energy and desire.

"Is your father still alive?" She smiled. And even with the sadness in her face, when she smiled her eyes opened wide as if to envelop the world.

"Yes," I said, feeling a warmth that I hadn't felt in a long time.

"Are you close?"

I hesitated. "I wouldn't say so. I'd been mad at him for a long time."

"Not any more?"

"I don't know."

"Why were you mad at him?"

"I don't want to talk about it."

"He left you, didn't he?"

"I said I don't wanna talk about it."

"Was that what you meant when you said we may have more in common than I think?"

I drew a deep breath and exhaled.

"I'm sorry," she said. "I don't mean to be so persistent. I feel things deeply, and I'm not afraid to express my feelings."

"Are you suggesting that I am?"

"No. I guess what I'm trying to say is that I really like you. And I'm curious. I suppose I want to know more about you than you're willing to share at this point."

"Why didn't you share with me the fact that Congresswoman Richardson was your aunt?"

"Who told you?"

"Was it supposed to be a secret?"

"No, not at all. It's just that many people don't know we're related."

"So why didn't you tell me?"

"I didn't think it was relevant. She will only tell you what she told me. To get over it. To move on. Yada-yada-yada."

"Do you think she knows who your father is?"

"She claims not."

"Do you believe her?"

She leaned her face to the side and sighed. "I believe she knows."

"Why wouldn't she tell you?"

"I don't know."

"Are you prepared to move on if I fail?"

She walked up to me and began to stroke my chest. "Right now I'm prepared to take you up on that proposition," she said. "Is it still on the bed?"

She slipped the dress straps off her shoulders and the garment fell to the floor. She was naked underneath. Other than a tiny scar above her navel, her skin was as even and shiny as marble. She turned and, without looking back, walked to the bedroom as I watched the weave and roll of the two perfect spheres of her ass.

I became one hungry puppy. All I could think of was lapping milk from the curve of her back. I wanted to nestle my head and go to sleep in the hearth between her legs. To feel the warm swell of her breasts, the wave and lash of her thighs around my waist.

I found her sitting cross-legged on the bed and fell into her outstretched arms. Gently, she pushed me onto the bed. She lay on her side next to me, caressing my chest for a while. I felt myself begin to relax, to smoothen out like a sheet in the wind, and closed my eyes. Immediately Anais' face flipped onto the screen of my mind. I opened my eyes to block it out. There was Precious leaning over me, her eyes moist, her lips parted slightly, her breath sweet as a chocolate.

"I was told once that the most intense sex comes when you feel totally overwhelmed and helpless. That's when you want to do the freakiest things. That's how I feel. Like being freaky," she said.

She unzipped my pants, then stood up and slid them down my legs. She nestled her face on my hip, and rolled her head over my groin with childlike exuberance. My dick was already a block of marble. Beginning with slow, soft kisses, she slurped along the surface of my skin, sending chills of pleasure to my brain. She slid up my body, biting, kissing the length of my torso until we were face to face. Hers was wrapped in a dreamy smile. I'm sure mine was too. I closed my eyes again. This time Anais didn't appear.

Back and forth Precious brushed her cheeks against mine, as if trying to imbue me with her scent. Her skin was soft and amazingly cool. It felt like I was being massaged by the wind. Silently, her tongue disappeared deep into my mouth. And like two sword fighters dissolving into darkness to outwit each other, our tongues locked in a fierce battle of passion.

We kissed for a long time, her body writhing on top of mine with mystical power and sensuality. My fingers fiddled with the curls of her pubic hair, then they honed in on the wet, pliant flesh beneath. First one finger. She moaned. Then two fingers. She wiggled around and bit my lip. The pain was brief and intensified my passion. I kissed her harder, my tongue becoming more insistent, wanting to expand in her mouth.

She slithered all the way up until her sex covered my mouth. With agonizing patience she teased my mouth with the meaty lips of her sex. Every time I reached for it with my tongue she'd take it away. Finally, I grabbed her hips and pulled her down to my face, darting my tongue inside.

"Lick me, baby," she cooed. "Lick me like you own me."

She made a strange sound, like a river deep in her throat was overflowing, and began to grind herself into my mouth. I held on to her ass as she rocked backward and forward, my tongue tapping out a gentle circular rhythm on her clit.

"Just like that, baby. Ooh, shit! Lick me!"

Her body stiffened for a moment, and she cried out as if she was about to come. But she rose up, slid down my body, and took me inside her. It felt like my dick was being swallowed in butter. She leaned over and her tongue vanished into my mouth again. I flipped her over so that I was now on top.

"Mash up the rasclot' punany, bwoy," she said, in a rich all-out Jamaican twang, reserved, it seemed, for lovemaking. "It's all yours. Mash it up."

Her skin was bright with a thin sheen of sweat as I slid into her again, finding myself inside a sheath of such heat, an inner space of such richness, that I no longer knew if what I was experiencing was real or a dream. She whipped her pussy up and around my dick, as I fought to stay in touch with her quick, powerful thrusts. I held on to her. She held on to me. We made love without inhibition, screaming and clawing at our demons, as if locked in a struggle to make sanity of our passion. We stayed locked all night and into the early morning hours.

# 14

❧ IT WAS DEEP into the day when I sprang from the deep
℄ chill of a dream with a terrifying knot in my stomach.
I thought I heard a jackhammer in the room but it was the
telephone. Frozen in a zone of disbelief, I waited for my
brain to catch up. Light seeped through the yellow venetian
blinds, giving the room a pale glow.

I dreamed I'd accidentally shot my brother instead of
the drug dealer he was buying cocaine from. What a
fucked-up thing the subconscious is. Nightmares are every
bit as powerful as reality. The phone stopped ringing.

"Blades?" Precious' whisper was barely audible from
the other room. Her head came into view at the door.

"There's a woman on the phone. Said her name is
Anais."

"Shit!" I grabbed the cordless from her, which she was

holding like a bomb. She looked apologetically into my eyes.

"Hello?"

"Who's that woman answering your phone?" Anais' voice was cold and hard.

"Her name's Precious."

"You fucking her?"

"Look, Anais—"

The next sound I heard was a deafening click. Precious was a few feet away, leaning on the doorjamb, one of my silk robes pulled around her like a blanket. I was naked. We looked at each other awkwardly.

"I'm sorry," she said.

"Not your fault. I don't think she was coming back anyway."

"I'm still sorry."

"What time is it?" I looked around for my boxers.

"Eleven."

I straightened up. "Eleven? You sure?"

"You were sleeping so soundly I didn't want to wake you."

I gave up searching for my shorts and looked up at her. Her dancer's neck seemed even more elongated and graceful this morning.

"Did anybody else call?"

"No. I'm making you breakfast. You like pancakes?"

"Yes, I do. I'll take a quick shower. If my partner calls, tell him I'm not gonna make it to the store until after lunch. His name is Leroy. And I love lots of butter on my pancakes."

She laughed. "How do you stay so trim eating like that?"

"I love butter. Only thing tasting better is you."

Her high-pitched laughter rang out furious as a summer shower. "You're such a flatterer. I bet you say that to all the girls."

"I don't remember any other girls before you. You erased my memory last night."

"Ooohh, lover boy. For that you get another taste after we eat. Unless you'd rather chocolate for breakfast."

"You shouldn't tempt me like this. How'm I gonna find time to look for your father?"

She patted my butt. "Maybe you can erase all that from *my* memory."

"Can I ask you a question?"

"Anything."

"Do you ever wear underwear?"

She laughed out loud. "Not in summer if I can get away with it."

I walked off to the bathroom, a fat smile on my face but with a weighty heart knowing that what little chance there was of Anais returning from the West Coast was now flattened.


IT WAS HOT in the kitchen so we decided to eat in the bedroom, where the air conditioner had been going all night. Dressed only in black boxer briefs I called Milo to tell him I wouldn't be in until later. Precious had not relinquished my robe and sat across from me, her back resting on the headboard.

She'd evaluated my CD collection and found it lacking in quality reggae music, but a few cuts had met her approval. A Beres Hammond joint was now playing on the stereo in the other room.

She stopped eating and stared off through the window. Sunlight filtered through the thin leaves of the tree outside the window to settle around us.

I put my fork down. "What's the matter?"

"I want you to know I don't often do this."

"Do what?"

"I got the impression you and your wife were separated."

"We are."

"But you still love her."

"It's very complicated."

"What's so complicated about love?"

I sat back. "If it's so simple why do people break up?"

"Men don't know their own minds, that's why."

"Oh, you subscribe to the 'men are children' philosophy?"

"Does she still love you?"

"I don't know. Like I said, it's complicated."

"Do I remind you of her?"

"Why do you ask that?"

"I don't know. We're both actresses. We both used to dance. What does she look like?"

"Do you really want to talk about her?"

"I'm sorry, but seeing the look on your face while you were talking to her was very upsetting."

I took a sip of coffee. I wanted to tell her that I wished Anais was out of my life, but what a lie that would've been.

She said, "I've been without a man for over a year. Not by chance. By choice. Do you understand what I'm telling you?"

"What about Jimmy?"

"What about him?"

"I thought you two were close."

"There's nothing between Jimmy and me, if that's what you're hinting at. You think I would fuck you if I was fucking Jimmy? Aren't you two good friends?"

"I'm not always sure about Jimmy. He can be a little erratic at times. He has a tendency of disappearing on me. I need to talk to him. Have you seen him?" I said. "I must've written down the wrong number. The number I called was disconnected."

"Not since the day he introduced us."

"Isn't that odd?"

The phone rang and Precious flinched. It rang for a

while as I imagined Anais' angry voice swelling in my head.

"Aren't you going to answer?" Precious said.

I picked up the phone. It was my mother.

"Carmen! Thank God you're there."

"What's the matter, Mom?"

She started to cry. Her voice faltered as she tried to speak through her tears.

I started pacing. "Calm down, Mom. I can't understand what you're saying."

She stopped talking. I could sense her gathering the storm of her emotions. When she started to speak again, her voice was soft but steady.

"Jason," she said.

"What about Jason?"

"He left for New York last night right after you did. He hasn't come back yet."

"That's only a few hours, Mom. Did he tell you where he was going?"

"He put on that shirt you brought him and said he was going to play baseball."

"He leaves Jersey to play baseball in the middle of the night and you let him go?"

"He said they have parks in New York with lights. How do I know? He hasn't called once. And I don't know why I didn't notice it before, but the small painting in the dining room next to your photograph is gone. It's worth about a thousand dollars."

"You think he took it?"

"Who else?"

It was a bad sign when recovering addicts began stealing. I was tempted to tell her we should let Jason fall on his own sword. But I knew what her response would be, and I knew I wouldn't be able to live with myself if I said that and something terrible happened to him.

"Is he driving his car?"

"Yes."

"I'll find him, Mom."

After I hung up I stood staring at a painting my father had given me before he went off to live in Barbados. The bright blue seaside scene, one of many he painted while he was there searching for his roots, held little cheer for me right now.

Precious came up behind me. She opened her robe and collected me to her sweat-glazed body, her breasts, like warm bread, pressing into the muscles of my back.

"You okay?" Her voice begged me to forget my concerns, to dismiss the world and sail off on her magical body.

"I gotta go out," I said.

"Where?"

"Personal business."

"Please, do you really have to? I don't want you to go."

I didn't want to turn around, to look into her eyes. It'd been so long since a woman pleaded with me not to leave her, my bruised ego was eager to pimp my brother's weakness for her embrace.

"Don't you have rehearsal today?" I said, still not turning around, afraid to present my vulnerability.

"I'm free for a whole week. My character has gone off to visit an old friend. And all my calls to the apartment automatically bounce to my cell. So I'm yours as long as you can stand me. How long will you be gone?"

"I don't know."

"I'll stay until you come back. I'll cook for you. Don't look so surprised. I didn't grow up with a silver spoon in my mouth."

I laughed.

"You're so beautiful when you laugh," she said.

"I bet you say that to all the guys."

"Only the ones who whisper my name in their sleep."

"Did I do that?"

"It was lovely."

I turned to face her now. Her eyes were full of passion and the darkness of her pupils was so pure they seemed to glow.

"There's a spare set of keys on top of the fridge in case you need to go out," I said.

"Just point me to the nearest fish store. Do you like fish?"

"Try Fish Tales. On Court Street. Just ask anybody. It's a neighborhood landmark."

I GOT DRESSED quickly, throwing on a pair of jeans, gray Perry Ellis polo shirt and sneaks. Precious was in the kitchen when I went to say good-bye.

"Hurry back," she said.

I kissed her. She clung to me.

"I'll call as soon as I can," I said.

She nodded.

I went out the door and down the stairs. On the first landing I peeked over my shoulder. She was still standing in the doorway, the robe open, watching me with a wide smile. I wanted to turn around.

# 15

A FRIEND OF mine—a former cop turned college professor—once said that we live in a nihilistic culture, a culture without feeling, where the quest for meaning, for truth and love, is meaningless because everything has been reduced to a game. Even ideology is a game. If, as Potts said, the rich are obsessed with playing the stock market and the rest of us with winning the lottery how can we expect to have a sense of loyalty, of fairness?

I was fifteen when my brother, then a junior at North Carolina, brought his girlfriend to spend a weekend with us on spring break. We lived on Garfield Place in Park Slope, one of the truly mixed neighborhoods in New York. Jason introduced first my mother and then my sister to his girlfriend. When he got to me he said: "This is Carmen, my brother."

His girlfriend said, "Oh, he's your adopted brother."

"No," Jason said. "He's my brother. Biological."

"But he's black," she protested.

"Nobody said he wasn't," Jason replied.

"Does that mean you're black too?" the girl said.

"Would you have a problem with that?" Jason said.

She didn't reply. I don't know what else was said between them in private, but a short time later, two days prematurely, his girlfriend left to take a flight back to Chapel Hill.

No matter what was going on in his life, I always felt that Jason loved me without reservation. And all my life I've tried to love him that way. At times it was difficult. Especially when I saw him so balled up on drugs he was unable to unbutton his own shirt. Through it all we've remained loyal to each other.

I suspected Jason had gone off to get drugs. This wasn't the first time I'd had to search for him. Most times, however, I'd had the vast resources of the NYPD at my disposal, including beat and patrol officers, as well as friends in undercover who would tip me off if they saw or heard anything. Quite a number of times I'd found him around 116th Street in Manhattan. I got the impression he was comfortable with the addicts and dealers in that area.

I drove around hoping to spot his car. Around two o'clock I hit jackpot, spotting the brown 1990 Honda Accord outside an abandoned building on 120th Street.

With a high fence around it, the building looked empty from the outside, but I knew not to let appearances deceive me. Addicts were famous for taking over abandoned buildings. I walked around to the front of the building, looking for signs of life inside. All of the entrances were boarded up, but a trail of empty beer cans and Burger King wrappers led me to a hole in the fence at the back of the compound.

I crawled through the space and up a flight of steps. The piece of plywood that had guarded the back entrance been ripped off and lay on the ground. Graffiti scribbled on it read *Death to the Diallo Cops*.

I walked into the dark building and stood still, letting my eyes adjust to the blackness. For a minute I considered fleeing the stench of rot and decay. The smell was overpowering, and I could not imagine Jason spending any time in this place. But this was the process. I had to eliminate every possibility before moving to the next one.

I called Jason's name as I explored each room. They were all empty of life but overflowing with blight. Carcasses of rats were nailed to the walls, as if the addicts had dedicated this as a museum to how low they had sunk. Makeshift beds made of boxes and crates cluttered one room. There was a room with books. Good literature was high on the minds of some addicts, it seemed. Soiled and rotten clothing had been trampled into the floor.

"Jason!"

"Will you shut the fuck up? I'm trying to get some sleep over here." The voice echoed from a deep chamber somewhere in the building.

"Where're you?"

"In heaven, muthafucker. Wanna know how I got here?"

I traced the voice to a room near the front. Sprawled on a bed made from IBM computer packaging filled with blankets and sweaters was a thick bump of a man. He was shirtless, and his head was covered in knots matted to his scalp with dirt.

"Who the fuck are you?" he said.

"I'm looking for somebody," I said.

"You've come to the right place," he said. "I'm waiting for Godot. He should be here soon."

"I'm looking for a big white guy. Over six feet. Two hundred and fifty pounds. Long hair. He's wearing a Dodgers baseball shirt."

He scratched his head. "Dodgers. Baseball. Duh! If you say Dodgers you don't have to say baseball. Capisce?"

"Capisce. Have you seen him?"

"You the police?"

"I'm his brother."

"You Blaze?"

"Something like that. How'd you know my name?"

"The nigga was here. Kept saying he got a brother who's black. Said your name was Blaze. We didn't believe him. You adopted?"

"Where's he now?" I said, ignoring his question.

"Maybe I know. Maybe I don't."

I took a twenty out of my wallet and held it in my hand. The addict's gaze shifted to the money, a lurid gleam in his eyes.

"Try Brooklyn," he said.

"What part of Brooklyn?"

"She said she was from the Marcy projects."

"She?"

"The bitch he with."

"Did he say why he was going to Brooklyn?"

"He didn't say shit. He and the bitch rolled me. When I woke up they'd bounced like Jell-O. But I got mines before she left." He smacked himself in a self-congratulatory manner on the thigh and rolled his eyes, laughing.

"Who's the woman?"

"A thief. Stole my money, the fat bitch."

"What's her name?"

"Said her name was Cherry. We met her in the park last night. I bet she lying. She definitely didn't feel like no cherry. More like a watermelon, you know."

"What'd she look like?"

"I just told you. Fat."

"Black? White? Short?"

"Fat short black bitch. That enough of a description for ya?" He looked at me with one eye closed and scratched his crotch. "Now you gonna give me that money or not?"

"Maybe I will, maybe I won't."

"You gonna try to shake me too, muthafucker?"

"I don't like you."

"Well, I ain't aiming to suck your dick neither."

"You spend too much time with your head up your ass, you know that."

"Go piss on yourself," he taunted. "At least I know who the fuck I am."

"You like being a crackhead?" I took a step toward him, my fists clenched.

"Yeah, I like being a crackhead. I'm a nigger crackhead and I like it."

"You're a nigger crackhead, alright."

"And you a nigger who think he white. I know all about your fucked-up family. That's all the nigger would talk about. Excuse me, your brother. Your mama likes black dick, he likes black pussy. And you like to pretend you're all one big loving family." He started to laugh.

"Fuck you."

"Your black-dick-loving mama."

I wanted to crank him, but I knew I would've probably killed him if I touched him. I turned and walked away.

"Hey, you cheap wanna-be-white muthafucker," he screamed.

I kept walking.


I CALLED TIM at the precinct as soon as I got outside. As I waited for him to answer the phone, I inspected Jason's car. Why did he leave it? Had it broken down? Tim picked up after the fourth ring.

"Detective Tim Samuel," he drawled.

"Tim, my man," I greeted.

"Not now, Blades. I'm busy."

"I need you, Tim."

"You always need me. I must be your wife."

"Who needs a wife these days?"

"I do. That's why I gotta go. I got somebody on the other line."

"Just listen for a second, Tim. I'm looking for my brother."

"Good luck. Bye."

"Tim, I need your help. He's in Brooklyn. Probably the Marcy Houses. He's with a fat black chick. Name's Cherry. Might be an addict. Or a prostitute. Can't be hard to spot a big white dude in the projects."

"You kidding me, right?"

"I wouldn't kid about something like this, cuz."

"I can't help you, Blades."

"I don't want to find my brother dead, Timmy."

"You need to have that boy committed."

"You're talking about my brother, Tim."

"If he were black would you be cleaning up after him like this?"

"Go to hell, Tim. I'll find my brother my damn self."

I SPENT THE next few hours walking around the Marcy Houses, located in the Downtown Brooklyn area, searching for Cherry and my brother. Many of the residents I spoke to—women and men in their sixties and seventies sitting out on benches in the tidy park next to the block of gray high-rise buildings—had lived there all their lives, had seen its rapid decline when crack became the hot business opportunity of the eighties, stirring the entrepreneurial spirit of everyone from grandmothers to kids not even old enough to have a wet dream. Some of them had witnessed murders, muggings; the sale of drugs in their hallways; seen addicts peeing in the stairwell; still they refused to leave. This was their home.

Their perseverance seemed to have paid off. Crime in the projects was down. Crack profits had dried up. The park was safe again for them to sit outside on a muggy day.

No one remembered seeing a man answering my brother's description with a fat black woman. And no one knew Cherry.

I left the Marcy Houses around four and dipped into a Caribbean restaurant on Fulton Street for a roti. I called my mother from there to see if Jason had come home. My mother was in tears. I tried to calm her down. She wanted to come to New York, but I convinced her it was best to stay home.

I called Precious. She was out. I left a message that I was going to Prospect Park and would be home by seven. It felt strange leaving a message about what time I would get home for someone other than Anais. At the same time, I was eager to get back to Precious.

# 16

**A GREAT DEAL** of creative energy had gone into an attempt to turn the Picnic House into a tropical retreat. It had failed. The big bright lilies and potted palm trees might've been enough to simulate the warm atmosphere of the Caribbean were it not for the pall on the faces of everybody in the room. They all looked like they would rather be someplace else.

This was to be a celebrity event hosted by Congresswoman Richardson to kick off the upcoming Labor Day festivities. Except most of the celebrities hadn't shown up. Still, it was an assembly of the most influential Caribbean people in New York. The congresswoman sat at the center table, flanked by her good friends Mary Bath, the Chairperson of the Caribbean-American Chamber of Commerce, and Ignatious Ralph, one of the people responsible for making the annual Caribbean-American Labor Day Parade a major political event.

I waited until Congresswoman Richardson had finished her welcoming speech, apologizing for the absence of the Mayor and other celebrities, and sat down. Away in the corner a steel band began to play. Jack Rosen, Brooklyn Borough President, was making his way to the podium. Through the maze of bodies, fruit-laden tables and palm trees in large green pots squeezed tightly together, I made my way toward the congresswoman's table.

About fifteen feet away the congresswoman's security, seated at a table to her left, intercepted me. But I wasn't about to be detained.

In a voice loud enough to draw everyone's attention, I demanded my release from the four officers who'd grabbed my arms and shoulders. The band stopped playing. Jack Rosen stood at the podium looking as if he'd just suffered whiplash in a traffic accident. The chaotic shuffle of chairs replaced the music.

"Vondelle," I yelled. "I need to talk to you."

The congresswoman stood up. She was a tall woman of very dark complexion and wore her hair pulled severely back into a tight bun. In a stunningly beautiful gold-and-black African-print dress that seemed to hug her body too snugly, she appeared ill at ease: as if the outfit had been selected by someone who didn't understand her taste. She picked her way through the network of seats and came up to me. Her eyes were animated, her heavily matted eyelids flickering madly like butterflies' wings.

"You'd better have a good explanation," she said through clenched teeth.

I started to speak.

She gave me the stop sign. "Outside," she snorted.

Her boys released me and I followed her outside. Behind me I could hear the shuffle of backsides reclaiming seats as Jack Rosen urged the guests to settle down.

Congresswoman Richardson walked a few feet down the paved path and stopped near the road, lighting a cigarette.

"What do you want?" she said. Her voice was choppy, icy cold.

"Do you know who I am?" I said.

She glared at me. "You're wasting my time, Mr. Overstreet."

"Your niece went to meet a man the other night and found a dead FBI agent."

She sucked ravenously at the Winston. "What's that got to do with me?"

"She went hoping to find her father."

She turned around. "Good-bye."

"She seems to think you know who her father is."

"Are you done?" She filled her mouth with smoke, then let it out slowly. Her hand trembled. She flicked the cigarette onto the ground and mashed it out.

"Why're you trembling?" I asked.

She pursed her lips with deliberateness. "You have no manners and I'm very angry."

Gabriel Aquia strutted from the Picnic House, ever Mister *GQ* in a fashionable gray suit, blue shirt and blue tie. You had to admire anyone who could dress like that in this heat. Standing a few feet away, he adjusted his glasses and cleared his throat.

"The guests are getting impatient, Vonnie," he said.

"I'll be right there, Gabe."

Gabriel stuffed his large hands into his pockets and waited.

"How you doing, Gabe?" I said.

Gabriel Aquia flinched. His face was pinched like he was trying to keep a fart from escaping. Then he turned and walked back into the Picnic House.

"If you know who her father is, why wouldn't you tell her?" I said.

Her brown eyes swept the ground. "Let's walk," she said.

Arms crossed over her bosom, she stepped onto the road, heading in the direction of the library. I walked beside her as skaters, joggers and cyclists floated by. To our right in Long Meadow Field, barbecue pits were going full blast. Picnic baskets were being emptied. Sun worshipers were getting burned. Volleyball and soccer players worked up a sweat. The air was dense with the green smell of freshly cut grass.

"You have some Caribbean roots, don't you?" she said.

"My grandmother was from Barbados."

"Ah, Barbados. Lovely place. You ever been there?"

"A number of times."

She reached out and touched my arm, squeezing gently. A smile swept across her face. "You should join us in the Picnic House. We have many Caribbean delicacies. We even have flying fish."

I laughed. "It's tempting, but I have somebody home cooking a meal for me."

"How very fortunate for her. Is it my niece?"

Her question caught me off guard, and I fumbled for a reply.

She laughed before I could respond. "How long have you known Precious?"

"Long enough to know she would give anything to find her father."

"Precious is a very complicated woman. Take my advice. Drop this matter. It will benefit no one. Whatever she's paying you, I'll double it."

"That wouldn't be ethical. Besides, I like her. If she wants to know who her father is, I think she deserves to know, don't you?"

She came to a halt. The park was bathed in an amber glow. A bright glaze masked the sky, and the tips of the trees glowed as if they were on fire.

"I have to get back," she said calmly.

"One last question."

"I have nothing more to say."

She turned and started to walk away.

"Can you get the Mayor to settle my case?"

She laughed. "I'll wash your back if you wash mine."

I watched her enter the shadows under the trees. I stepped off the road onto the grass and made my way to my car.

# 17

AN AMBULANCE AND two fire trucks blocked my street, so I parked a block away on Union. The cops had cordoned off about ten feet of sidewalk opposite my building. A man with his head wrapped, working on the fire escape on the adjacent building, leaned over the metal railing waving to workers below. Curiosity seekers sat sipping water in the gardens across the street.

I tried to tell a rookie securing the perimeter that I lived in the building, but the youngster puffed up his chest and pointed me to his superior, who was smoking a cigarette halfway down the block. Then I spotted a uniformed cop I worked with briefly in the Seven-One. His name was Paquito Torres, a rangy Dominican brother with a long face and an appetite for pork chops to match. He turned around when I touched his shoulder.

"Blades, what's up with you, brother?" He grinned cheerily, flashing fresh white teeth, and clasped my hand tightly in small sweaty palms.

"Doing okay, Paco. What's going on?"

"Still trying to represent, brother."

"When're they gonna let you out of those bibs?"

He laughed. "Any day, now."

"You said that last time I saw you. When was that?"

"A year ago. Central Park. I was doing the Sting concert."

"Yeah," I said. "Think of the money you'll save."

"I'm ready, man. Can't stand this fucking uniform."

"What's going down?"

"You live here?"

"A year now."

"I thought you lived in Queens."

"My wife went west in search of a gold statuette. I ended up with more space than I needed."

"It ain't criminal to be alone, man."

"Feels that way sometimes, though. So why the artillery?" I said.

"Homicide."

"Who?"

"I don't know. I'm just a perimeter junkie."

"Can I go in?"

"Sure, follow me."

As we entered the building, my neighbor from across the hall, Mrs. Galloway, an old woman in a green dress and slippers whose hair color ranged from beehive gray to purple on any given day in the week, was being helped through the door by two officers, I presumed to the ambulance waiting outside.

"Mrs. Galloway? Are you okay?" I said.

Her deeply wrinkled face was blank and ashen. She looked at me as if staring into a dark deep well.

"Shock," one of the officers said. "She found the body."

"Where?"

"Four-B."

My lungs became instantly sealed with lead. I couldn't breathe. I thought my heart was about to explode.

Two at a time, I bounded up the stairs, the thud of my shoes on the wooden steps shattering the hush in the narrow stairwell.

The door to my apartment was open. I rushed in. A female detective knelt in the kitchen beside a body. Another detective, a slender black man, stood inches away.

They heard my wheezing and looked around. I moved forward. The black detective tried to block my progress, but I threw him aside like a piece of used tissue and rushed to the body on the floor. The kneeling detective stood up and stared at me with sharp, focused eyes. She was a big woman, a head shorter than me, with the girth of a football lineman.

She stepped aside and I knelt beside the body.

Precious lay on her side in a bed of dried blood, which had caked the color of mud. My robe was wrapped grotesquely around her. She'd been shot in the head. Her twisted face was blotchy and puffy as though she'd been beaten with a crowbar.

"You recognize him?" the black detective said behind me, speaking to his partner.

"The famous Blades Overstreet," the female detective scoffed.

I got up from the body and dropped into a black straight-back chair. The female detective loomed above me like a spreading oak.

"I'm Sergeant Romano. He's Detective James," she said.

"What's her name?" James said.

"Precious," I said. "Who did this?"

The two detectives looked at each other and shared a private chuckle. I was too shocked to care that it might've been at my expense. Why would anybody kill Precious? She was too beautiful to die this way.

"Precious what?" James asked.

"Just Precious," I said.

"What kinda name is Just Precious? Was she a prostitute?"

I glared at him. He held my threatening gaze without flinching.

"Don't you watch TV?" Romano said to him. "She's on the soaps."

"Who's got time for that shit? Were you fucking her?" He persisted, staring at me with cold, egg-colored eyes.

"That's none of your goddamn business," I blurted out.

"There was a murder in your kitchen, pus-brain. Whatever you did with the bitch is now our business," he said.

I lunged at him. Romano stepped between us and grabbed me in a half nelson, sending me face first into the fridge door. Her thick arm, bulging against the seams of her blue shirt, felt like a chunk of wood against my neck.

"Relax," she said.

She held me until my breathing calmed, then released me, standing close to see if I would resume my attack on her partner.

"Sit down, Blades," said Romano.

I stared past her at James standing next to Precious' body. He had a tight face, scrupulously clean-shaven with bushy eyebrows and the tensed feral look of a fox. I saw the muscle mass in his bony jaws contract and relax as he breathed heavily.

I still wanted to hit him, to get him away from Precious' body.

My menacing stare was beginning to antagonize him. He took a step toward me, beckoning with outstretched arms. "Come on, bitch! You wanna piece of me?"

Romano held me securely by the neck before I could move, pushing me roughly toward a chair. I refused to sit down, and for a while we tugged each other around the room like tired tango dancers. Exasperated, she released me.

"Are you going to calm down?" Her puffy eyes were red.

"I'm calm. Just keep that animal away from me before I rip his tongue out," I said.

Romano turned to her partner. "Relax, Bernie."

"He ain't a cop no more. We don't have to coddle him," James screamed. "He knows the deal. Let's take his ass to the precinct."

"For what?" I said.

"Anything. Suspicion. Who gives a shit!"

"You take me from here, you better have a reason, otherwise I'm gonna have my lawyers so far up your ass you're gonna be begging for Ex-Lax," I said.

James rushed at me. Romano tackled him and held him in her beefy arms.

"Let me go," James screamed.

"What the hell's wrong with you?" Romano said.

"He's mad because he can't get off the plantation," I said.

"Fuck you, you traitor," James shouted.

Romano released him, and he sulked off to the window that looked out onto the backyard, chewing on a hangnail on his thumb. Romano came up to me.

"What was she doing in your apartment?" Romano asked.

She was so close to me I could smell her cigarette breath. Her spicy deodorant stung my nose.

"She was a friend. I left her here to go take care of some business."

"When was that?"

"Around twelve."

"Where did you go?"

"Around. Manhattan mostly."

"Anyone saw you leave?"

"I don't know."

"Was she alive when you left?"

I looked at her sharply. "Very much so."

"When did she get here?"

"Last night."

"So she spent the night?"

"Yes."

"Who else knew she was here?"

"I don't know."

"There was no sign of forced entry."

"What're you trying to say?"

"I don't have to spell it out."

"I didn't kill her."

"Right now you're a suspect. The only suspect."

She questioned me for another fifteen minutes before the coroner arrived to take the body. The two detectives left, taking Precious' belongings wrapped in plastic bags. I was alone with the dried blood and the chalk outline of her body on the tiled floor. That's when I broke down and cried like a child.

# 18

TWO HOURS LATER I still hadn't cleaned up the blood. I drank beer after beer until I felt myself slipping into a reverie that I hoped would lead to sleep.

The apartment had been ransacked. But I was too shocked to pay much attention to it, much less look to see if anything was missing.

There were three messages on my machine, all from my mother. I was too weak to call her back. All I could think of was finding a way to forget. A way out of this nightmare. My head and stomach began to ache. Then I started to feel the coarsening of anger. Someone had walked into my house and committed murder. Destroyed the tranquility I'd tried to create for myself in this chaotic city. My home had been desecrated, and somebody was going to pay.

I called the Great Wall Chinese restaurant on Court

Street and ordered shrimp in black bean sauce. They said it would take fifteen minutes.

Longing for the illusion of cleanliness, I took a shower and changed into khaki shorts and a yellow tee, just in time to hear the doorbell. Slipping on my sandals, I stumbled downstairs. I realized I was drunk or close to it. The Hispanic delivery boy was waiting in the vestibule, a red baseball cap dangling, peak backward, on his head. The meal was ten dollars; I gave him fifteen.

His bike was tied against the rail ten yards away; a rusted lump of iron that could've been mistaken for discarded junk. I held the bag in one hand as I stared at it as if hypnotized.

For a fleeting moment a light flared in my skull, as if some prehistoric memory of the origin of man had suddenly been implanted in my brain. The alcohol-induced light turned gray, then it dulled to nothing.

I ran after the delivery boy as he wheeled away. Looking scared, he hopped off the bicycle.

"Do you speak English?"

He nodded.

"How much for the bike?"

"Qué?"

"Your bike. I want to buy it. How much?"

He hesitated, looking at me as if my head was full of snakes. I reached into my pocket and pulled out sixty dollars.

"Maricón," he muttered.

He grabbed the money, jumped on his bike and sped off. I limped after him cursing, too intoxicated to run, finally giving up at the intersection of Bond and Sackett, about two and a half blocks away.

Exhausted, I sank down onto the sidewalk. There was no rational explanation for what I'd just done. What was I going to do with that rusted piece of shit? I didn't want to go back to face Precious' blood. I didn't want to have to clean it up.

I opened the plastic bag and took out the white bowl of shrimp. The rice came in a thin cardboard box. They'd sent white rice instead of brown. I thought for sure I'd ordered brown. I hated when they did that. The shrimp were overdone and the sauce too oily and bitter. After a few mouthfuls I threw the rest in the street.

As I walked back, the warm night air touched my face and I experienced a surge of energy. I thought of the light that had just flashed in my head. Was I about to lose it?

I stood outside my apartment building in despair about going back inside. I didn't want to talk to my mother. I couldn't talk about Jason now. I was too angry. Precious' death made me angrier with Jason for letting us down once again. I was grieving for Precious, but it felt as if I should really be grieving my brother. Without our will, we are no more than a lump of coal or a block of rusted metal, like the delivery boy's bike. My brother, shooting heroin or cocaine into his veins, or shoving his dick into some bloated crackhead, was as dead as Precious lying in the morgue because he'd surrendered his will. I hated my brother for being so weak. At least Precious had fought to stay alive. But as much as I wanted to, I still could not hate Jason.

I started to walk again. Moving like the dead in a horror flick, oblivious of the world around me, I headed up Court Street. Night buzzed around me. Lost in the jungle of my own pain, I saw flashes of light and blurred images dancing around, but nothing registered in my mind. I didn't know where I was going and I didn't care.

Somehow I managed to cross Atlantic Avenue against the light without getting squashed by cars and trucks thundering in both directions. Meandering through the tiny streets of Brooklyn Heights, I found my way to the Esplanade.

Filling the night like the roar of a stampede, the rumble of traffic on the BQE seemed to bring me to life. I stood leaning on the rail, dazzled by Manhattan's million lights reflecting off the shiny black face of the East River. Behind me, on the terrace of one of the apartments, a group of people was howling to Frank Sinatra tunes. They sounded drunk. They sounded happy.

I left the Esplanade when a young couple chose the bench behind me to get their freak on. My wandering became aimless again. I started down the clean cobblestones of Hicks Street in the direction of Atlantic Avenue. Gardens thick with shrubs and flowers drifted by, and the fragrant flowers of the leafy linden trees hung in long-stalked clusters, floating soft sweet aromas in every direction. I paused to inhale the rich, haunting scent, wishing I was far away in the country.

A silent squadron of mosquitoes swooped down from the branches above my head. After their first sortie, in which I sustained one sting, I moved briskly on. I'd just crossed Atlantic Avenue when a black sedan with tinted windows pulled up ahead of me. As I drew abreast, one man in a dark-colored sweat suit jumped out and stuck a gun in my face before I could react.

"Get in the car," he whispered coarsely.

Surprise and panic stopped me dead. But only for an instant. My street-cop instincts immediately took over. The man was very close to me. Too close. A bob of my head was enough to distract him. I slammed my hand down hard on the gun. Off-balance, the gunman tried to aim. I crashed the heel of my hand into his neck and snapped my knee viciously into his groin. He crumpled to the ground.

Another man jumped from the car. I turned to run. His voice barked behind me.

"Easy muthafucker, or you're dead!"

I froze with my hands in the air.

He came up behind me and pushed me into the metal grating of a closed deli, jamming his gun into my neck. The cold shock of steel against my ear sent my body limp. My eyes and head were throbbing, but I tried to relax. His body was pressed close to mine. He stunk of pizza and beer.

"You think you're Jackie Chan, eh Blades?" Pizza-Breath taunted. "Well Jackie Chan this muthafucker."

He jammed his knee wickedly into the small of my back. My chest slammed into the corrugated gate, blasting the air from my lungs. Then he grabbed my head and smashed it into the metal gate.

I was dazed but conscious. My mind struggled to focus. He knew my name. Was this a robbery? Who the hell was this cheese-guzzling scab?

"Get in the fucking car," he hissed.

Like a mosquito's sting his spit splattered against the back of my neck. Desperate for breath, I inhaled deeply.

"You heard me, muthafucker?"

"Who're you?" I managed to whisper.

"Wrong move. Simon didn't say you could speak."

He cracked my head against the fence again.

"Okay, okay," I cried.

Holding the gun under my chin, he led me to the car. As if it was on a timer, the back door opened the moment we got there. I was shoved inside. Stubby was coiled in the far corner, his face dark and swollen from our last encounter.

Stubby spat in my face. To retaliate then would've been stupid. I casually wiped the spit from my forehead, staring at him as he unwrapped a fat cigar.

He sniffed the stogie, rolled it under his nose then bit the tip and spat it in my face. "You're a pussy, Blades, but not good enough to get one of my cigars."

He laughed at his own joke. Fear was beginning to crawl up my bowels. Of all the nights to get drunk, I had to pick one when Stubby came crawling out of his sewer looking for me. In Stubby's eyes burned a dark fire, a look I'd seen humble many an overconfident dealer.

"You think I'm going to kill you, don't you, Blades?"

I didn't answer.

He sniffed the cigar again, more slowly this time. "Are you scared?"

"Takes more than your ugly grill to scare me," I said.

"You should be scared, muthafucker. I could crush you with my bare hands. But I have something special planned for you."

He began bobbing his head, nodding to himself. He addressed Pizza-Breath, who I now recognized in the light as the man with the gargoyle ears. "Where's Noodles?"

"Left that nigga rolling around like a break-dancer. Blades got him in the nuts."

Stubby put the cigar in his mouth. "You're lucky he didn't fuck you up too. I taught this nigga everything he know, then this muthafucker turned around and tried to shake his dick in my face."

"Let's be truthful here," I said. "I pissed on you."

Stubby snorted. "That you did, Blades."

"Let me shoot him, Stubby."

"Shut up. Go get Noodles."

Pizza-Breath got out cursing.

"I wouldn't think of running if I were you, Blades. Simon ain't too fucking bright. Shooting a man is easier for him than eating pussy."

Stubby took a brown paper bag off the floor and reached inside. He pulled out a bar of soap.

"You know what this is, Blades?"

I didn't answer.

"Answer me, nigga!"

I refused. He slapped me across the face. The blow caused my head to swivel around so hard I fell back against the seat.

"See this bar of soap, Blades?" He tried to laugh but a snarl came out. "I've been carrying this around for six muthafucking years. I knew it was you who set me up, muthafucker. And I might've forgiven you. I understood how you felt. Stupid as it was, I understood your crusade. You never understood the problem wasn't the dealers but weak muthafuckers like your brother. You were out to save

the world. But I hold you responsible for what happened to
me in the joint. One evening I was in the shower. A bunch
of cocksucking road runners I'd sent up jumped me.
Caught me off guard and knocked me around. I was half
conscious when they shoved a bar of soap up my ass. Then
they took turns raping me. Gave me the muthafucking
virus. That's right, Blades, I got the virus. I got it in jail. I
got it because of you. You understand what I'm saying,
bitch? I can't forgive you for that. I've taken care of each
one of those muthafuckers that jumped me. When I got out
of jail I just wanted to kill you. But that seemed too easy.
I'm glad I waited."

Simon returned with Noodles, still writhing in pain.
They got into the front seats, Simon behind the wheel.

"Sad what happened to your girlfriend, ain't it,
Blades?" Stubby said.

"Did you kill her?"

He started to laugh. It was a heavy laugh, lazy, like
sludge going through a sewer. "Give me a light, Simon."

Dark face beaming as if he was about to get laid, Simon
whipped out a lighter and lit up the car yellow. I could see
Stubby's face clearly now, round, sweaty and swollen. He
puffed twice and the cigar glowed. His swollen lips twisted
in a freakish grin as he blew smoke in my direction.

"Did I kill her?" His laughter filled the car like a cannon
blast. I could see his whole body shaking from his mighty
heaves.

"Why, I thought you killed her, Blades." His chest rat-
tled with laughter again. This time Simon joined in, and
Noodles, whimpering like a spayed puppy, did soprano on
their a-capella performance.

"Just about now the cops are pulling a thirty-eight out of
a Dumpster on Ninth Street. Guess who it's registered to,
Blades? After they run ballistics they'll find it's the same
gun you used to chop the Fed. By tomorrow every cop in
the city will be jerking off on your picture."

I filled my lungs with air. This was it. Stubby had busted his nut. I kept reminding myself to breathe and relax. This wasn't the time to go crazy. Let Stubby settle into his after-climax glow.

"I'd like to feed your brains to my dog, myself, Blades. But I'm gonna give you a choice. Which is more than you gave me. I want the laptop you boosted from that apartment. Give it to me and I'll let you go. You can take your chances with the Mayor's boys. Refuse and go straight to dead."

"I don't know what you're talking about."

"Is that your final answer?" He puffed a few times, filling the car with thick gray smoke.

I didn't reply. He slapped my face.

"Answer me when I talk to you," he screamed.

Hot tangy breath rushed out of his mouth. I kept my face turned to avoid my eyelashes getting singed by the smell coming up from his bowels.

"Can I make a suggestion?" I said.

"Bitch, the only thing I wanna hear from you is where that laptop is."

"I'd recommend a good dentist. Your mouth needs scrubbing. And a good laxative to cleanse you, my friend."

Stubby's eyes wobbled in their sockets. Then he grinned, showing new white dentures. "Simon, let's take this muthafucker to the morgue."

Simon started to cackle, head bopping up and down with glee.

"Shut the fuck up and drive the car, you idiot," Stubby growled.

Simon ceased his antics immediately, like a wound-up toy that had suddenly run out of batteries. The car lurched forward, then gradually, evenly picked up speed. Stubby kept looking at me as if expecting to see fear in my eyes. I leaned against the seat, absorbing his curiosity.

I knew the door on my side wasn't locked. I had already

formed a plan of escape in my mind. The car turned down
Kane and stopped at the light on Court Street. I looked out
the window. At the cinema on Court Street a large crowd
was gathered outside. I don't know what was playing, but
the line snaked down the block.

I waited, my eyes directly on Stubby's face. My stomach churned with fear, but I tried to keep it out of my eyes.
No way would I give him that satisfaction. The car turned
right onto Court Street. Exactly what I was hoping for. As
we approached the cinema, I opened the door and threw
myself onto the sidewalk. I landed hard on my shoulder
and rolled to a stop.

The shocked crowd shrank back. I heard the squeal of
tires as the Lincoln screeched to a halt. I was already on
my feet. I rushed into the crowd of moviegoers. I didn't
see, but someone must've gotten out of the car with a gun
because the crowd began to scamper. Women were screaming around me.

I raced through the crowd and away into the night.

# 19

I OWNED TWO guns: a nine-millimeter Glock auto and a .38 semi. As soon as I reached my apartment I called my old friend, Noah Plantier, who kept both of them. Once a cop himself, Noah had been in a theater group with my father back in the seventies. Noah was now a theater professor at City College, where I'd taken a few classes.

His phone rang a number of times before the machine came on. I left my mobile number and hung up. If Stubby wasn't bluffing about this gun—and my gut told me he wasn't—I wanted to know if it was the gun Noah had been holding or another gun someone had managed to register in my name. With the kind of identification required and background checks done by the authorities, it wasn't easy to register a gun under someone else's name. But it was something Stubby could pull off. In any event, I was taking no chances staying in the apartment tonight.

I made two more calls: one to Tim Samuel, the other to Trevor Lester. Neither was home. I was annoyed that I hadn't heard from Trevor. There might be something on that computer to help me out of this mess. I wondered how Stubby had found out about the computer. T-J perhaps? That meant she was probably one of his girls. And her presence in that apartment across from the FBI agent might not have been a coincidence. Why was Stubby after that laptop? And if, as he hinted, getting revenge on me was merely opportunistic on his part, what then was the primary motive behind these murders?

Changing into black jeans and a gray short-sleeve shirt, I grabbed my car keys and whatever money I had stashed away inside my Bible, and left the apartment.

It was minutes to midnight when I phoned Milo from the car.

"Blades, boy, what happen?" Milo's voice slurred like he'd been drinking. "Why you calling me this late?"

"I'm coming over. Make some coffee."

"All I got is Nescafé."

"That'll do."

MILO LIVED ON Rugby Road and Avenue H. As I picked my way through traffic on Ocean Avenue, I could hear music exploding from mass camps along the way, filling the night like a tropical breeze. The noise and the bright neon signs along Ocean Avenue gave the night a gaudy vibrancy, a reminder of what separated New York from other cities. Pre-Carnival revelers mingled and milled about the street, moving slowly, dreamlike, as if emerging from a long slumber to prepare for the event that would crown the New York summer.

It took half an hour to reach Midwood. I parked on Avenue H across from Milo's building—a large prewar red brick complex of about twenty apartments. I crossed the tree-lined street and rang the bell. I was tensed and breathing hard, even though I'd only walked a few feet. When Milo buzzed the door open, I fell into the lobby with naked relief.

The marble lobby was brightly lit. Two ceiling-length mirrors filled one wall. A group of sharply dressed young men speaking Creole were huddled together against the wall near the bank of elevators, preening in the mirrors. As I stood waiting for the elevator, I caught a faint whiff of ganja coming from a ground-floor apartment.

Two men stepped into the elevator behind me. I hadn't seen where they'd appeared from, and I felt my heart quicken. My senses were on full alert.

We reached the sixth floor and I got off. I heard the elevator door close behind me and breathed a deep sigh. Christ, I was getting jumpy. My stomach growled, but it wasn't hunger.

Milo's apartment was at the end of the corridor. I was about to knock when he opened the door dressed in gold-and-purple Lakers shorts and a vest.

"I heard the elevator," he said.

Milo's two-bedroom apartment had been taken over by Carnival. Wire, shiny multicolored cloth, sequins and paper covered just about every square inch of the living and dining rooms. Half-done costumes hung from hangers. Bent wire and remnants of cloth were heaped in corners. The smell of glue, sweat and alcohol permeated the apartment; Milo himself smelled as if he'd fallen into a vat of Old Oak. A strained, fever-pitched voice screeched one of the latest soca tunes through Milo's tower speakers.

"Perfect timing. I just done make the coffee, eh, man," he said.

Around Milo's neck hung a bright red cloth tape measure.

"You ain't getting too old for this shit, Milo?"

"'Til I die, Blades. 'Til I die. When Carnival come, I is everything. Designer. Tailor. Seamstress. Iron-bender. Superman. I don't sleep. Just me and my music going all day and night. It's the best time of year."

"I wish you'd work this hard at the store"

"How would you know? You hardly there."

I maneuvered my way through the jungle of cloth to the kitchen. I filled one of his *Trinidad Is Carnival* mugs with coffee and returned to the living room to find him on hand and knees snipping slinky purple cloth.

"Boy, I have to get these costumes to the mass camp by Sunday night, else I dead, eh," he said.

"Looks like a lot of damn work for one day, Milo."

"But I enjoy it, eh. When I see these costumes on the Parkway, is pride I feel, eh. Pride. When you see women dancing in your costume. Oh God, boy. That is the feeling. Nothing else can compare."

I shrugged and sat on the edge of the sofa, sipping my coffee.

"You need to come dance on the Parkway, boy," said Milo, looking up at me. "You need to jump in a band."

"Right now I need to jump in a bed."

He sat up and turned to face me, grinning and rubbing his weary-looking eyes. "Boy, you the strangest man I know. You the only man would drink coffee before going to sleep."

"Not now, Milo. Don't needle me. I'm drowning in shit."

Milo dropped the scissors onto the floor and stood up. The grin had faded from his face. "What's going on, boy?"

"Nothing for you to worry about."

"I is your partner. If you got problems, it sure to affect the business."

I told him what I could, leaving out the part about framing Stubby six years before.

"I need a drink," he said after I'd finished my story.

"Don't forget you gotta open the store tomorrow," I said.

He crinkled his eyes and went to the kitchen, returning with a bottle of Old Oak rum and a short glass. In the oversized shorts his skinny legs looked like a bird's.

He sat on the floor and poured a drink. "Blades, man, you can't come here and scare me so."

"It's all in your mind, Milo."

"That's your answer to everything. Man, if your mind so powerful, how come you can't get over your wife? That's where this whole thing start."

"How you figure that?"

"You still heartbroken. That's why you in this mess. You was using this woman to get over Anais."

He tilted his head back and gurgled the brown liquid down his throat, letting out a hoarse breath of fire.

"Shut up before I call Immigration and have your ass shipped back to Trinidad."

"How come you can't get over Anais if your mind so damn strong?"

"I ain't even hearing you, Milo."

"I seen this woman on TV. This Precious. She's very pretty, but the only reason you sleep with her is because you can't get Anais."

I rested the cup on the floor. "What you want me to tell you, Milo? That I still love Anais? That I can't seem to get over her? I don't know how to stop loving the woman, Milo. Are you happy now?"

I stared at him, angry with him for making me admit something I'd been trying to ignore. Silence anchored itself between us. He began to cut a pattern from a piece of silver cloth that looked like foil.

"I'm going to sleep," I said, and walked away.

"Hey, Blades."

I stopped and turned to face him.

Putting the scissors down, he tossed the silver cloth into a basket on the sofa and got up, inching around the piles of cloth until he was in front of me.

"Your mind can't do something you don't want it to do. I've watched you ever since Anais left. You don't really want to forget her. You fighting pride so hard you hardly living. Come to the Parkway, man. Come back to life."

"I don't see your apartment overflowing with lovers," I said sarcastically.

"Then you blind. Look around you. Every one of these costumes in here is a person who appreciates me."

"I have my family for that."

"Who? Your cokehead brother who don't know his ass from his mouth? Your white sister who wouldn't care if your black ass disappear tomorrow?"

"Milo, you better slow your roll before I bend your skinny ass around one of these wires. First of all, Jason's sick. And second, Melanie is not my *white sister*, all right? She's my sister. Get that through your fucking coconut."

"That girl don't like you. She hate the fact that she got a black brother."

"Maybe, but she's still my sister."

"Your sister? What kinda sister that? I wouldn't want somebody like that to be my sister."

"It's my problem, not yours."

"I know how it burns you up, Blades."

"Don't worry about what burns me up. Just make your stupid costumes."

"It ain't no more stupid than you thinking that girl will ever accept you."

I pushed him. He stumbled backward and fell onto a heap of cloth. He grabbed his scissors and jumped up, waving the scissors in the air.

"You can't bully everybody, Blades," he said, his voice rising with urgency and passion. "You can't beat up everybody for telling you something you don't want to hear. It'd be nice if things were as simple as you make them sound. Melanie is your *white* sister whether you want to hear it or not. That's the way America see it."

"Well, fuck America. Fuck everybody. You don't know my family. I don't see my family that way. I don't see my sister that way."

"That's your choice, Blades. If you wanna stay blind to who she really is, fine. But as your friend I telling you that you can't have it both ways. Just because she's your sister don't make her holy."

"Leave me alone, Milo. I don't meddle with your family. Don't meddle with mine."

I retreated to the bedroom and closed the door behind me.

# 20

❧ I OPENED MY eyes to the sound of loud chanting. I lay
motionless, waiting for my mind to focus. The sound
seemed to be coming from far away, and at the same time it
had such a surreal sweetness I could easily have been
dreaming. Slowly, my mind embraced daylight and reality.

Rain was falling against the window in rhythmic sheets,
the loud echo resonating like choral chants. As I listened, I
felt a kind of spiritual longing to be in the rain, dancing,
waving my hands and singing. I didn't know why I felt that
way. Like I needed to release something deep from within
my heart. What Milo said the night before came back to
my thoughts. I tried to push it from my mind.

Milo hollered from the living room. "Blades! Come
here, man!"

Before I could move, he appeared at the door, excitement shining in his eyes. "Blades, come quick! The Mayor is on TV. He's talking about you."

I didn't rush. I was quite familiar with the Mayor's diatribe. He was a man unable to admit that he was wrong about anything. I put on my pants and went into the living room.

The Mayor stood in front of a line of microphones, his patented comb-over barely managing to cover his scalp. One side of his mouth sagged heavily and his lips crimped at the edges, making his long slit of a mouth droop like someone who'd suffered a stroke. His wide-set horse's eyes bulged with glee as he enthralled the reporters.

"I'm not surprised that this individual is a suspect in a pair of rather brutal murders," he was saying. "I tried to tell you all before. But you wouldn't listen. Blades Overstreet is unstable. Three years ago I suggested that he needed professional help. For him to think that what happened to him then was anything more than an accident was ludicrous. This is a man who once expressed a desire to kill his superiors. Clearly this is a man who shouldn't have been a police officer, given the right to carry a weapon. We try to hire the best people for a tough job. It's not a perfect process. Now it looks as though he may've killed not one but two people, including an FBI agent. We found some rather disturbing pictures on his computer. The same kind of pictures found at the scene of the FBI agent's death. I don't want to speculate, but therein may be the motive for these killings. I promise you we will bring this confused man to justice."

Milo looked stupefied. "He's crazy, that Mayor."

"There's gotta be a law against maniacs getting elected to office."

"You want some coffee?" Milo said.

"You bet. Black."

Milo, still dressed in the clothes from last night, headed to the kitchen. I wondered if he'd slept at all.

The Mayor's news conference was continuing. He was answering questions about who he would be supporting in the upcoming congressional elections.

Just then there was a loud banging at the door.

"Open up! Police!" a voice barked from outside.

Milo ran out of the kitchen looking like he'd crapped in his drawers. Signaling to Milo to stall them, I rushed to the bedroom. I stumbled into my shoes and was about to leave without my shirt when I spotted it under the bed. Shirt in hand, I opened the window. The banging had gotten louder. They were busting the door down.

The window opened onto a huge oak tree, the nearest branch to me being about three feet away. Fifty feet below was a railway track. If I timed my jump well, I could catch onto a branch and climb down.

I jumped from the window. But the branch I grabbed was thick and wet. My fingers slipped and I lost my grip. My momentum sent me hurtling into the branches. I banged my head against the trunk and was stunned momentarily as I slid out of control, finally coming to a stop wedged in the *Y* of two branches.

I struggled to catch my breath. There was no sign of cops below. I reached up and grabbed the branch above me. My head was spinning, my heart exploding in my chest, but I'd suffered no broken bones.

I scuttled down the wet knobby trunk, jamming my thumb on a jagged branch. When I got within range, I jumped to the tracks. Every imaginable type of refuse lay beneath my feet. Keeping my eyes peeled for an outlet to the street, I ran down the canyon of debris, sidestepping bottles, cans, clothes, rotted tires, trying to ignore the stench. It was hard to believe these tracks were still used.

The rain was steady but not hard. At the first clearing, I clambered up the embankment, laying in the wet grass like a wild animal, scanning the street for cops. My lungs were pasted to my ribs, and I was wheezing like a 1960 Thunderbird on a hot summer day.

Putting on my shirt, I ducked under the perimeter fence separating the tracks from the houses and stepped onto the street. I looked up at the street signs to see where I was. East Seventh Street and Avenue H. My car was six or seven blocks east. Drenched, I walked briskly along Avenue H toward Rugby Road. My palms were slick with dirt and blood. I dried them on the side of my pants.

I reached Coney Island Avenue and crossed the street, walking under the arched canopy of trees that lined the street to Westminster Road. I got no farther. There was a line of police cruisers, two emergency service units and five unmarked cars down the next block.

Quickly, I walked back toward Coney Island Avenue, trying to think of what to do. I was concerned about Milo. In my haste I had forgotten my cell phone. There was a subway station nearby on Newkirk, and I headed that way.

I got some change and called Milo from the train station. He didn't pick up. I assumed the police were still questioning him or had taken him away.

FIFTEEN MINUTES LATER I was sitting hunched over on a Manhattan-bound Q train, my head resting heavily in my hands. The exertion on an empty stomach and the realization that I was a hunted man had drained all my energy. The adrenaline I'd used to escape had dissipated, and my head now felt as if it'd gotten in the way of a Mark McGuire home-run swing.

The train gradually began to fill up. I had lost count of the stations, but we were still in Brooklyn. A plan was beginning to formulate in my head. I would get the D train in Manhattan, heading for the Bronx. It seemed like a good place to begin, since that was where Noah lived.

Noise erupted around me with the suddenness of a car crash. Above the murmur of shuffling paper and subdued coughs, a shrill voice slammed my eardrums. I looked up to catch the offending mouth attached to a plump black woman with tiny fish eyes. The object of her wrath was a flat-faced, stocky man with slight blond hair and eyebrows thick as lawn grass.

When he replied, his thick European accent made it difficult to understand what he was saying, but Bessie Smith, cursing him in A-minor, seemed to have no such problem.

In the few moments that had gone by, they had fired enough invectives and racial epithets back and forth at each other to kill any peace treaty. But when the woman called the man a "Russian thief" and the man retorted in a high-pitched voice that she was an "ignorant monkey," blows began.

I couldn't tell who struck whom first, but the woman was getting the worst of the exchange. I got up and pushed my way past a scrawny white man and stepped between the two tongue-weary combatants. The woman was huffing as if she'd just run the New York Marathon. Froth swelling at the corners of the man's wide mouth made me think of a horse after a race.

The man stared at me with wild green eyes. I could tell he wanted to push me out of the way to get at the woman, but he didn't dare. I met his stony stare with a cold reverb of my own. We were locked in a stare-down, like a horn riffing to the bebop of the piano.

Other black women on the train applauded my action. In their eyes I was the black archetype that they could only dream about: a strong black man protecting a black woman from the wrath of the white monster. In my mind I was just trying to stop these two fools from prolonging my nightmare. If word filtered to the conductor that there was a fight on the train, the cops would be here sooner than I could spit.

Above my head they continued to shuttle words like *monkey*, *Russian mobster*, and *cocksucker* back and forth. Everybody, black and white, and Latino too, were begging them to shut up already.

We reached West Fourth and the black woman got off, but not before challenging the man to join her on the platform. He declined with a condescending snarl that she was too ugly to be seen with. The train pulled out of the station, and I moved away from the green-eyed troublemaker to stand at the far end of the train.

It's startling how swiftly bad news travels, how easily stereotypes become archetypes. Even before some immigrants come to this country it seems as if they already know that before they can taste that elusive delicacy called the American Dream they must distance themselves from America's nightmare: its *niggers*.


THE RAIN HAD abated slightly when I got off the D train at Yankee Stadium in the Bronx. Raindrops like soft kisses on my skin raised the hair on my neck. By the time I reached Noah's apartment, the rain had melted away the memory of my train ride, and I was back to the ugly reality of my present dilemma.

# 21

✿ NOAH PLANTIER WAS a man of uncanny self-control,
a true friend, blessed with great patience and integrity.
Once he was paid $200,000 to write a movie script about
drug dealers and cops. When he turned over the script, the
producer told him the black people sounded too intelligent
and asked Noah to fix it so they sounded more *street*. Noah
tore up the script and returned the money.

He'd spent many years as a cop before retiring to study
theater and film, going on to get a Ph.D. During that time
he began researching his roots. He discovered that his
great-great-grandfather had come from Haiti and that
somewhere in the process of assimilation the original family name of Plantier had been changed to Planter. Noah
promptly contacted a lawyer and had his last name
changed to Plantier.

It was at Noah's suggestion that I started taking courses at City College when I left the NYPD. I took one of Noah's playwriting courses and enjoyed it so much I considered enrolling full-time. Then Anais and I began our descent into marriage hell and I changed my mind.

Anais, with wide eyes always bright with optimism, was raised to expect riches from the world. And that is what I tried to give her until I got shot. The anger I felt never abated. It was as real as a cobra slithering up my back. I grew fat on its venom and poisoned our marriage with my daily tirades at the Mayor, the Commissioner and the press. Therapy didn't help. It was like getting my dick sucked by a piranha. Not that I was ever really predisposed to the idea, but I tried. I told the doctor about the recurring bad dream I had about killing some member of my family in an accident and that some days I felt like picking up a gun and going down to One Police Plaza and taking everybody out. She wanted to put me on Zoloft. I refused to go back. Hell, everybody has bad dreams. That didn't make me psychotic. Anais and I would argue about it for hours, and when we got tired of fighting, we would make love. It was a crazy marriage.

Anais did her best to brave the storm, but I refused to come in from the cold. Revenge was my goal; my marriage be damned. I was so upset that Detective Pagano got such little time, I went out and got drunk the day he was sentenced. What else happened that night, I don't remember. Anais was gone when I woke up the next morning. She'd left a cryptic note: *Gone to be a movie star.*

Shortly after that Noah separated me from my guns. I told him about a dream I had in which I'd shot myself accidentally in the head. He asked me if I'd ever thought about shooting myself. The answer was yes. After Anais left. He drove to my house that day and took my guns.

A month later I took off to find my father.

* * *

I WALKED THROUGH the rain to Noah's co-op in the shadow of Yankee Stadium. After I rang the bell, he came to greet me at the entrance, and we walked side by side to his second-floor apartment. His casual greeting told me he had not yet heard the news.

Noah's apartment was beautifully laid out and decorated. The man had taste, let me tell you. After unearthing roots in Haiti, Noah and his wife went one step further and made the pilgrimage to Africa that all progressive, educated middle-class blacks presume they have to make to be hip. And like all the others, had returned with the requisite treasures. The apartment was saturated with art: stunning African sculptures and masks of which Noah and his wife were rightly proud. The heads in green or shiny white stone from the Shoshona tribe of Zimbabwe were magnificent. Paintings on the wall reflected a wide selection of African-American art, from Beardon to Reid.

"Where's Donna?" I asked when we got to the living room.

"Man, you got to be kidding me. You standing here dripping water on my expensive carpet and asking me about my wife with a straight face?" He began to laugh. "Get your black ass into the bathroom and dry yourself."

That was my man Noah. His home was indeed his castle. And he would be the first to tell you the same. He'd moved from Harlem to the Bronx in his teens. When the redevelopment of Harlem began and whites started moving uptown, Noah flew into motion.

"Harlem is the cultural capital of black America," he told me. "I was born there. And I ain't letting white people come uptown and strip Harlem of its cultural identity. No way."

He and his wife bought a brownstone and were waiting for the refurbishment to finish before moving in.

I came out of the bathroom with a towel wrapped around my waist.

"I guess you need to borrow some clothes," Noah said.

Noah was shorter than me, but not by much. He had a dark, serious face and intense eyes the size of golf balls. I often joked that he reminded me of James Baldwin, which was ironic because he once ran a playwriting workshop under that name. He claimed he maintained his athletic body from thrice-a-week sex.

"A pair of jeans and a tee-shirt would be good," I said.

"I'm still waiting for my parka you borrowed last fall," he said.

"The dog ate it," I joked.

"Yeah, well, you train that dog to see my shit and leave it."

"He left with Anais."

"Sensible dog," he said and disappeared into the bedroom. He returned with a pair of jeans and a white shirt.

"I'm sorry, but you're gonna have to go without shorts. My boxers wouldn't fit you in the front," he joked.

"Yeah, I hear when you pass sixty your balls begin to swell and shit."

"Your ass better be thankful I'm not sending you out in the rain naked."

"You love me too much to do that," I said.

"Not if you keep cracking on my age. I'm fifty-five years old, muthafucker. You want some coffee?"

"You bet."

"Black, right?"

Without waiting for my reply, he left. I got dressed quickly and went into the kitchen, where Noah was pouring coffee into two mugs. His kitchen had been recently redesigned with a new floor and a black granite-top breakfast table. I sat at the table.

"What the fuck you doing here, anyway?" Noah said.

"Did you check your messages?"

"The shit's broken. We were out late last night visiting Donna's relatives. Actually she was picking up stuff to take to Dominica. I just got back from the airport. You know how it is with these West Indians. They can't go home without taking half of New York back with them. And they could be here a hundred years, they're still calling the place they were born home. Donna's been here for forty fucking years. All her family is here. The only thing they got back there is a shack. But every year she gotta go back to make sure the shack's still there cause that's where she was born. I stopped going after I hit fifty. I told her I can't take shitting in an outhouse at my age."

I sipped the coffee. Noah was in one of those moods when he'd start riffing in that poetic cadence of his about anything that came to his mind. It could be his wife, his friends at the university, the state of black America. Anything. And he was always funny. I hated to break his rhythm.

"I'm here for my guns, Noah."

He broke off what he was about to say, the smile frozen for a moment on his face, then it melted like ice cream on the side of a building.

I quickly brought him up to speed on the events that were preventing me from living the happy, quiet life for which I yearned.

After I finished, he got up, focusing his deep, intelligent eyes on my face, his mouth twitching nervously. I could sense a flame igniting beneath his dark leathery skin as I watched him struggle to keep calm. He drew a deep breath and walked to the stove.

"You hungry?" he said. "After the shit you just told me, I'm liable to go a little crazy. I hate being angry on an empty stomach. And I'm starving."

"Am I taking a big chance here?" I laughed.

"Man, that ain't even funny. You know I'm a gourmet cook. You don't wanna fuck with me right now."

He scrambled some eggs and made fresh coffee. I manned the toaster.

"How you like your toast?" I said, dropping two slices of wheat bread into the toaster.

"Brown."

We ate in silence. I was anxious to see if my guns were still here, but I didn't want to rush Noah. If my guns were missing, I'm sure he'd have a good explanation.

Halfway through the meal he got up and left the room, returning a short time later with a black shoe box. He set the box down on the table and lifted the lid. The expression on his face changed immediately. Eyes downcast, he pushed the box across the table to rest in front of me. It was empty.

"What the fuck's going on, Blades?"

"You tell me, Noah."

He looked at me, his lanternlike eyes hazed over. "What're you thinking?"

How could I suspect Noah? I might as well suspect my father. I trusted this man with my life.

"Nothing," I said, averting his gaze.

"Look at me, muthafucker."

I looked at him again.

"I want to know what you're thinking," he said.

"I ain't thinking nothing, Noah. I just wanna know where my guns are."

He got up. "Well, you can see they aren't here."

"Yeah, I can see that."

"So what do you think? You think I gave them away?"

"I don't know."

"What the fuck you mean you don't know? I want to know what you're thinking."

"Somebody used my guns to commit murder, Noah. And now the NYPD is looking to use me for target practice. Somebody else is going to feel my pain."

"And that somebody else is going to be me, is that what you're saying?"

"I don't believe you'd do anything to hurt me, Noah."

He stared at me expressionless. A taut vein pulsed in his neck. "I'm sorry, Blades. I don't understand how this could've happened. I've got a state-of-the-art alarm system."

"Perhaps you should invest in a good guard dog."

He tried to smile. "That company's gonna feel my pain too."

"Did you tell anyone my guns were here?"

"Not a soul."

"When's the last time you saw Stubby Clapp?"

"That ass-wipe? Not since you redid his furniture."

I took a sip of coffee. It was cold.

"Whatever you're cooking up, I'm in," Noah said.

"No, you're not. If anything happened to you I'd have to shoot myself before I faced Donna."

"It ain't up for debate."

"You bet, because your creaky ass is staying right here where Donna left you."

"I told you not to crack on my age."

"I need a gun and a car. Can you swing that?" I said.

He paused, thinking.

"And a phone," I continued.

He left the room. We had eaten only half our meal. I tested the coffee. It was lukewarm. I got up and started clearing the dishes from the table. Noah returned with a blue-face plated phone. He had changed into what looked like traveling gear: jeans, baseball cap and shoes.

"Where're you going?" I asked.

"Taking you to get a piece."

THE RAIN, COMING down hard in thick white sheets, made visibility low. The slick roads had a surreal sheen from the focused headlights of slow-moving traffic.

We were sitting in Noah's 4x4, waiting for construction vehicles that blocked the street to move. Water trickling along gutters sounded like thousands of rats scurrying around. Yellow neon signs ahead in the middle of street warned motorists to reduce speed. Around us the wet black buildings fit snugly together like old women shuffling through the storm.

I felt exhausted, and in a part of my mind I was hoping we wouldn't have to move for a long time. Noah sat at the wheel whistling a tune.

"So how's your father doing?" Noah said.

"I don't know."

"Where's he now?"

"I don't know."

"You don't know or you don't want to tell me?"

"I told you . . ."

". . . You don't know." He looked at me and smiled.

"That's it."

He resumed the whistling. He tapped the steering wheel as he whistled. Then he stopped. "Do you miss being a cop?" he said.

The construction vehicles began to move, and Noah let the Jeep roll gently down the street.

"Sometimes," I said.

"I was a cop for fifteen years, and to this day I still don't know how I managed."

"That's just it. You manage. You have to."

"You had it easy compared to me."

I looked at him. "It's still tough in there for us."

"Was like getting fucked in the ass for me."

I laughed. "I don't know what that's like."

"Sure you do. It's what's the City tried to do to you and your family after you got shot. But you made it out. With all your faculties."

"Almost didn't, though."

"Why'd you do it? You had a choice. You had college. Why?"

"Does it matter?"

"You're a strange bird, Blades. I wouldn't have done it if I'd had your choices. I had a baby. I needed a job. It was either be a Panther or a cop. Your father went the other way."

"Now he's forever on the run."

"Funny thing is, I made that decision for my son. And he grew up to despise me. Don't even talk to me now. Ain't that something? He's a big shot these days. Always in the news. But he doesn't call me. He calls his mother at her school to avoid talking to me. But you know what? I don't regret it. Being a cop. It helped me control my anger. I was an angry young man back then. There was some serious shit going on. We had Malcolm getting killed. Martin. Medgar. Black people were being targeted by every kind of yahoo racist who was blowing up black churches, kidnapping children. The Panthers were recruiting. You couldn't trust anybody. Not even your best friend. Being a street cop forced me to think about consequences. If I hadn't been a cop, I would've been a killer. I would've killed somebody. I swear."

I said, "Do you write plays about that life?"

"I write plays about people I grew up with. Normal people."

"When's the last time you did one?" I said. "A play."

"Producers don't want to do my work. I don't write about pimps and whores and addicts. I write what I know. Black people striving to live normal, decent lives. America doesn't believe that kind of black person exists. Nobody's going to be pulling a gun and *muthafucking* throughout my play just so white America can have an orgasm. You ever heard of the African gray parrot?"

"What's to hear?"

"There're no leaders among them. They're all equals. True democracy. The problem with people is that they can't be happy unless they know there's somebody somewhere worse off than them. They gotta think they're better than somebody to be happy. Everybody wants to be a top dog. The poorest, worst-educated piece of white trash can still feel good about himself because when he turns on his TV and sees the way black people are depicted, he can say: 'At least I ain't like them niggers.'"

We had driven about half a mile. Noah pulled up outside a bodega on Webster Avenue, parking close to the curb and next to a hydrant. He opened his door and I did likewise.

"This one's private," he said. "Benito don't like strangers."

He left the engine running and hopped through the rain into the bodega. I fiddled wearily with the radio dial, passing up rock and hip-hop for sports talk. I quickly got bored with that and started scanning the stations again, settling his time for news.

Noah came back shortly with the *Daily News* protecting his head from the rain. He got into the Jeep, cursing.

"Fucking rain."

"That was quick," I said.

He flapped the newspaper on the floor in front of him to shake off the water. "Too many people in the store right now. He told me to come back in ten minutes. What's this shit you listening to?"

"News."

He flipped the station to an easy-listening music station. "You want news, read the newspaper. The radio in my truck is for music."

"Well, since you got the newspaper, tell me what the fuck is going on."

He looked at me and smiled, an honest, friendly smile, showing all his teeth. Then he opened the newspaper. "Let's see. The police found that fucker who bombed that black church in Atlanta. The one who escaped from jail."

"Gene Kurtz?"

"Yeah, that Nazi. Found him dead in Prospect Park with his eyes blown out. Guess the next swastika he'll be kissing is the one on Hitler's ass in Hell. A new poll says that Congresswoman Richardson will win reelection with ease. And in another poll, most people think we should rebuild the Twin Towers. What about you?"

"I agree. What about you?"

"I don't care."

We fell into silence. Noah flipped the pages of the newspaper quietly, his lips pursed, his head bowed. Ten minutes later he got out and ran into the bodega once more.

I leaned forward to flip the dial to WINS but stopped myself. A group of cornrowed youngsters came skidding toward the Jeep, playfully kicking up waves in the river that ran through the street as they passed a bottle in a paper bag back and forth. The gloss of rain was so thick I couldn't make out their faces, but they seemed to be having fun. They passed the Jeep and out of my thoughts when, out of the corner of my eye, I saw a shape moving to my left.

Someone was trying to jimmy the door on the driver's side. I slithered over behind the wheel and slipped the vehicle into gear. The group ran off.

Noah returned five minutes later. I was still sitting behind the wheel. He got in the passenger side and laid a snub-nosed .38, a box of shells and an ankle holster with Velcro straps in my lap.

I hefted the loaded gray pistol. It felt heavy, foreign.

"Whatever you do, bring my truck back in one piece." He winked.

"What's the number?" I said.

"The number?"

"The cell you gave me."

"Oh. It's taped to the back of the phone."

# 22

I DROPPED NOAH off and managed to pinch my way through traffic over the bridge to Manhattan. I tried Jimmy's number. Still disconnected. Beginning to get the feeling I wasn't going to hear from Jimmy again. Tim was next on my list. He wasn't around either. Then I called my mother.

"Carmen," she cried. "Where're you? The police were here this morning. And the FBI. It was like an invasion. What is going on?"

"What did they tell you?"

"That I should tell you to give yourself up. I can't deal with this, Carmen. Jason's disappeared, and now you're in trouble. I am going crazy."

"I have to go now, Mom. I'll call you later."

I hung up without waiting for her to say good-bye. I couldn't stand to hear her break down.

Creeping down the waterlogged FDR I tried to fit what pieces I had of the puzzle together. Why would Stubby put a hit on a Fed? He should know that you'd stand a better chance stealing the crown jewels than getting away with the murder of an FBI agent. Those guys hunt you to your grave. But there was one sure way, of course. Have some-one else take the fall. And there I was, right on cue, stumbling head first into their noose. But why was Edwards killed? And why was he in trouble with the Bureau? Bressler had said it was bigger than a murder. What did he mean? And was Precious just an innocent victim in all this? None of it made sense, and I could feel myself getting more and more frustrated.

I called Trevor. After about five chimes he answered, sounding groggy and tensed.

"Whaddup, cuz," I hailed.

"Yo, Blades, are you in jail? The cops answered your phone. Gave me the fucking third degree."

"Any day now you might see me on 'America's Most Wanted.'"

"Dang! This shit's whack. We gotta talk, yo. Somebody slammed my condo."

"I'll meet you at the Bridge in half."

THE BRIDGE DINER sat on the wing of the Brooklyn Bridge across from a park. I arrived ten minutes before Trevor and sat by the window. The rain was bringing a white wind on its tail, which whipped against the window in heavy swirls.

Trevor arrived in black baggy jeans and a red water-proof windbreaker, tugging nervously at the gold ring hanging from his left earlobe.

"Whaddup, babe?" I greeted.

We pounded and he sat down, after looking around anxiously. He tried to smile, but it soon faded into a grin that was somehow earnest and suspicious at the same time. He shed the windbreaker and slung it over the back of his chair. Underneath he wore a gray oversized Yankee baseball shirt.

I smiled in an attempt to relax him. "How's that queen of yours?"

"Safe, for now."

Our waitress came, a painfully thin young woman who walked in a stiff, upright manner. I ordered coffee. Trevor asked for a buttered croissant with ham and cheese. She batted metallic eyelids at Trevor and left.

"You sounded like you just got up," I said.

"Fuck the small talk, yo. What's bubbling?"

"The police think I killed a couple of people."

"You kidding, right?"

I shook my head.

"Man, what the hell you got me into?" he said.

"I'm sorry, man."

"They shot my wife's dog, man! Muthafuckers destroyed all my shit and shot Jordan. Is that all you got to say? 'I'm sorry'?"

"What else can I say?"

"You realize how close Pat and I came to being iced, cuz?"

"Trevor, look, I'm sorry. I didn't realize this shit was going to become hotter than a hooker's ass. I didn't mean to put you and your wife in danger."

"What about her fucking dog? Her dog's dead."

"I'll get her another dog."

"She don't want another dog. She loved Jordan."

"We'll get a dog named Kobe. She likes Kobe, doesn't she?"

"You think this is a joke? If my wife didn't insist on playing one of her games last night, we'd both be dancing with the Devil about now."

"What kinda game?"

"Every once in a while she likes to pretend she's a hooker."

"You know what, on second thought, forget I asked."

"Well, I gonna tell you, cuz. Because it saved our life. She likes to stand on a street corner, you see, dressed in a skimpy outfit. And I'd watch from a few blocks away in my car as she toys with the men who pull over. She'd always set the price too high so they'd eventually have to drive off."

"What would happen if an R. Kelly or Mike Tyson bubbled up in a Six-fifty, spitting crazy game and enough money to buy her for a week?"

"What?"

"What if—"

"I heard you. What would R. Kelly be doing driving around Brooklyn looking for pussy?"

"What about Mike Tyson?"

"Man, why you always gotta be so fucking contradictory? Mike Tyson is too short. She'd find a way to get rid of him. Then I'd drive up and we'd agree on a price and she'd get into my car and go to a hotel. And that's what we did last night. This morning we came home to find the place wrecked and Jordan dead."

"What about the laptop?"

"You must've been born on the twenty-ninth of February, man. I was having some trouble with one of my servers, so I took the laptop to a partner of mine. He's still working on it."

"You sure?"

"Spoke to him just before you called. He's still working on your shit."

"Oh, Trevor, man I love you, kid."

"Just don't hug me, alright? I don't feel very brotherly toward you right now."

"Where's Patricia?"

"I put Patricia on a train to DC a few hours ago."

"Why didn't you go with her?"

"'Cause. How else you gonna get your shit? Besides, I got me a loaded forty-five. I hope those muthafuckers who trashed my place come back. I'll be waiting."

The waitress returned with our order. Before she left she took another long look at Trevor.

"I'm married," Trevor said, tilting his chin in a laconic pose.

She smiled and walked off.

I wrote my new cell-phone number on a napkin, folded it and handed it to Trevor. "Let me know the minute I can check that computer, Trevor."

The veins in his neck pulsed as he chewed vigorously on his croissant, his elastic cheeks ballooning with food. He looked at me, swallowing hard. "They're doing their best, kid."

The rain had peaked and the dark clouds were beginning to drift westward leaving thick patches of gray scab. People were taking back the streets with frightening speed. A couple strolled by, arms interlocked at the elbows, and I suddenly thought of walking with Precious along Tenth Street after our meeting at the café in Manhattan. I wanted to just sit there and daydream, but I forced myself to get up. I had a job to do. Her killer was still walking around and she wasn't.

# 23

THE LATINO DOORMAN who pronounced my name as if it was a fire got up from his seat behind the desk when I entered through the open glass door. He smiled exuberantly as I approached, as if eager to have a little more fun with my name.

"Blades," he greeted.

I smiled. "Yes, that's it."

"I practice," he said.

"Very good. Where're you from?"

"Honduras. I been here in three mons."

"Months," I corrected, exaggeratedly mouthing the word to emphasize the action of the tongue slipping between the teeth to produce the *th* sound.

He smiled and shook his head. "Yes. I have practice English." He looked at me thoughtfully, then slowly and silently practiced what I'd just done until he felt he'd mastered the technique. With a confident smile, he said, "Months, yes?"

"That's it."

"Thank you,"

"Is anyone in C-Four?"

"No. Policía."

"Police?"

"Yes, police. They two hours gone."

"I want to go up," I said.

"She no there."

"I know." I slipped a twenty-dollar bill into his hand. "Can you open it for me?"

"You policía?" he said.

I nodded and walked off toward the elevator.

THE APARTMENT WAS immaculate. Arranged in a spiraling long-neck pink vase, the flowers blooming in the living room on a black brass stand were still fresh. Must've been bought the day she died. Everything in the room was perfectly placed, as if Precious had been expecting a photographer for a layout. I looked around, marveling at the exactness of it all, from the choice of the vase to the placement of each painting on the wall.

But I hadn't come to pay homage to Precious' design talents. I followed the brightness of the polished floor to the bedroom, which was not so deliberately organized. Clothes were scattered about, along with partially opened packages, catalogues and books.

The old-fashioned four-poster king-size bed made of dark wood was positioned majestically in the middle of the large room directly in view of the window. Directly behind the bed was a tall potted palm tree which bloomed in rich green. Next to the bed was a round mahogany pedestal table. On top of that was a lamp with a Tiffany shade, an old-fashioned clock and candles. White underwear lay on the unmade purple sheets. Were these the underwear she'd taken off before coming to my house? I picked them up and sniffed them. Her smell flowed urgently back to my senses.

I sat on the bed, underwear in hand, dazed into memory. It felt like only a few moments ago we'd kissed and held each other. What if she'd lived? Would she have fallen in love with me? I with her? I wanted to run from the room, her presence there too strong and painful. She'd been in my life only a short while, but the waves she'd created were still cresting and breaking over my head.

I went to the window and looked out. A gray curtain was still drawn across the sky. I stood there for a long time, feeling the pull of some unknown energy inside the room wanting to keep me there.

On the dresser and on the wall above the bed were a number of framed pictures of Precious with famous people—Magic Johnson, Harry Belafonte, Sidney Poitier—and a picture of her with Vondelle Richardson.

I opened drawers, emptying the contents onto the bed. More photographs, maps, paper money and coins from different countries. Precious traveled a lot, it seemed.

There were two ample walk-in closets. Both were crammed with clothes and shoes bearing the labels of famous designers. On the top shelf of one of the closets I found a small black purse, which contained letters from friends, expired contracts, titles to three cars and a birth certificate.

She was born Precious Kenya Appleton in Kings County. Her father's name was missing, but her mother's wasn't.

I folded the document and was about to put it back into the purse, then I changed my mind, deciding to take it with me. I didn't know why Precious had lied about her mother, but I intended to find out.

\* \* \*

THE SKY WAS the depressing color of drain water from a rain-washed New York street. Instead of cleansing the City of grime, the rain seemed to have flushed the sewers right into the street. A raw sickening smell bled in through the open window of the Jeep. Black sludge tumbled along the road's edge, the sound of water rushing under the street, as mighty as a waterfall.

There was only one journalist in New York I knew well enough to trust. Semin Jhoti wrote for *The New York Times*. During my ordeal she was the only writer who didn't seem interested in sensationalizing my story. Her series of articles on racism in the NYPD won a Pulitzer Prize. She interviewed me several times, and we developed a close friendship, so close that Anais became jealous.

Heading over the Brooklyn Bridge, I called Semin and asked her to do some digging for me. On everybody. From Congresswoman Richardson to Agent Edwards. I had no idea what I was dealing with here. Precious had lied to me. Jimmy Lucas had disappeared. The land was shifting under me, and I didn't like the feeling of being caught in a mudslide. Two people were dead. The only link seemed to be my gun. And the identity of one man. A man the congresswoman had known intimately.

# 24

THERE ARE SOME women in whose presence your brain just turns to mush. What it is about them that causes this chemical chain reaction in your body is a mystery. Be it the glint in their eyes when they look at you, the way they smile at you as though they can see into your heart or the way they draw you into their space, the power of their spirit is so enduring you imagine yourself being a part of their domain, imagine yourself affecting their lives. But thinking you have that much power is as much a fantasy as being in a room with Sharon Stone crossing and uncrossing her legs with no panties on.

Precious had had that effect on me. Now it was clear where she got that quality: her mother.

The Lefferts-Prospect section of Brooklyn was a leafy

five-block area of well-preserved one-family brick houses contained by Flatbush Avenue to the west and Nostrand Avenue to the east. I was standing in the ground-floor living room of Congresswoman Richardson's two-story house, a large, high-ceiling cottage on Maple Street, watching her descend the stairs. The maid who'd let me in had disappeared somewhere; I didn't see where to because my eyes were fixed on the figure dancing down toward me.

Halfway down the stairs Congresswoman Richardson stopped and smiled. In the cool light, her skin was especially dark and glossy. She wore a potato-colored knee-length cotton dress arrayed down the front with crisp gold buttons. The dress was fastened halfway up her chest, exposing the dark palate of her cleavage. Today her hair was down, and the neck-length braids, generously sprinkled with silver, framed an unlined face that had a youthfulness that most women her age would've considered unfair. The matching African necklace and bracelet of black beads were almost lost in the luster of her skin. In her right hand, as though it were a prize, she held aloft a glass containing a dark golden liquid.

"Mr. Overstreet, you are either a brave man or very foolish coming to see me." Her clear voice resonated like the strike of a pinball.

I walked to the foot of the stairs. "You look stunning as always, Ms. Richardson."

She smiled and lifted her chin slightly. "What a flatterer you are, Mr. Overstreet."

"Please, call me Blades."

"Are you as dangerous as your name sounds?"

"Depends."

"On what?" She winked with a flirtatious smile.

Her waggish manner puzzled me. Perhaps it was all an act, still trying to keep up the pretense that she had been nothing more than Precious' aunt.

"Depends on if you like danger," I said.

"What do you think?" She had reached the foot of the stairs. "Do you think I like danger?"

"Yes, I think you have a wild side."

She smiled. I didn't want to continue this game. I wanted to talk about Precious but was somehow powerless to shift the conversation in that direction. Her eyes were fixed on my face with a deep interest, like a child staring at a fire.

"You have very interesting bone structure, Blades."

She reached out and touched my cheekbones, a gentle massage rather than a caress. After a few seconds, her face seeming to bow under the weight of a private thought, she stepped back and sipped from her drink.

"I used to know a man with cheeks like those," she said.

"Precious' father?"

My attempt to fluster her did not work. Other than a soft smile playing at the corners of her mouth, she was unmoved.

"Why don't you come upstairs? It's much cozier."

She turned and ascended the stairs, as aloof and as bewitching from the back as any woman I'd ever met.

I stood at the bottom of the stairs watching her. She reached the top and turned, arms outstretched, beckoning me to her. I approached her, drawn by her smile and august presence as a storm to the sea. I must've had a bewildered look on my face.

"Don't be afraid, Blades," she said. "I won't attack you."

She led me into a large room made intimate by the aroma of fresh roses. I saw them, long-stemmed, white, yellow and red, set about the room in vases on tables and in window alcoves. The room appeared to be used as a study. Next to an oak cabinet, two ceiling-high bookcases were crammed with books, papers and magazines. There was a phone on the desk, a laptop and one of those all-in-one printer/fax/copier machines. The window behind the desk was closed, but trees were visible through the clear panes of glass.

"Is it too early for you to have a drink?" Congress-woman Richardson asked. She was standing at the open cabinet uncorking a bottle of scotch.

"If it's not too early for you, I can manage."

She turned to me with a wet smile on her lips. "Spoken like a man."

"Straight. No ice," I said.

"Just what I expected. For the record, I have mine the same way."

She refreshed her drink first, then she poured mine and handed it to me in a short, heavy glass, continuing on to the couch, where she sat, drawing the dress close to her lap. Her back was straight, her profile that of a proud high priestess presiding over a ceremony.

"Come sit next to me, Blades."

Her eyes glinted with a strange sad fire. It was then I knew it was all an act. Before I could sit she made a wide sweep of her arm, catching my hand in hers and drawing me down to the couch.

"Do you like my house?"

"It's amazing," I said. "I didn't realize there were such beautiful houses in this part of Brooklyn."

"Thank you. There's only one thing missing." She looked around as if expecting someone to materialize from the space around us.

"What's that?"

She sipped her drink and held my gaze. "Precious was really my daughter you know."

I squared my body to face her. She let go of my hand and stood up. Slowly she crossed the room and stood with her back against the window. She sipped niggardly at her drink.

"This is a very big house," she started. "I never intended to spend my life in it alone. And let me tell you, it gets terri-bly lonely in here. This house belonged to my father, who was a teacher. He left Jamaica when I was ten and never came back. I didn't see him again until I was a woman. By then I'd grown to hate him. He left this house to me when he died. At first I thought of selling it. But the first time I walked into it I fell in love with it. I wanted to leave it to Precious, but she told me point blank she wanted nothing from me."

My eyes left her face and roamed the room to the many pictures of her with important world figures: Nelson Mandela, Kofi Annan, President Clinton. She and her daughter shared the taste for the spotlight.

"I need your help," I said.

She swirled the whisky around in the glass, her face strained and intense. "I told you not to follow Precious into this maze. I can't help you."

"I didn't kill your daughter, but I think you know that. Does the name Stubby Clapp mean anything to you?"

"Never heard of him."

"I think he killed Precious."

"Who is he?"

"Someone I worked with some years back. He's out for revenge now."

She was smiling, a kind of delicate web to hide her pain, then she looked away to focus somewhere outside the window. "I wish she and I could've found a way to be friends at least."

"Who is her father?"

With a sharp twist of her head, her dark eyes converged again on my face. "How do I know you didn't kill her?"

"I had no reason to."

"You've never killed anyone?"

"Self-defense."

"Violence is in your blood."

"What do you mean by that?"

"You've killed. That makes you violent in my book. If you killed once you would kill again. You should've taken my advice. Now Precious is dead. And the police said you killed her. Why should I believe you and not the police? I don't know anything about you other than that you've killed before."

I stood staring at her, unable to refute her words.

"You should go, now, Mr. Overstreet."

"Why did you pretend to be aunt and niece?" I said.

"Precious was legally adopted by my sister. I was her aunt."

"What's going to happen to her daughter?"

"What daughter?"

"Doesn't she have a daughter in a home?"

"Precious having children?" She laughed. "Did she tell you that?"

I didn't answer. Jimmy Lucas had played me in more ways than one.

"Precious didn't want children," Vondelle said.

"What are the funeral arrangements?"

"Her body will be flown to Jamaica in a few days."

"Are you going?"

She didn't answer, having withdrawn into an armor of silence behind aloof eyes. Her detached stare knifed through me with the bitterness of winter cold.

I wanted to grab her and shake her until she spoke up. There was no rule that said a mother should shed tears for her children in death, but Vondelle Richardson could've acted like she cared.


HUNGER STABBED AT my ribs like a George Foreman jab. But in this neighborhood it was a welcome sensation. I left the Jeep on Maple and walked toward Flatbush in search of food.

It was after two P.M. Humidity had put a stranglehold on the day. Near Flatbush Avenue, barebacked youths in Chloé sunglasses had found a way to neutralize the moisture by opening a hydrant. Girls with bad perms, wearing doorknob earrings, danced in the middle of the street to ca-

lypso music from a boom box on the sidewalk. Carnival
was in the air, as palpable as the dampness.

I'd been using gum to forestall the craving to smoke. As
I walked slowly along Flatbush, I stuck a piece of peppermint gum into my mouth. The taste was particularly offensive today, but it was either that or light up.

I spotted a Golden Krust restaurant across the street.
There was a line to get in, but I didn't mind waiting for a
good patty.

Inside, customers leaned over each other's shoulders,
shouting orders to a frenzied staff who found it difficult to
keep up. Bob Marley posters plastered the walls, and his
wailing voice could be heard over the sound system. With
two or three people shouting at the same time, the shoe-
box restaurant had the atmosphere of a marketplace, and
the air inside, choked off by the crowd, was a heavy mish-
mash of competing aromas: beef, chicken, shrimp, curry,
pepper and various cheap knockoff colognes.

I ordered two veggie patties and sorrel. My grandmother used to make sorrel that always made my mouth
run water. Her ruby rich drink, melded by an assortment of
spices, left such sweetness lingering on the breath that
hours later when I remembered the taste, my mouth would
water. I didn't expect that today, but I wouldn't have complained if I got such a surprise.

It took fifteen minutes to get my patty. I took a bite before snaking my way through the throng. I smiled. The
patty was outstanding. Now if the sorrel could be half as
good. I took a sip. No such luck. Ah well, there was always
next time.


HAD THE PATTY not been so tasty, drawing my focus away
from the street, I might've seen Romano and James before
they rushed up on me. I would've noticed them crouching
through traffic, holding Glocks at their sides in conceal-

ment more from the crowd on Flatbush than from me. When I did spot them they were crouched in shooting position, close enough for me to see glee in their eyes.

"Stop! Police!"

I dumped my food where I stood and leapt in front of a moving car. The driver swerved and hit a truck going in the opposite direction, setting off a chain reaction of cars and trucks smashing into each other. The mad panic that followed was enough of a diversion for me to dash through a group of women huddled together outside a hair salon, too deep into their conversation to do anything but throw up their arms in fright as I busted their gossip ring.

I heard the two detectives screaming.

"Stop or we'll shoot! Police!

"Stop muthafucker! Police!"

Keeping my head low, I sprinted along Flatbush, veering off onto Lincoln Road crowded with kids playing on the sidewalk. Hurdling a kid on a tricycle, I raced across Ocean Avenue against traffic and into the verdant Prospect Park.

There I looked back for the first time. No one had followed me into the park, but I did not slow down. With its constant patrol by cruisers, Prospect Park was no place to hide. I had to get out as soon as possible. In no time the ghetto birds would be circling overhead.

I charged up the hill through thick grass and pigweed, no match for my bulldozing feet, past the memorial to a Maryland regiment that fought with George Washington in the War of Independence and through a trap of maple and sycamore trees, racing across the sun-scarred lawn, skipping around and over bare-chested sun gods and their whining whippets, and past the Tennis House before exiting the park near the Bandshell at Ninth Street. I slumped onto a bench, gasping for air. The smell of freshly cut grass piqued my nose. Sweat streamed from my brow, making tiny puddles on the cement beneath me. Looking down at my feet, I saw tufts of green stalks stuck to my shoes, along with tiny red and purple spikes, fragments of flowers and other plants I'd destroyed in my flight, I suspected. Pity I couldn't charge the City for mowing the grass.

I picked debris from my shoes and from around my ankles. Up above, a brick-red–breasted bird on a branch gulped down a wet scarlet berry, shook its wings and was gone into a gray sky. In its wake came a swarm of monarch butterflies, their black-veined wings stiff and beautiful in the sunlight. I got up and started walking toward Grand Army Plaza. My breathing soon returned to normal, but my ribs hurt, and so did my knees. As I neared the Plaza I unclipped my phone to holler at Tim Samuel. His phone rang four times before he picked up, answering in a muffled voice, as though his mouth was full of food.

"Tim?" I said, unsure.

"Blades?"

"Whaddup, cuz?"

"Not your tail, that's for damn sure. The Mayor's got anybody that can shoot straight out hunting your ass."

"What can I tell you, Timmy? I was voted most likely to lead in my senior class."

"Your bowl's about ready to overflow, cuz. They raided your apartment. Found pictures on your computer."

"Yeah, I heard."

"Who told you?"

"The Mayor."

"You talked to the Mayor?"

"I caught him throwing up all over the press this morning."

"Did he say that they're the same pictures they found near that agent's body?"

"I'm being set up, cuz."

"Tell me where you are. I'll come get you. You don't wanna end another Diallo."

"Sorry, Tim. Can't do that. But I do need your help. Find my brother."

# 25

AFTER I HUNG up I felt totally disheartened. When I was a boy, my mother used to read poems to me all the time. Some she wrote, others by poets she considered great. There was one in particular she read to me often. I still remembered bits of it. It was a poem about the different masks of life and the struggle an individual undergoes to find himself. As I encountered fierce opposition from my mother over my decision to drop out of college to become a soldier, I reminded her of that poem. It was time to embark on a quest that I could not experience in college, I told her. And she agreed.

I was about to embark on another quest. The forces I was up against were still unknown to me, but it was becoming clear that this conspiracy to trap me was more elaborate than I could've imagined. Stealing my guns was good work, but planting pictures on my computer took some imagination and indicated a level of sophistication and technical skill way beyond anything Stubby could be accused of. Perhaps I was wrong, but I didn't think Stubby was that smart.

Not knowing where to turn now, I opened my wallet, aimlessly flipping through business cards and telephone numbers, hoping that somehow, by some unimaginable magic, one of these numbers would spark my brain to converge on a theory to explain what was going on.

I paused on Gabriel Aquia's card. His gallery wasn't far away on Sixth Avenue. Perhaps, if nothing else, he could help me untangle the Precious and Vondelle knot. Limping across the street, I made my way along Union.

The day was still dreary. Dull, stiff clouds parked overhead like a tarpaulin over a greenhouse concentrating the heat below. The air was smothering; the dense clouds seemed to be emitting some kind of energy-sucking vapor. I hadn't stopped sweating. I sniffed my armpits. Finding a change of clothes would be my immediate mission.

On Seventh Avenue I slipped into a Gap store as a chain of patrol cars screamed up the block with lights and sirens going berserk. I had about $600 in my pockets. Deciding to change my appearance a bit, I picked up a pair of baggy jeans, an oversized Hawaiian shirt, a baseball cap, a pair of Calvin Klein boxers and a red bandana. After changing in the fitting room, I dropped the Gap bag containing my dirty clothes in the garbage can outside the store.

Across the street I spotted a diner, which looked dramatically out of place in this neighborhood of upscale restaurants and chic boutiques. From the outside it had the appearance of an old social club frequented by wise guys, its muted interior lighting making it difficult to see inside from the street.

I was still hungry, and it seemed the perfect place to eat. I also had to use the bathroom. I entered and sat at the counter. The room was freezing and had an odor of bug spray.

Casually, I glanced around. Five men sat huddled together like a family of penguins at a booth in a far corner. There was no sign of life from any of them, as if they were meditating on the nature of cool. A waiter came over and I ordered Swiss cheese and turkey on rye and a Coke.

"Where's the bathroom?" I asked.

"You gotta pay first," said the cashier, sitting a few feet to my left behind the register. Her red heart-shaped mouth moved in tight choreographed circles, twirling a piece of gum like it was a baton.

"What?"

"You heard me. Pay first before you can use the bathroom. People like you come in here all the time and try to pull that trick."

"People like me?" I said incredulously.

"You want to use the bathroom, you gotta pay first."

If I didn't get to a bathroom soon I would burst into a geyser of urine; getting angry wouldn't help the situation. I paid the four-fifty and followed the direction of her silver nail-polished finger to the back of the diner.

The john was locked. I looked over to the cashier, who was watching me, smiling conceitedly. Then I saw her hand dip under the register and a buzzer sounded.

"Push the door," she hollered.

I pushed the door and presto, it opened. What a tiny shithole. No bigger than a litter box. Smelled like it too. I did my business quickly, ran water on my hands and bolted for the hallway, where I dragged deep on insecticide.

The cashier had left her station and was in a brisk conversation with the waiter. When she saw me, she stopped talking and went back behind the cash register.

I walked back to the counter where my food was waiting, but I had lost my appetite. I took one bite and left the rest.

* * *

GABRIEL AQUIA'S GALLERY occupied the top floor of a
two-story building, above a Korean nail salon on Sixth and
Union. I climbed the stairs and entered the modest-size
gallery. Before me was an impressive collection of African
masks and sculptures, and a few paintings, all manner of
headrests, fabrics, scarves, wooden bowls and other imple-
ments that most unsophisticated Westerners, like myself,
would assume were used in day-to-day life in an African
village.

A woman in a body-fitted black dress and matching
choker, her hair twisted and spread in thick spikes, glanced
up from her magazine and eyed me with sloppy insolence,
her hawk nose pointed downward, as if she thought I
couldn't possibly be here to buy anything.

"Is Gabriel Aquia here?" I asked.

"Do you have an appointment?"

"Tell him it's Blades Overstreet."

She made an attempt to smile, baring her teeth quickly;
they were long and crooked. She hid them again behind
purple lips. Just as she turned away, Gabriel Aquia came
out of an office behind her, shaking the hands of a tall white
woman whose smile seemed painfully false. The woman
passed me without acknowledgment and went out the door
and down the stairs. When Gabriel saw me, his expression
turned grim, his dark reptilian eyes furtive and anxious.

"Mr. Overstreet, you buying or selling?" His leaden
voice cracked with insincerity.

"How about a trade?"

"Come into my office. Let me take a look at your mer-
chandise."

He stared intently at his attendant, as if trying to send a
telepathic message. She maintained an appearance of in-
difference, settling behind a desk flipping through pages of
*Vogue*.

I followed him into the large office painted a cream lively and dramatically decorated with art-deco prints and man-size plants. A coffee-colored sofa stretched out against one wall; several gold disks occupied the space above it. He sat behind his long cherry desk.

"What can I interest you in today, Mr. Overstreet? I just received a nineteenth-century Punu mask from Gabon. Great condition. I was thinking of adding it to my personal collection, but I'm willing to offer it to you for cost."

"I feel so special."

"But you are." He smirked and picked up the phone.

I reached down and lifted the .38 from my ankle. "Put the phone down."

He stared at the gun, then at me, trying to smile. His self-confident smirk had deserted him.

"No need for that. I just want to tell Regina to hold all my calls."

I sat at the corner of his desk. "Keep your fingers away from the phone."

He shifted in his seat and tapped his fingers on the desk. "Sure thing."

"How long have you known Vondelle Richardson?"

"We've been friends a long time."

"Did you know Precious was her daughter?"

He hesitated, slicing his gaze toward the door.

"Can I call you Gabriel?" I said, moving closer. I still couldn't stand his damn cologne.

"I insist."

"Everybody I've met in the past two days seems to think there're no consequences for lying to me. I promise you, Gabriel. There are consequences."

"Are you going to shoot me?" he said.

"Who is Precious' father?"

"I don't know."

"Remember what I said about consequences?"

"What do you want me to do? Make up a name because you have a gun?"

"Why did you come to my office?"

"Vondelle was concerned that Precious might've hired you to sabotage her campaign."

"Why would Precious want to do that?"

"You don't know Precious."

"You didn't answer my question."

He tried to get up out of his chair. I grabbed his shirt, pulling him back down.

He leaned his body away from me, his knobby lips pink as salami against his muted dark skin. "How do you think Vondelle knew that Precious had hired you? Precious called and told her. She wanted to make her mother sweat. Their relationship was hell. Precious would've done anything to destroy her mother's campaign."

"Why wouldn't she tell Precious who her father was?"

"I don't know. I don't get involved in their family secrets. You should ask her."

"She calls you Gabe?"

"So what?"

"Sounds like you and her got some secrets of your own."

"What're you implying?"

"Nothing. I know that some men dream of fucking their mama."

"Looking at you one would not think you'd be so uncouth."

I stepped away from him. Gabriel's eyes contracted, and his craggy brow knotted as though a huge carbuncle had appeared on his forehead. I could tell he was trying to figure out what I was going to do next. He straightened his shoulders, trying to look brave, but I was done with him.

"What cologne do you wear?"

"Drakkar Noir. Why?"

"It stinks," I said.

Stuffing my gun back into the holster, I breezed out the door. I knew that Gabriel Aquia would call the police the minute I stepped out of his office. I hailed the first livery cab and directed him to take me to Maple Street.

# 26

COMING BACK TO get the Jeep wasn't that much of a risk. I had little respect for the NYPD's ability to track me down. They were such bunglers it wouldn't have surprised me if they were busy dragging the lake in Prospect Park, thinking that I may've accidentally drowned. I'm sure the only reason they found me on Flatbush was that Congresswoman Richardson had dropped a coin.

As expected, there was no sign of surveillance around the Jeep, so I got in and drove off, making the first right onto Bedford Avenue and then turning down Empire Boulevard.

Spotting a McDonald's up ahead, I pulled up to the drive-thru window and ordered a crispy chicken fillet and a Coke. The attendant seemed as disinterested in what he was doing as I was in looking at his face. This was my third attempt to eat lunch today. Would this be a charm?

I drove away after making sure the order was correct, snapping into the sandwich with the savagery of a pit bull. With no clear purpose I cruised east along Eastern Parkway, bopping my head to Ornette Coleman's wicked sax on WBGO.

In two days the West Indian Carnival Day Parade would transform this street into a mall of music, food and half-naked flesh. Side streets would be jammed with burnt-out revelers, artisans and one-day entrepreneurs. Milo had tried many times to get me to don costume and jump in his band, but I'd resisted. Standing on the side like the other tentative souls, to watch the colorful costumes and listen to the pulsating music while stuffing myself full of channa, roti and sorrel was enough for me.

I passed Utica and was about to loop around the tennis courts at Lefferts Terrace when a face came to me. It was a round face with clear, dazed eyes. I'd seen the face five days ago, in one of those disgusting pictures ringing the dead agent's body. The nameless face stayed with me as I downshifted to stop at the light, and then it was nameless no more.


MY WIFE HATED cleaning. So did I. When we lived together in Rosedale we paid a woman from Brooklyn to clean and do laundry twice a week, and sometimes she would surprise us by cooking dinner, but that wasn't part of her regular duties. Her name was Lusca Morris. She was a genuinely wonderful person. Lusca had come from Belize on a temporary visa and never returned. One morning she came to work with red, swollen eyes. She'd been up all night crying. Her thirteen-year-old daughter, Serena, hadn't come home from school. Afraid to go through official channels because of her immigration status, she asked me to help.

I took her to the precinct to file a missing person's report, assuring her that there'd be no repercussions because of her lack of a green card. Then I tried to trace Serena's movements that day.

The day before Serena disappeared she and her mother had visited the offices of the Caribbean Agency for Immigrant Rights (CAIR), to inquire about an upcoming green-card lottery. Serena left school at 2:30 the next day. Her mother had told her to pick up some documents from CAIR on her way home.

According to CAIR, Serena never made it to their office. In fact, they had no record of any visit, including the prior one. And they couldn't find the forms Lusca and her daughter had filled out. This made me suspicious, and I had planned to run a check on them. That night I was shot.

Lusca came to visit me in the hospital. Her face was full of concern for me, but her heart was joyful. Serena had come home. Apparently she'd gone on a joy ride with friends to Atlantic City for the weekend. As Lusca put it, her relationship with her daughter was rocky, and Serena was known to go off and do wild things from time to time. Before I got out of the hospital, Lusca stopped working for us. She called to say she had found a better-paying job. We never heard from her again.

The face that came to me was Serena's. I was quite sure of it. I was surprised it took me this long to remember her face, since I'd often remarked on her beauty to Lusca. Perhaps it was because I hadn't seen her in a while, but once the face came back to me, there was no mistake whose face it was.

I had to find Serena. When she worked for us, Lusca was renting a basement apartment from a Barbadian couple, the Bradshaws, in Flatlands. But I had no idea if she still lived there or even if she was still in New York City.

I tested 411. They had no listing for Lusca Morris. Undaunted, I made a right turn onto Buffalo. Flatlands was about twenty minutes away.

WITH ITS CRISP lawns and flower gardens, the block of charming, brightly painted two-family homes looked to be well maintained. Lusca had lived in a half-brick house, painted pastel green on the lower level and yellow on the upper level, in the middle of the block.

I rang the buzzer for the basement. No one answered. The owners of the house lived on the first floor. I rang that bell. A dour-looking woman with dark rings under her eyes opened the door and peered through the grill of the iron guard gate.

"Hello, Mrs. Bradshaw." I greeted her with a smile.

She squinted as if trying to make out my face in the sun.

"My name is Blades Overstreet. You have a tenant, Lusca Morris, who used to work for me a while back."

Her face lit up at the mention of Lusca's name. "Oh, of course. Lusca. You said your name was Blades?"

"Yes. Lusca used to work for me. The police officer from Queens. You may've seen me bring her home."

"Oh, yes, Blades, I remember you. The police gentleman with the pretty wife."

Her face quietly turned blank. I could almost hear the chaotic wheels of her brain racing as she tried to recall where she'd seen or heard my name recently.

"Does Lusca still live here?"

"I sorry, but I cooking right now. I can't talk to you," she said in her thick Bajan accent.

"Mrs. Bradshaw, it's very important that I speak to her."

"She ain't here. She gone."

"She doesn't live here, is that what you're saying?"

"Look, Mister Blades, I don't know nothing 'bout where she is. I don't want to get involve in nothing."

"I know you've seen my face on the news. I didn't do any of those things. That's why I'm here. I need to speak to Lusca. She might be able to help me prove I didn't kill those people."

She looked at me, her eyes narrowing with doubt.

I tried to hold her gaze and spoke with a steady, plead-ing voice. "A few years ago her daughter disappeared for a few days. Do you remember that?"

She stared at me, expressionless. But at least she hadn't moved. She was still listening.

I continued. "Lusca had asked me to find her, but I got shot and was in the hospital. There may be a connection between Serena's disappearance back then and the mur-ders. I need to find Serena. I need to talk to her."

"They left."

"When? Where did they go?"

"I don't know."

"Please, Mrs. Bradshaw. My life may depend on it. Did she say anything at all about where she might be going?"

"You not a policeman no more?"

"I resigned a few years ago."

"Why they say you kill those people if you didn't do it?"

"I swear I didn't do it."

"I remember you used to bring Lusca home. You seemed like a nice gentleman."

"I'm not a murderer."

"After her daughter came back, she say to me that she got to leave. She ain't give me no reasoning. She just say she got to find another place to live. She didn't leave her address or nothing, but she owed me some money and a few months later she send me a letter with a money order. I think I still have the letter. Wait. Let me see if I can find it."

She turned away from the door. Apprehension gripped

me. There was no way of knowing if she would call the police while I waited. I tried to listen for her voice on the telephone, but the hiss of vehicles behind me created too much background noise.

Five minutes passed. I began to panic. Lines of sweat blistered my brow. The urge to turn and run began to season.

The door opened again. The short dark woman unlocked the gate and squeezed her way out onto the steps with the help of a canary-colored cane.

"Sorry I take so long," she apologized. She looked up at me from a stoop, her shoulders hunched as if she was in pain.

I said, "Are you alright?"

She smiled and handed me a piece of paper. "Yes, I fine. I had a knee operation months ago, but it don't look like it want to get better. Every day it still stiff stiff. Thanks for asking. Here's the address that was on the envelope."

I took the paper and thanked her. She watched me walk off and did not return to her house until I had reached my car.

# 27

LUSCA'S ADDRESS ON Butler Street was in my backyard, so to speak, a mere six blocks from President.
How we'd never run into each other, I don't know. It was
even possible that we shopped at the same supermarket. As
I drove along Utica Avenue, I had to smile to myself at the
irony.

The Gowanus Houses were a high-rise block of gray
buildings near the Gowanus Canal, stretching from Wycoff
to Douglas. As with most housing projects in the city, it
had been preyed on by drug dealers when crack ruled, at-
tracting the kind of lower animals, too gutless to slit their
own throats and end their miserable lives, who instead
turned other people's misery into gold, weak people into
lost souls.

I parked two blocks away on Bergen. Approaching the

Gowanus Houses on foot was a descent into chaos. The odor of ferment and decay swayed on the dusty air. Bins had long been overrun by trash, which hadn't been collected in days; streets and sidewalks had become overwhelmed by dirt and garbage. The parade of men and women into the liquor store on Hoyt Street was as steady as a January snowstorm. I glimpsed a bundle of shriveled bodies huddled outside around a bottle of gin, their hearts in their throats, waiting patiently for their chance to kiss the bottle's mouth and release the genie inside.

On the other side of the street youngsters who may've once respected those now feeding their dreams to the colorless genie in the square bottle bantered with youthful vigor. Men in Versace shirts and Hilfiger jeans wedge themselves between shiny new SUVs, an unceasing anger bubbling just below the surface of the bragging and posturing.

In the tiny park at the edge of the complex, distracted parents howled wearily, unable to trap their darling little elves who chased each other into the street, darting in front of cars with mischievous glee.

As I crossed the park I spotted Lusca sitting alone on a bench, a brown paper bag in her lap.

She looked in my direction and seemed to recognize me, rising from her seat with excitement, then, just as quickly, as if she might have mistaken me for someone else, sat down again, elbows planted on her thighs, eyes swallowing me as I walked toward her.

I reached her and paused a few feet away, our eyes measuring, reacquainting. She wore a burgundy velour jogging suit several sizes too big, her slight frame swallowed up in the mass of cloth. She'd lost a lot of weight. I remembered a more robust figure, not large but lively, with a laughter as unpredictable as the fragrance of wild flowers.

She smiled with difficulty and embarrassment, her haggard face telling stories of struggle and loss, of dreams unlived.

"How're you, Lusca?"

"Just fine, Mr. Overstreet." She always called me Mr. Overstreet. "Just fine. Sitting here enjoying the sunshine."

A lump rose in my throat. It was dusty in the park. Her face was dirty and smudged like it hadn't been washed in days.

I said, "You know, I live just down the street from here."

"Oh, that is good. That is good. We almost neighbors, then."

"Yes. Imagine that. How long you been living here?"

She leaned back to appraise me, her face suddenly becoming agitated. "Why you come here bothering me?" she said.

Caught off guard, I fumbled for words. She was drunk. Her cavernous eyes devoured my face like she was trying to put a spell on me. Her eyelashes were clumped together as if pasted with glue.

I sat next to her. She stood up, calling out to a little boy playing in the sand with a group of other kids.

"Malcolm, don't let me have to come and get you."

The kid turned, his face remote with surprise, then, when Lusca sat down again, he returned to his sport, hitting one of the other children with a tiny plastic bucket.

"That's Serena's boy." She looked at me as though I should've known that piece of information.

"Where's Serena?"

Her face became obscure again, lost in a thought that seemed to have taken her a thousand miles away.

"I would like to talk to her," I said.

"You can't," she said.

"It's important."

She turned to me, staring wildly. "Can you talk to the dead?"

A few feet away a couple stopped their conversation and turned to eye us suspiciously.

"Are you telling me Serena is dead?"

She looked at me with a disoriented expression. She was jacked way up, but I wasn't sure if it was alcohol alone or drugs as well.

"How old is Serena's boy?" I said.

She smiled and her eyes sparkled briefly. It lit a small fire in her face, and the corners of her mouth relaxed. "He's almost three." Her voice hopped cheerfully, and for the first time she laughed. "He can spell his name already. And he can count backward from ten. He's going to be a genius."

Head first, the little boy was now surfing the coiled slides, hotly pursued by his friends.

"Is Serena dead, Lusca?"

Her face turned to stone; the spark vanished from her eyes. She leaned back, drawing the paper bag to her lips. Half her face disappeared into the bag, and when it appeared again a dark glaze had descended on her face like the final curtain on a play, her lips pasted white with froth.

"I miss my baby," she said, sighing deeply.

A tear broke loose, hanging in the web of her eyelash for a second, then dissolved.

"What happened to her?"

Her body was still, her face blank as night. Then, with a backhand swipe, she cleaned the froth from her mouth and began to speak.

"She didn't want to have him, but I don't believe in killing, so I told her no. It happened when Malcolm was only months old. I had gone to the Pathmark on Smith Street. Only a block away. The two of them were on the bed sleeping. So peaceful. I was gone for about half an hour. When I walk through the door I heard Malcolm crying. I called out to Serena. When she didn't answer I put the bags down and went into the bedroom. I don't know what got into her mind. I didn't think she would ever do anything this crazy."

She paused and looked out across the playground for

Malcolm. He was back to playing in the sand with his bucket.

Lusca continued. "She had climbed up on a chair and tied an electric wire around the ceiling fan in the bedroom. When she jumped off the chair the whole thing came down. The fan was heavy. They said it hit her in the temple. There was blood all over the floor. I called the ambulance, but they couldn't save her."

"Was she depressed?"

"After what happened to her, what do you think?"

"You mean having the baby?"

"She was raped."

I watched as she fought valiantly against the rising flood of emotions threatening to break loose. She bit her bottom lip, her face set hard against the dark wash of memory. As though something was lodged in her craw, she gulped repeatedly, then she coughed and spat a wad of phlegm on the ground.

"I'm sorry, Lusca. When was she raped?"

"Don't pretend you don't know."

I looked at her, stunned.

She continued before I could speak. "She told me she went to Atlantic City. It was only after she found out she was pregnant that she told me the truth."

"Who did it?"

She looked at me and shrugged. "Your friends."

"My friends?"

"Your police friends. She was blocks away from home when a car stopped in front of her. Two men got out. One was a police. The other was Immigration. They told her she had to go with them, that I had been arrested. They put her in the car and drove off. But instead of taking her to the station, they took her to a house and told her that if she didn't do what they say I would be deported. They took pictures and made her have sex with different men."

"Why didn't you tell me this before?"

"I didn't want nothing more to do with no police. That included you. How did they know I didn't have my papers? The only person who knew that was you."

"You think I had something to do with this?"

"Tell me how did they know then? I kept to myself. Nobody don't know my business. You were the only person I told."

"Was she sure they were cops?"

"They had badges and guns."

"I had nothing to do with this, Lusca. You gotta believe me."

"Why should I believe you?"

"Because I would never do anything to hurt you."

"She was only thirteen. Why they had to do that to her?"

"Did you ever go back to CAIR?"

"CAIR?"

"Did you ever go back to them? I went to see them after you came to me. They didn't have any of the forms you said you filled out."

"That's crazy. Me and Serena sat there for half an hour filling out forms for the green-card lottery."

"Did Serena stop there that evening after school?"

"I don't remember." She began to sob. "She was only thirteen."

I took her bony hand in mine. "I'm really sorry, Lusca. I'm going to find the people who did this. I promise you."

I had $200 left in my pocket. I knew she was a proud woman and might refuse charity, but I offered it to her anyway. To my surprise she accepted without protest. She thanked me and squeezed my hand hard. When I got up to leave, she rose too.

My every step across the litter-strewn courtyard was filled with guilt and anger. I'd failed her. She came to me for help and I'd let her down.

But I wasn't about to fail again. And I wouldn't fail Precious, either. I was determined to get her killer.

# 28

I SHOULD'VE GOTTEN into the 4x4 and driven off. Instead I sat in the car feeling sorry for myself living on the run like a criminal. No more than ten blocks away from my home and I couldn't go there. What would I give to be sitting in my own living room or kitchen or bedroom, listening to Mingus or Nina Simone. To be able to open my fridge, get a whiff of the aged blue cheese I kept in a blue plastic container. To be able to sip beer in my underwear or watch a baseball game, or even jerk off fantasizing about making love to Anais in the shower. Crazy shit like that.

Daydreaming left me vulnerable to the surprise attack from Bressler and Slate, who'd crept up to the car without my noticing. The front passenger door flew open and I was staring down the barrel of a nine-millimeter Smith & Wesson.

"Don't even breathe," Slate hissed.

I checked the rearview mirror. Bressler had taken up a firing position behind the car, feet braced, gun cocked and aimed at the back of my head.

"Nice and slow. Hands on your head," Slate said.

I hesitated, still trying to calculate a way to escape.

"Don't even think what you're thinking," Slate snapped.

I raised my hands slowly and clasped them on top of my head.

"Good boy."

I wanted to kick his teeth in for that.

"Now get out. No sudden moves. Keep your hands where they are."

"How the hell am I supposed to do that?"

"Now, Oreo-face!"

I swiveled around and slid across the seat. When I felt my feet touch the running board I leaned my body out of the truck.

Bressler holstered his gun and came to assist his partner. He pushed me facedown onto the hood. Locking his knee between my legs from behind to force them apart, he frisked me. A few feet away, Slate watched with gun cocked as his partner lifted the snub-nose from my ankle. He ejected the clip, putting it into his pocket before tossing the empty semiautomatic to Slate. Then he wrung my hands behind my back and clamped stainless-steel bracelets to my wrists. The cold metal pinched into my flesh. Bressler straightened me up and swung me around to face them.

"They're too tight," I said.

"Too bad, asshole," Slate said, his face red and swollen from the heat.

Neither of them wore a jacket; both wore short sleeves. The underarm of Slate's gray shirt was oily with sweat.

A small group of onlookers had gathered at the corner. Bressler waved his FBI badge and told them to move on, but in New York it took more than a badge to scare a crowd.

"You're making a mistake," I said.

"And what would that be? Not cutting out your nuts and feeding those stray dogs the other day?" Slate said.

I looked at Bressler. "Is he jealous?"

Slate grabbed my throat, slamming my head hard against the side of the 4x4, and began to squeeze, his wild boar eyes constricted to slits. My knees slackened as my muscles started to melt. Firecrackers were going off in my chest. Noticing the crowd edging closer, Bressler tapped Slate's arm and he released me. I bent over, gasping for air.

They led me to their car parked two lengths behind the Jeep. Bressler pushed me to lean onto the side of the Buick while he opened the back door.

I turned my face to stare into his gray eyes. "You've got the wrong man."

Bressler squinted and smiled slyly. "Where have I heard that before?"

They shook their heads and looked at each other with perverse smirks.

"I didn't kill him!"

"Save the crying for your mama," Slate growled. "Get in the car."

"Somebody's gone to a lot of trouble to set me up," I said.

Slate stepped forward and grabbed me by the shoulder and head, attempting to force me into the car. I planted my feet, refusing to bend my back, making it impossible for him to move me.

"Help me here, goddamn it," Slate screamed at his partner.

Bressler took hold of my legs, and together they thrust me inside like a piece of furniture, banging my head on the door casing. Slate got next to me; Bressler eased behind the wheel and slammed his door, cursing.

"Listen to me for a fucking minute," I screamed, desperate now. It was over for me if they got me to jail.

Bressler sighed loudly, fidgeting in his seat as if he was sitting on coals.

"I just came from talking to a woman whose daughter went missing for a couple of days four years ago. She's from Belize and used to work for me when I was a detective. She didn't have her papers and was afraid to file a missing person's report, so she came to me for help. I began asking some questions. That same night I was shot. Her daughter came home the next day, and that was the end of that. So I thought. One of the pictures I saw next to that agent's body was this woman's daughter."

"I thought you weren't there," Slate mocked.

"This woman just told me what really happened when her daughter disappeared. She'd been kidnapped and forced to have sex, which was videotaped. I know somebody planted pictures on my computer. That's why I believe Agent Edwards' killer might be the same people who kidnapped this girl."

"How much more of this whining are we going to listen to?" Slate said.

"Finish your story, Blades," Bressler said.

"I'm now convinced more than ever that my shooting three years ago wasn't an accident. It's possible it was a hit. This woman said her daughter was kidnapped by cops and INS agents. I believe the man who shot me may've been involved in the kidnapping."

"This is crazy," exclaimed Slate.

"Can you prove any of this?" Bressler said.

"Not yet. But Troy Pagano is in a federal prison. Should be easy to get him to talk," I said.

Slate began to laugh.

"What's so funny?" I said.

He turned to me, his puffy cheeks woven with tiny purple veins. "I guess nobody's bothered to give you the news. Pagano's been out on parole since July."

I fell back onto the grease-stained seat, a sudden transcendent flush of anger flooding my brain with such fury that I became dizzy. I closed my eyes, hoping to block out the memory replay of being shot, to which my brain had fast-forwarded. The man who shot me was out on parole and nobody had bothered to tell me.

I heard Bressler's voice, but it seemed to have taken on the quality of bright white light, revolving on top of a tall building, flashing messages that I couldn't decipher.

"Blades?"

I opened my eyes. Bressler was looking at me, his eyes opened wide as if he was staring into a mirror in a funhouse.

"Do any of you have kids?" I asked.

Bressler turned back to face the street. "I've got two girls."

"How old?"

"Twelve and ten."

"The woman I just spoke to, her name is Lusca Morris. Her daughter's name was Serena. I knew her. She was a beautiful girl. Thirteen years old when they took her off the street. Today she's dead. Killed herself. After giving birth to a boy. She killed herself because she couldn't live with what they did to her. This little boy was a constant reminder of the terror, and she couldn't live with it. Now if you think I could do that to a young girl, you should just shoot me now. Make it look like an accident. I don't care. But just do it. Because anybody who would do that doesn't deserve to live."

Slate got in my face, his mouth so close to mine I thought he was going to kiss me. "Nice performance raghead, but we're not buying it. An FBI agent is dead. Do you understand what I'm saying? And you're our man."

"I believe him," Bressler said.

Slate turned to face his partner. "You what?"

"What were you doing in that apartment?" Bressler said.

"Making a drop," I said.

"A payoff?"

"Precious was supposed to meet somebody in that apartment to exchange fifty thousand dollars for some information."

"What kind of information?"

"About her father."

"Who's her father?"

"I don't know. That's the feed she was buying. Perhaps her father was an agent or an ex-agent or an informer. Look, Bressler, I think I know who killed Edwards though I don't know why. A pimp named Stubby Clapp is trying to set me up. Were he and Edwards involved in anything?"

Bressler looked at me and smiled confidently. "Tell you what, Blades. We'll make you a fair trade."

"I'm listening."

"Edwards stole a laptop with some sensitive information from the Bureau. We believe you have it. We want it back."

"I don't have it."

"Too bad." He started the car.

"Wait! What was the trade?"

"Your freedom for the laptop." He shifted the car into drive.

"Wait a minute," I said.

He gunned the motor then turned it off. The engine groaned to a halt with a percussive clickity-clack as if parts were falling off.

"I don't have it, but I know where it is."

"Then let's go get it."

"Can you take these cuffs off?" I said.

"After we get the computer."

"Come on, man. These shits hurt."

Bressler hesitated a moment, then without turning around he said to Slate, "Take off the cuffs."

Slate did not move. He stared at the back of his partner's head as if it were a hypnotist's light.

Bressler turned around. "Give me the damn keys."

Reluctantly Slate fished the keys out of his pocket and dropped them into the palm of Bressler's hand. Bressler got out and walked around to my side. He opened the door and stepped back as I slithered out. He grabbed the cuffs and I heard the metallic click and felt the pressure dissolve from my wrists.

"Thank you," I said

He stared at me, his lips crinkled at the edges. "If you're lying to me, Blades, you're gonna wish you weren't born."

I stuffed myself back into the car, manipulating my wrists to restore circulation.

TREVOR'S HOUSE WAS only five minutes away on the other side of Atlantic Avenue. The block was almost empty of cars when we got there, but Bressler chose to double-park next to a blue Mazda in front of the building.

Slate and Bressler got out and waited on either side of the car as I edged myself out of the backseat. Walking in front of them I crossed the street and went up the steps. The boughs on the trees along South Portland began to bend. Ah, a breeze! I felt it creep under my shirt, filling it for a brief moment with life. Then it was gone, like an embarrassed lover from a tryst.

I rang the doorbell. Knowing Trevor, I had some idea what might happen next, so I stepped back and to the side in anticipation of the door opening. He must've been waiting near the door because it opened almost immediately. His gun was pointed directly at Bressler's chest. The two agents dropped to their knees at the same time, groping at their waists for their weapons. I sprang inside and slammed the door behind me.

I dragged Trevor to the floor as the agents opened fire from outside. Bullets ripped through the door, burrowing into the walls above our head. When they paused to reload, I jumped up.

"Let's go!"

We ran out the back door and into the yard, trampling Trevor's summer growth of tomatoes and beans. We vaulted a low fence and into the neighbor's yard, sprinting through their garden before busting a gate to exit onto the street.

"Put that thing away!" I screamed.

Looking stupefied, Trevor stuffed the .45 into his waistband.

The Fulton Street subway stop was a block and a half away. We raced to the station and bounded down the stairs, vaulting the turnstile as a train screeched to a stop below. Making it to the platform just as the door began to close, we squeezed into a car and stood gasping for breath.

"Who the fuck was that?" Trevor said, wheezing.

Passengers were staring at us. I looked at Trevor and noticed that the gun butt was visible above the waist of his jeans. I grabbed his arm and started walking to the next car.

"Pull your shirt out," I whispered to him.

We got off at the next stop, Hoyt-Schermerhorn.

"Where's your car?" I said as we ran up the stairs.

He stopped on the stairs, hunched over. "In front of my building."

"We can't stop. Come on."

"Man, can't you see I'm trying to catch my breath."

"Catch it somewhere else. Come on."

"What the fuck's going on, Blades?"

"That was FBI you just drew on. This whole area is going to look like the training ground for an invasion in about ten minutes. Let's go."

He straightened up. "FBI! You let me draw on the fucking FBI?"

We reached the street. Hanging back at the mouth of the

train station I looked around for any sign of Bressler and Slate or a livery cab.

"I can't believe you let me draw on the FBI," Trevor moaned, leaning against the handrail.

"Coulda been worse, son."

"Worse? What could be worse?"

"You coulda shot one of them."

"Has anybody ever told you that you're a jerk, Blades?"

"I don't listen to gossip. Gimme the piece."

He hesitated.

"Come on, give me the gun," I said.

Sweat ran down the side of his face. His eyes narrowed to slender grooves, and his face became a dark valley of competing emotions. He exhaled deeply, trying to steady himself, then pulled the .45 out of his waist and handed it to me. I pushed it into the back of my waist.

Seconds later I saw a black Lincoln with livery plates. Stepping into the open, I raised my hand. The car stopped and we got in. I directed the Hispanic driver to Bergen Street, where I'd left the Jeep.

"I don't like you anymore, Blades. You got people breaking into my home and the FBI shooting at me. What's next? The Marines?"

We rode the rest of the way in silence.

"You got money in your pocket?" I said to Trevor, as the driver pulled up next to the 4x4.

"About a hundred bucks," Trevor grunted, his mouth compressed into the shape of a horse's ass.

"Take care of the fare," I said.

"What am I supposed to do now?"

"Whatever you do, don't go home," I said and got out.

I watched the Lincoln drive off. The sky seemed to be swaying like a blanket. A ghetto bird appeared out of a cloud and hovered above the buildings.

I smiled and opened the driver's door of the Jeep.

# 29

I DROVE ALONG Atlantic Avenue more vigilant than ever. How long would it be before some crazed cop got a good shot at me? And what about Troy Pagano? Would he try again now that he was out? Panic pinched my gut. My whole body tingled from the burden of knowing that the man who tried to kill me was now free. I've had drug dealers shoot at me—more out of fright than anything—because they knew I was coming to get them. Call me hypocritical, but a fellow cop crossing that line curdled my stomach.

I tried to call my mother but the cell phone had died.

AS NIGHT APPROACHED, Fulton Street's pulse quickened with that of the rest of New York. The sky had turned scarlet as if it had been dipped in blood, and it seemed to stretch to infinity. Streetlights began to pop on, like bulbs on a Christmas tree, neon signs suddenly becoming vivid, sensual, alerting the uninitiated and experienced alike to the hidden magic of this city.

I was hoping that CAIR's offices were still open.

The lights at the corner of Fulton and New York were out. Under normal conditions it was a difficult intersection to maneuver. From there, traffic turned ninety degrees left or right, or in a third direction: a thirty-five-degree right onto Thompkins. Angry, confused drivers swore as pedestrians crossed the street ignoring their honking as if, to them, the absence of traffic lights meant the area had been turned into a street mall.

The clang of iron gates signaling the closing of various stores ricocheted around me. Up ahead, multicolored streamers outside Burger King flipped giddily in the fat wind. The sky hung low over the city, and the dirt-brown buildings were now camouflaged a passionate red.

I parked on Fulton opposite a packed Chinese take-out restaurant and walked to CAIR's ground-floor office, half a block away in Restoration Plaza. It was still open.

When I walked in, a young man in linen pants and white shirt looked up from his paper-cluttered desk. He had the lean muscular frame of someone who worked out.

I introduced myself using a bogus name. In an accent as melodious as a spring shower, he told me his name was Panama Nelson.

"Is June Coxman here?" I asked.

The youngster directed me to sit and scooted off to an office in the back.

I scotched at the corner of his desk. There was one other small desk in the room, and a subway map of New York City hung on the wall, along with pictures of Marcus Garvey, Malcolm X and Dr. Martin Luther King.

Wearing brown slacks and a wheat-colored shirt with a

brown tie, June Coxman followed the youngster out of a back office. He had a plump greasy face the color of weak tea and his oblong bald head shone brightly like the dome of the Temple on the Mount. The rest of his body followed the general rule that fat was easier to accumulate than muscle. When he saw me his face froze.

"What can I do for you, Mr. Stewart?" he sang as he waddled toward me.

"Actually the name is Blades Overstreet," I said. "But you know that."

He glowered at me through uneven slits. It appeared as though one of his eyes was swollen. But it was hard to tell. His entire face looked like a bruised cantaloupe.

Panama returned to his desk, busying himself shuffling papers. June took a sip of something from a paper cup he was holding.

"You do remember me, don't you?" I asked.

"Excuse me?" His tried to sound nonchalant, but his voice quivered, a telltale sign of nervousness.

"I was here a few years ago."

"You expect me to remember that?"

"I questioned you about a girl who'd disappeared."

"You a cop?"

"Then I was."

The phone rang. Panama picked it up on the second ring. The conversation was brief. After he hung up he stood up and whispered something to Coxman, who bobbed his head. Then Panama picked up a knapsack and went through the door.

"So what do you want?" Coxman said in a voice that came from the pit of his stomach, bringing with it the sourness of his lunch. He sat down in the chair Panama had vacated and rubbed his cheek. Blood rushed to the spot. He reached for a pen and pad and began scribbling.

"Do you know a man named Troy Pagano?" I said.

He looked up. His eyes were an unnatural gray. He

stopped scribbling and straightened up in his seat, rubbing his cheek again as if it was the Rosetta Stone.

"Who?"

"How about Stubby Clapp, do you know him?"

"If this is a pop quiz, gimme a clue. What are they famous for?"

"Kidnapping little girls."

"So why're you asking me about them?"

"I was told they were friends of yours."

"You've been misinformed."

"I'd like to see Serena Morris' file."

"That name don't ring a bell."

"Do you remember the names of all the people who come through here?"

"Our files are confidential anyway."

I reached into my waist and pulled out the .45. He stiffened in the chair, his eyes roaming furtively from the gun to the cold fire in my eyes.

"Let me tell you about Serena Morris. She killed herself. After your friends kidnapped and raped her and made her pregnant. She was a nice little girl. Her mother brought her here from Belize because she thought they could build a life here. And they came to you for help. And how did you help them? You shit on their dreams."

"You don't know what you're talking about. We've been serving the Caribbean community for eight years without one complaint. We must be doing something right. So why don't you get out of here waving that gun around like some damn lunatic before I call the police."

I grabbed his tie and pulled. His head jerked backward like he'd been smacked in the face. I cocked the gun inside his nose cavity. His jaws tightened; his eyes opened full bore.

"Get me Serena's file before I turn your nose into the Holland Tunnel."

"The files are over there." He nodded his head in the direction of a filing cabinet directly behind him.

He stood up. Too quickly. I reacted just as quickly, backhanding him with the butt of the gun. Blood squirted from his busted lip painting the front of his shirt crimson.

"Are you crazy?" he screamed, holding his mouth.

"I'd just as soon get my mack on with you. I don't care. No more sudden moves."

He walked to the back of the room. I stayed close to him. His body had the odor of fish exposed too long in the summer heat. When he reached the filing cabinet he drew the drawer out slowly. He searched one then another. After a few minutes of this, he glanced at me, his eyes limp and scared.

"I don't see it. How long ago did you say she was here?"

"You're not making me smile."

"I can't find a file for somebody who's never been here." He spat blood contemptuously on the floor.

His arrogance set off a keg of anger in me. I brought my elbow down on the back of his neck, and he crumpled to the floor like a punctured blimp. I hunched over him, sickened by his smell and by the blood gushing from his mouth.

"You need to understand what's going on here, Juney-boy. Every cop in the city is having wet dreams about putting a bullet in my brain. I ain't going out like that. And if I gotta go, I'm taking the garbage out first, you being the first bag of shit to hit the sidewalk if you don't find a way to make me smile."

"Then fuck you, alright! Shoot me if you want."

My instinct told me his bluster was a result of fear. Not of me but of someone else. My guess was that the bogey man of his dreams would be Stubby Clapp. I decided it was time to hasten the onset of his nightmare.

"What'd you do with the files?"

He swallowed hard, his Adams apple ballooning like a lizard's sac. "Why're you running up on me like this, bro?"

"I ain't your bro."

"I told you this is a legit business."

"And I'm the Pope."

"That's your problem, not mine."

I slapped him. "Where's Stubby Clapp?"

"I don't know who you're talking about."

"How many girls have you helped him kidnap?"

"I bet you ain't so tough without that gun." He tightened his jaws arrogantly.

"Oh, you do, eh?"

"Yeah, I do. "

I eased up off him and stuffed the .45 into my waist.

He got to his knees. As he began to straighten up, I jerked my knee up, quick and hard under his groin. He squealed like a woman in childbirth and slumped to the floor.

"Give Stubby a message for me. Tell him instead of soap I have a stick of dynamite for his ass the next time I see him."

I left him groaning on the floor.

# 30

I GOT INTO the 4x4 and rolled down the window. My stomach began to snap at me as I waited to see what Coxman would do. The temptation to get out and order from the Chinese restaurant quickly passed. From where I was sitting I could see the inside; it was no bigger than a coffin. Either the food was great or dirt cheap; the place was still packed. Its grimy graffiti-scarred walls looked like they hadn't been painted or cleaned in years. I decided my hunger could wait.

Two feet away, in the doorway of an abandoned building, a drunk, bleeding from a cut above his eye, struggled to get to his feet. At a phone booth next to the Jeep a skinny man was shamelessly begging for pussy. A smile sneaked across my face as I listened, letting my mind roam back to the first time I seduced Anais. It was inside the foyer of the apartment building where she lived on Fifty-seventh Street in Manhattan. She made me get down on all fours and lick the back of her knees right there before she would let me upstairs, even before I could kiss her. It was the funniest, most romantic thing I've ever done.

Twenty minutes later Coxman came limping down the sidewalk. He crossed the street like a man with a purpose, got into a red, late-model Audi parked opposite a bridal store and drove away. I followed several car lengths behind.

Coxman turned right off a filthy Fulton Street, choked with traffic; I followed, keeping my distance as he turned onto Thomas Boylan Avenue. Now I knew where he was going and could follow at a safe distance. For someone who'd never heard of Stubby Clapp, Coxman had found out about his restaurant mighty quick.

He pulled up outside Clapp's Palace and, moving as fast as his rubber legs would propel him, stumbled inside. I parked about twenty yards away. Stubby was too smart to be at this location knowing that I'd tagged him here once before, so I waited.

A green Supra passed me and pulled up behind the Audi. A woman got out and then leaned back into the car to say something to the driver. When she straightened up again I recognized her. T-J, the prostitute from St. Johns Place. She turned, and after pausing a second to light a cigarette, went into the diner.

Coxman's visit was brief. Five minutes later he staggered out again. This time followed by Simon, he of the pointy gargoyle ears. I slipped the automatic out of my waist and placed it on the seat beside me.

The two of them got into Coxman's Audi and drove off. I followed at what I thought was a discreet distance. When they slowed down to merge onto Linden Boulevard, I braked to keep my spacing. That's when the Supra rushed up beside me. I turned to see Noodles, a fleecy smirk on his face, training a large pistol in my direction. I mashed the gas pedal to the floor and ducked.

*Pop! Pop!*

The left rear window shattered, spraying nuggets of glass onto my neck. I flew ahead weaving in and out of traffic with the Supra stuck to me like Velcro. The Audi was still in view up ahead. I checked my rearview mirrors again. Noodles was lining up another shot.

Gripping the steering wheel tightly, I swerved left abruptly, funneling the 4x4 into a tight opening between a truck and a car. I checked for Noodles. Didn't seem like he made it through the opening, but I couldn't tell where he was either.

Damn! Traffic was beginning to slow down.

*Pop-po-pop! Pop!*

Frantically I checked my mirrors. The Supra was on my right, sandwiched between a Bronco and another car. Noodles seemed to be firing indiscriminately at anything in his way. The sound of broken glass filled the night as he shot out someone's window. It wasn't mine. Drivers began to honk their horns in panic. Some were driving onto the median to get out of the way of flying bullets. I swerved into the right lane, cutting off a truck, and climbed the median crossing over into the narrow access road. To my left Noodles was attempting the same maneuver at about eighty miles an hour. The low-chassied Supra failed to make it over the median, its underside scraping along the concrete, sending a shower of sparks into the air. Then it careened off the median, out of control, bounced off an eighteen-wheeler and flipped into the air. When I checked my mirrors again, the car was skating on its top like a turtle slaloming on its back.

I took several deep breaths, spat out the window and sped on. A spasm of electricity flew through my body. The tension made my gut hurt. I dragged air into my lungs in short frenetic gasps.

Brooklyn had given way to Queens when I merged back onto the highway. I'd lost the Audi. I was now speeding along North Conduit Avenue, which fed into Kennedy Airport. I was doing seventy-five, zipping past cars, but I had no idea where I was going. I was still shaking. Taking deeper breaths to calm myself, I slowed down and turned onto the exit before the airport.

Chances were, Coxman hadn't been speeding to catch a flight. I coasted along the poorly lit street with nothing but grass and low-slung warehouses on either side. At the intersection, I stopped on red. Leaning my head forward onto the steering wheel for a moment's relief, I happened to glance to my right. At the end of the next block I saw a Mobil gas station and what looked like a red car. The light was still red, but eager to get a better look at the car, I edged through the intersection, turning right and parking next to a chain-link fence in the shadows of an oak whose branches stretched across the street.

It was the Audi. With his jeans slung low across his ass, Gargoyle stood outside eyeing the gas meter. The spigot was lodged in the Audi's tank. I doused my lights.

I wanted a cigarette. I was out of gum and my throat was parched. My calves and bladder ached. I hated this shit.

I tried not to think of the pain in my bladder as I watched Gargoyle remove the spigot with a violent rattle as if he was angry at having to pump gas. For a second I closed my eyes and thought of Anais. What was she doing right now? What would she do if she knew how much trouble I was in? Would she pity me? Would she laugh in my face if I called and told her how much I missed her?

When I opened my eyes, Gargoyle had finished his job. He got into the car and slammed the door. The Audi pulled away from the station, pausing briefly to let a truck go by, then zipping across the street, turning into eastbound traffic. I tagged behind.

At the next light the Audi turned left and drove along a

narrow, dimly lit street next to a large park. The arching branches of ancient oaks, some as thick as a tank, met above the road, forming a dark tunnel. I slid through the damp channel of trees behind the Audi for another ten blocks before Coxman made a sudden right turn and slowed down, coasting to a stop behind a white Escalade in front of a large brick house with a lawn, surrounded by trees. I killed my lights and drifted to within fifty yards before I stopped. I could almost smell Stubby.

Coxman and Simon got out. Waving his hand in the air, Coxman said something to Simon, and the gargoyle got back into the car and slammed the door. Coxman hobbled up the steps to the house. I waited a few minutes to see if he would come out again before springing into action.

I got out and relieved myself against the side of the Jeep. Then, with the automatic at my side like a trusted sword, I crept up on Gargoyle. He was so short I could barely make out the outline of his head. The fool hadn't locked his door. When I grabbed and pulled, it opened. He bolted upright. My elbow crashed into his jawbone. I felt the crunch as his jaw broke. He flopped down on the seat.

Grabbing his do-rag I jerked him upright, corkscrewing my gun into his right ear.

"Who's inside?" I snapped.

"Your mama. I fucked her last night." He tried to spit blood at me. I dragged his head out the door and his crimson spittle fell harmlessly onto the ground.

There were times when a man needed to be humble. This was such a time for Gargoyle. Here I was feeling bad that I'd broken his jaw, and he still sought to disrespect me.

I smacked him behind the ear with the gun butt, hard enough to keep him eating Advil for days but not to knock him out. His head sagged and went limp. I slapped his face and he jerked upright. I dragged him from the car and closed the door.

"Let's go, Spock."

I nudged him forward. Each time he bucked I jammed the gun into his ribs and he straightened up. He stopped and spat onto the ground, cursing. I suspected his jaw was swelling fast; soon from now he wouldn't be able to open his mouth to speak. I kicked the back of his leg and like a mule he jerked and started walking.

At the front door I crouched behind his tortoiselike frame. Except for one light coming from a back room, the house was dark inside.

"You got a key?" I asked.

He flinched, but was silent.

"Answer me, shithead," I said.

"What the fuck I look like? The super?" He mumbled with difficulty.

"Press the bell."

He spat on the ground. It was a mixture of blood and phlegm.

"Do it," I hissed.

He jammed the buzzer with angry energy. A voice inside the house swelled, erupting in curses, then I heard the hushed pounding of heavy feet on carpet as someone hastened to the door. I hunkered down behind Simon, my arm locked around his neck, the gun nozzle sealed into the small of his back.

"You know what to do. Get cute and I cap your ass right here," I said.

"Who is it?" said Coxman from behind the door.

"Open the door," Simon said.

"I told you to stay in the car," Coxman said.

"Man, open the muthafucking door before I break the shit down."

Coxman cursed some more, then the door opened. He stood in the doorway, a nervous lump, his eyes shadowed by the largesse of his cheeks. Before he could speak, I rose up with the speed of a snake, wrenching Simon's neck

sideways as hard as I could. I didn't know if I broke it, but
he fell in a heap to the ground. I instantly shifted the gun to
Coxman's head. He stiffened. I hated being this close to
him. His smell made it hard for me to breathe.

"Not a sound," I said.

Coxman stared at me, stricken, his eyes washed in fear.
He took a look at Simon and his face contracted. Blood
oozed from the corner of Simon's mouth.

"Is Stubby here?" I said.

He nodded and glanced off to the left toward a door
leading to the back of the house.

"How many people down there?" I said.

For a moment he stood breathing stiffly, as if waiting for
a translation. Light streamed from the back room, and I
could hear voices in the basement below. The room was
large and had an air of affluent living: sumptuous red sofa
and love seat, modern European lamps, prints of black and
white photographs of snow-capped trees and bridges by
Ansel Adams.

"How many?" I pushed the gun like a bayonet into the
folds of his flesh.

"Five."

"What're they doing?"

He gulped. "Making a movie."

"Let's go," I ordered.

Woodenly, he shuffled off. I stayed close, trying not to
breathe too deeply. We entered the kitchen. It was empty. A
door leading, I presumed, to the basement was open. Faint
voices rose from below. I couldn't make out any of the
voices distinctly.

Then I heard a girl's tiny wheezy voice. It was a
shielded cry, one that was being forced back in fear.

Keeping Coxman in front of me I crept through the
kitchen to the top of the stairs. They were bound to hear me
coming down the stairs, but my options were limited. We

were still on the top rung when Coxman transformed himself into Spiderman, leaping to the bottom of the stairs in
one jump.

"Stubby!" he screamed.

I squeezed the trigger. The .45 jerked. A bullet ripped
open the back of Coxman's head. He was dead before his
head hit the floor.

The lights went out below. Screams and quick snappy
orders signaled the ending of the party. I leapfrogged the
remaining stairs, landing in a crouch beside Coxman's
crumpled body.

The room was black. I couldn't see anything. A door
opened and closed. A quiet whimpering began. Gradually
my eyes regained focus in the dark. There was no one in
the room save for a little girl on the bed.

I jumped to my feet, reaching the back door in two
strides. I peered around the side of the house.

The *vroom* of a large engine being gunned into action
broke the warm nighttime silence. I stepped outside, gun
held tightly in two hands, advancing cautiously until I
could see the area in front of the house and the street
clearly. A car squealed away from the curb. I raced down
the driveway in time to see the Escalade gobbling up real
estate down the street.

There was no point following them. I returned to the
basement and flicked on the light.

The trembling little girl curled up on the bed was naked.
She was crying, making little muffled noises. Her body
shook with a stubborn rhythm, as if under some mechani-
cal power. I couldn't see her face well, but I guessed her
age to be about twelve or thirteen. She wore long exten-
sions woven into tiny braids. The room was stocked with
digital video-recording equipment: three cameras, one on a
tripod, one laying on the floor and another on the bed near
the little girl's tiny feet.

An old couch was propped against the wall, along with

two other broken chairs. The room had an odor of stale urine, and the warped wallpaper was stained with mildew.

"Where're your clothes?" I said to her.

She didn't answer. Her muffled crying turned to sobs.

"Get your clothes. I'm taking you home."

She didn't move. But I couldn't wait around for her to figure out she'd been rescued. Neighbors might've heard the shooting and called the police. I pulled the sheet from under her and threw it around her body.

"Listen to me," I said. "Everything's okay. You're safe now."

She sat up, taking deep gulps of air into her lungs, but she simply couldn't stop shaking.

"What's your name?" I said.

For the first time she faced me. Her round tiny face was blotchy around the cheeks, like someone had been pinching her roughly. Her eyes were red funnels of fear.

"What's your name?" I said again.

She remained silent, glaring at me with a vacant intensity that only asserted her pain and fear.

"Where do you live?" I tried again.

"Rutland Road." Her voice trembled.

"Your mother's there?"

She nodded.

"What's her name?"

She stared at me without answering.

"Okay, let's go. The bad men are gone. I'm taking you home," I said.

Wrapped tightly in the white sheet, she got down off the bed, her tiny body lost in the swirls and folds of cloth. She looked like a trick-or-treater in a Halloween costume. We exited through the back door.

The houses around were dark and silent. Bowed tree limbs hung across the street as we walked briskly under the shadowy canopy to the Jeep. In the distance, police sirens scorched the night with a profane noise.

As we drove she sneaked bewildered glances at me from time to time. We left Queens and were driving along Linden Boulevard in Brooklyn before she spoke again.

"Who you?" Her voice was soft, like air rushing out of a tire.

"Don't worry. I'm not going to hurt you."

She fell silent until we reached Rockaway Boulevard.

"What's your address?" I said.

"Three forty-five Rutland Road."

"That's near Flatbush?"

She nodded.

"You Trini?" I said. I could tell by her accent.

"Yes."

"My partner's from Trinidad. He used to be a singer. You like Calypso?"

She shook her head.

"No, why not?" I said.

"I like reggae and hip-hop."

"You sure you're Trini? You can't be Trini."

"I was born in Diego Martin."

"How long were you in that house?" I said.

Her body swelled as if it were a balloon as she struggled to fight back tears. She pulled the sheet tighter and looked out the window without answering.

"Where did they take you from?" I said.

"He came to my house in a big white car."

"Who?"

"The man with the gold teeth."

"Was your mother there?"

"Yes."

"And she let you go with him?"

She looked at me, then straight ahead and started speaking in a blank monotone.

"She told me I had to go. That I was supposed to go to work for a woman. But when I get there they say that me and my mother here illegally and that if I don't do what they say I would not see her again. That Immigration would put her in jail and send her back to Trinidad. And that if I told anybody about what happen in the house, the police would come and send me back to Trinidad too. Then they make me take off my clothes."

"What's your name?"

"Carmen Belmont."

I smiled. I'm such a sucker for girls named Carmen.

# 31

❧ CARNIVAL CAME EARLY to Carmen's home. No more than five seconds after her mother gurgled a phlegm-filled "Who there" over the intercom in reply to my impatient pressing of the buzzer and heard her daughter's "It's me. Carmen," she came bounding down the stairs.

There was crying in the hallway, joyful screams in the elevator and loud laughter in the small apartment. Carmen's aunt had been left sitting in the kitchen with chemicals in her hair. By the time Carmen's mother remembered, the chemicals had burned her sister's scalp white.

Hugging and crying went on for some time. Then someone arrived with food and drinks: roti and callaloo and rice and peas. And the calypso music started. I was glad for the food. After downing my third Carib beer, I pulled Carmen's mother, Phyllis, aside to get her story.

Her ordeal started about a month ago. She worked in a little auto supply store on Utica Avenue, owned by a friend of a friend. One evening Immigration and the police swooped in and arrested her. The three men, two blacks and one white, were all in plainclothes. One black man was broad with a bald head, the other young and good-looking. The white man was tall with gold-rimmed glasses and wore cowboy boots.

She had no idea how they found out she didn't have her papers. They put her in the back of a van and drove off. All she could think of was her daughter. She began to cry. The bald-headed man kept screaming at her to shut up. When she did manage to calm down, they started their questioning.

They asked her all kinds of questions, from who was the last person she had sex with to when she was born. How did she get into the country? Did she pay to get her visa? Did she know it was a crime to stay in America without the right visa? And so on. She began to cry again. She asked them what would happen to her daughter, but they refused to answer.

They pulled up outside a precinct; she was too scared to notice which one. The two black detectives got out and went inside. The Immigration guy began to talk to her in a friendly voice.

"Listen, I know you don't want to be deported. Your daughter is in school. I know you like it here. My friends went inside to see if there's any space to hold you here overnight. If not, we gonna take you downtown to the Immigration detention center. Once you're in there you don't get out. I can help you, if you're willing to help me."

She looked at him, drying the tears from her eyes.

"This is just a job to me," he said. "I don't care if you stay in this country. I don't have a problem with immigrants. Legal or illegal. My great-grandfather came here from Ireland. He didn't have a visa to stay. But three generations later we're all still here. You can be back home in fifteen minutes. But here's my situation. My wife, she runs a little business. How old is your daughter again?"

"Thirteen."

"What's her name?"

"Carmen."

"Carmen? That's a nice name. Anyway, my wife, she runs this business, you see. She hires people to go out and clean other people's homes. You know, middle-class fuckers who wanna play they're rich. Too lazy to clean their own houses. Anyway, it's hard for my wife to find people. She tried hiring Polish immigrants but they're too organized. They want eight, nine dollars an hour. More than fucking minimum wage. Imagine that. But see now, if she was to hire your daughter, she could pay her below minimum off the books and that would work for all of us. Everybody would benefit. Carmen would only have to work weekends. She could make some money for herself. Teenagers always want stuff. Music, clothes, jewelry. You wouldn't have to worry about buying her things. And my wife would do okay too. We would all benefit. And I might even be able to help you get your papers. See what I mean. We all benefit."

She was too stunned to say anything.

He touched her arm. "So do we have a deal?"

She searched his green eyes. "You serious? You would let me go?"

"Give me your word and you're free. One thing I know about West Indians. They're very trustworthy. I think I can trust you, can't I?"

She nodded.

He pinched her cheek, as though he was playing with a child. "If you try to double-cross me, realize that we found you once and we can find you again. And I wouldn't be so nice next time. With all the shit going on with immigration you don't want to go into the system. You'd never get out."

She wanted to slap his hand away from her face; instead she forced a smile. "And all I have to do is let Carmen work for your wife?"

"That's all."

"And you'll help me get papers?"

"We can arrange that."

They shook hands, and he got behind the wheel of the van and drove her home. Before she got out, he said she would hear from him in a few days.

She didn't hear anything for about three weeks. Then someone called and asked if Carmen could work the next week. She said yes.

Last night a man with a soft voice called. He was polite and friendly. He said someone would pick Carmen up the next day and would bring her back home. His reassuring voice made her feel comfortable letting Carmen go. A white truck showed up next morning at seven o'clock. The driver, a dark, short man with gold caps, said Carmen would be back by four.

When six o'clock passed and Carmen didn't come home, Phyllis got worried. She had no idea where they'd taken Carmen to work. They'd given her a number, but when she called, it rang and rang. By nine o'clock she was in tears but was afraid to call the police.

Even before she confirmed it, I suspected that she'd visited CAIR's offices a few days before she got picked up.

I told her to take Carmen to the hospital and have her checked out and despite her fears, to call the police. Then I gave her the name of a lawyer who, I told her, would help her if she got into any trouble. She smiled at me and in her weak smile I saw that she would do neither of the things I suggested.

I left the apartment around midnight. Cruising along

Flatbush going nowhere in particular, I began to feel the effects of the night's exertion and the alcohol. I felt lethargic and dopey; my back and shoulders ached. Where was I going to sleep? Night would guard me from the NYPD. Until tomorrow.

# 32

LEAVING THE JEEP in an alley instead of the hotel parking lot, I registered at the Marriott in Metro Park as Earl Lovett and got a room with a mini bar. The first thing I did, even before I checked the bed, was to plug my phone in to charge.

Relieving myself of the automatic, which I placed on the pillow, I threw myself fully clothed across the king-size bed and closed my eyes. Fifteen minutes later I was still rolling around like a bowling pin. My eyes burned as if sprinkled with lye. I could not relax. My mind, rebelling against sleep, buzzed and crackled like a short-circuited bulb.

I got up and called my mother. She began to cry as soon as she heard my voice.

"Oh, Carmen, where're you?"

"Don't worry, Mother. I'm fine."

"How can you say that? My God! Jason is out there. God knows where. He could be dead. And you? You're wanted for murder. And you tell me not to worry?"

"I can't talk now."

"Please, Carmen. Don't hang up. I need to talk to somebody."

"Gotta go, Mother."

"Carmen, please."

I hung up. Calling her on the hotel phone was risky. The consequences could be my freedom, but I wanted to hear her voice, let her know that I was okay. I'm sure her phone was tapped, but I wasn't on long enough for them to trace the call. I walked to the window and looked out. Below, Adams Street was deserted.

I wished I knew where Trevor was. Would I be able to get to Stubby and Troy Pagano before the police got to me?

It was obvious that Stubby was involved in some kind of child-porno ring using the threat of deportation to corral scared young girls. But how big was it? Had Agent Edwards been part of Stubby's crew? Is that why he was iced?

If Stubby wanted to get into the porno business, why kids? He had a stable of prostitutes. Why not use them? Then I remembered seeing T-J going into Stubby's place. I checked the clock. It was three o'clock. I grabbed my keys and the .45 and left the room, hoping T-J wasn't one of those vampire prostitutes who worked until the sun came up.


THE AREA WAS still very much alive. Bars on Utica Avenue were still open, and young men lingered at street corners. When I parked outside 724 St. Johns Place, it was three-twenty. The door to the courtyard was closed, but the lock was broken. I walked in and crossed the courtyard. After buzzing several apartments, including T-J's, I waited to see if the tactic, which usually worked in large ghetto apartment buildings, would be successful. Presently, I heard the electronic *bzzzz* of the door unlocking. I was in.

There was a sign saying that the elevator was out. Wearily, I climbed the ten flights, which left me out of breath by the time I reached T-J's apartment. There was a strange quiet in the narrow hallway. I felt as if I was in a prison.

I pressed the doorbell. There was no answer. I pressed it again.

"Who is it?" T-J's voice gurgled from deep inside the apartment.

"Blades Overstreet. I have to talk to you."

"Do you know what time it is?"

"I saw you earlier tonight and wanted to talk to you but it wasn't a good time."

I heard her footsteps approaching the door. A few seconds later, the bolts clacked and the door opened. T-J's face was covered with green stuff, I imagined some kind of facial scrub. She had a towel wrapped around her, a toothbrush in her hand.

"Can I come in?"

She looked up and down the hallway. Then she stepped back. I entered and she closed the door.

"What's this about now? You came back to give me some private dick? Well, I'm not in the mood now, thank you."

"Are you one of Stubby's girls?"

"Who?"

"I saw you with one of his boys tonight, going into his restaurant."

"What're you? My pimp? Have you been following me around?"

"You didn't answer my question."

"I don't have to answer you, muthafucker. Get out!"

"Did you know that Stubby was going to park that agent?"

"Get the fuck out my house, limp-dick muthafucker! Who you think you are, coming here accusing me of shit?"

"I'm not accusing you of anything, but being an accessory to the murder of a federal agent can get you slapped on the barbecue pit without the sauce. Think about that."

"I shoulda dropped a coin on your ass when I heard your voice just now."

I saw a shadow out of the corner of my eye. I looked around. It was a young girl, about fifteen or sixteen. She was tall, wearing pink shorty pajamas.

"What's going on, Mom?" she said, squinting.

"Go back to bed, Adora," T-J said.

"Is everything okay?"

"Yes, now go on back to bed."

"Who's that man?"

"Girl, I said get back to bed!"

Screwing up her face and rubbing her eyes, the girl turned and disappeared.

"What about your daughter?" I said. "All the sacrifice you've made for her. Are you willing to throw that away? Stubby is a fat piece of shit. He kidnaps little girls. Children. Forces them to do porno videos. You wanna protect scum like that?"

"Save your sermon for next Sunday, preacher. You don't know shit, understand. You don't know Stubby. You don't know about when I was in the hospital for a month fighting for my life. Who convinced me not to give up. You don't know about my bills taken care of. My daughter's private piano lessons paid for. So don't come lecturing me about the devil, okay. Now get out!"

She opened the door.

I grabbed the door and slammed it shut.

"You wanna hear a fucking sermon?" I shouted. "Listen to this. I knew one of the girls Stubby kidnapped. She was thirteen. Coulda been anything she wanted. Had her heart set on being a doctor. Now she's dead. Now tell me how you would feel if that girl's name was Adora."

T-J turned her head, averting my gaze.

"It's nice that Stubby helped you through a bad time. But you know what, I don't give a fuck about that. He's still a rat. And I'm going to squash his head until every ounce of slime runs out."

I ripped the phone number off the back of my cell phone and held it out to her. "If you change your mind and want to talk to me, here's my number."

She refused to look at me or take the piece of paper. I let it fall. It floated to the ground, landing on her foot. Then I stepped into the hallway and heard the door slam behind me.

I ALMOST BROKE the bar in my room that night. In between drinks, I caught glimpses of movies on cable. In between glimpses of movies, I dozed and hallucinated about making love to Precious on the roof of my apartment building. She was crying and wanted me to stop, but I couldn't. As dawn grew, Precious' face dissolved away, and I dreamed of running with Anais on a deserted beach while bullets kicked sand around us.

# 33

MY EYES DIDN'T open again until four o'clock the next afternoon. My stomach hurt, my lips were welded together, my mouth raw and full of mucus. Moving like a phantom, I made it to the bathroom. I didn't know if I was still drunk or dead. I looked at my eyes in the mirror and flinched. They were red and leathery, as if all my blood had flowed there and stopped.

I managed to shower without swallowing the soap. My mind was a fog and my stomach was as empty as a right-wing think tank. After I dried off, I realized I had no clean clothes. I put my pants on without shorts and ordered coffee, eggs and grilled salmon from room service.

I then called Semin Jhoti.

"Blades, where the hell are you?"

"Can't tell you that, Semin," I said, happy for the concern in her voice.

"Are you safe?"

"I'm okay."

"You better stay that way."

"You got anything interesting to tell me?"

"Lots," she said.

"That's what I wanted to hear."

"Just a second. Let me get my computer."

I lit a cigarette as I waited for Semin to return but snuffed it after one drag. Semin came back sounding purposeful and businesslike.

"Blades, I don't need to tell you how to live your life, but aren't you worried that the police might shoot first and ask questions later?"

"I'm watching my back."

"How can you watch your own back?"

"You learn to do it in Undercover."

"I worry about you, Blades."

"Thanks, Semin. I'll be careful. Let's start with Agent Edwards. I understand that the FBI was getting ready to scalp him."

"Yes. My sources tell me that there was an investigation into the selling of information."

"What kind of information?"

"Agent Edwards was part of a countermilitia task force. The FBI seems to think he might've tipped some militia members suspected of weapons and drug trafficking to impending FBI raids. On at least two such raids the suspects managed to slip away and were in Mexico hours before the FBI arrived."

"What would be his motive?"

"Gambling. He was in the tank for several large ones."

"Have you heard anything about computers missing from the FBI?"

"No. Is this something you know about?"

"A little."

"A little? Come on, Blades. Out with it."

"Not now, Semin. What else you got on Edwards?"

"Went to Georgetown. Graduated with a law degree. He lived on Long Island. A wife and a little girl. Had a lot of debt."

"Did you talk to his wife?"

"She's gone into hiding."

"Okay, let's move to our congresswoman."

"Well, she went to school in the south. Was active in the civil rights movement. Owned her own financial consulting business and was very outspoken in the community about immigration issues, which led her into politics. Never married. No children. Rumor is she likes younger men. In fact, she almost lost a city council reelection several years back because of a scandal when she allegedly called a campaign worker a fag because he spurned her advances."

"Anything connecting her to Agent Edwards?"

"Not that I could find."

"What about Gabe?"

"Gabe?" She chuckled. "You mean Gabriel Aquia? Is he a friend of yours?"

"Oh yeah, we're kindred spirits."

She laughed. "I know you too good to believe that. Gabriel Aquia is one interesting subject."

"How so?"

"The man has his fingers in so many pots I'm surprised he can still wipe his ass. He either owns outright or is a partner in about three or four businesses. A small import-export and shipping concern, an African art gallery, a recording studio, and he's always flying out of the country."

"Where to?"

"Europe, mostly. Africa. The Caribbean."

"How often?"

"Three . . . four times a week. He gets around. But here's

really what makes him interesting. All that stuff I just mentioned is minor compared to his latest venture. This is a man about to hit the lottery. Jump into the big-money leagues. What do you know about empowerment zones?"

"They empower nobody but the rich."

"Close. Gabriel Aquia is the owner and president of a company called the Aquia Development Group. It's a real estate development company but hasn't really done any big projects so far. A few renovations here and there. They refurbished Restoration Plaza. Nothing major. The rumor is that Aquia Development is the frontrunner to get the contract to develop some Brooklyn waterfront property along the East River and also the redevelopment of Fulton Street in Bedford Stuyvesant. We're talking malls, restaurants, a cineplex, condominiums. Those areas were declared empowerment zones a few years ago by President Clinton. But the Mayor and the Governor have been squabbling over control and have only recently agreed to cough up their one hundred million to match the three hundred million put up by the federal government. Along with that, the City is kicking in another fifty million to build a park. Aquia Development had already snapped up a number of old warehouses along that waterfront for about four million dollars at auction and some abandoned buildings along Fulton for one million and stands to get the kind of tax-break incentives worth a fortune. In fact, construction on a shopping complex budgeted at a hundred and ten million dollars could begin on one of the sites as early as next year. It could turn a small developer like Gabriel Aquia into a multimillionaire overnight."

"That's Congresswoman Richardson's district, isn't it?"

"What's more, she's head of the board of New Bedford Empowerment Corporation, the nonprofit corporation that will handpick the developer."

"Where did he get the kind of money to buy those warehouses?"

"I guess his other businesses are doing well."

"That's a little too well. Is he married?"

"The man's a loner. Lives in Westchester. Just bought a home in Harlem. No wife. No children. His father came from Ghana. He dropped out of school at fifteen, later got a G.E.D. before joining the Army. He rose to the highest NCO before getting discharged for fighting. He enrolled in NYU and finished a degree in computer technology in three and a half years with a three point seven five GPA."

"So he's also some kind of computer geek?"

"He's a bright man."

"When was he in the Army?"

"Eighty to eighty-six."

"What company?"

"Bravo Company. Fifth Platoon."

"That's the same company Stubby Clapp was in."

"Who?"

"Somebody I know."

"Blades, when are you going to tell me what's really going on? You promised me a story. I don't want to have to take it from your hospital bed again, you know."

"Don't worry, Semin. You'll get your story. And I don't intend to be in the hospital for anything other than to give blood."

She laughed. "Take care of yourself, Blades."

"Keep your cell phone on. You never know when I might be calling."

She laughed again. "Bye, sweets."

After I hung up I went to the fridge, searching for juice. The only thing I hadn't finished was the bottled water. I opened one just as room service arrived.

As I ate, I mused on the information Semin had given me. Gabriel Aquia was a man of many surprises. And I'd allowed his *GQ* mannerisms to fool me, thinking he was just style and bullshit. He was obviously an ambitious man, someone to be reckoned with.

* * *

AFTER MY MEAL, I called my mother again to see if she'd heard from Jason. There was nothing new on that front. She told me Melanie had called saying she was concerned and would be flying back from California. That surprised me. And I was touched, but I told Mom to call Melanie back and tell her not to come. That everything would be okay. Then I hollered at Milo. He was in surprisingly good spirits. Frankly, I was disappointed. I thought he would've been more concerned about me. The police had been to the store a number of times, but business was going on despite the intrusions.

The next two hours were spent shopping in the Fulton Mall, where I also got some cash from a machine. I went back to the hotel, got rid of the clothes I'd been wearing for the past twenty-four hours, and dressed in baggy black jeans and a loose-fitting blue polo shirt picked up at Macy's.

It was now nine o'clock. Anxious for any lead on Troy Pagano, I tried to get in touch with the guys from our old Undercover outfit. I hadn't kept up with either Nelson Rodriquez or Evan Miguel. Using the little acting skill I'd picked up standing in for actors in the James Baldwin Playwriting Workshop run by Noah Plantier, I called the 103rd Precinct, where Nelson Rodriquez had been transferred after my shooting, pretending to be an old high school friend. Apparently Nelson Rodriquez had left the department. I called information and got four listings in Manhattan for Nelson Rodriquez. The third one of those numbers was for a bodega in Washington Heights. A little girl answered the phone. Then someone took the phone from her and said hello. It was Nelson. After a lengthy preamble, he told me he got injured in a fall from the second-floor fire escape of an apartment building while chasing a drug dealer. He bought a bodega and now spent his days trying

to prevent kids from stealing his candy. Evan Miguel had
been killed in a boating accident in Puerto Rico. I asked
him if he'd heard that Troy Pagano was out. Troy had
called him once, he said, ironically to ask about me. He
hadn't left a number, which didn't surprise me. But Nelson
knew that his brother, Rudy Pagano, a detective in the 1st
Precinct, hung out at the Blue Girl on North Moore Street.

MINUTES LATER I was rumbling over the metal grating of
the Brooklyn Bridge in the 4x4, stealing glances at the
hypnotic Manhattan skyline. At the speed I was going, the
lighted skyscrapers looked like exploding fireworks. Beneath me, traffic whirred in waves up the FDR.

If Rudy Pagano happened to be at the Blue Girl, he
most likely would be in the company of other cops. To separate him from his friends wouldn't be easy. But what
choice did I have?

I parked the 4x4 across the street from the Blue Girl, a
safe distance from a hydrant, leaving little space for another car. I didn't want the Jeep to be hemmed in, just in
case I had to make a quick getaway. Then I crossed the
shadowy street.

Many of the old factory buildings of this once-thriving
manufacturing area had been turned into lofts for yuppies
and washed-up movie stars, with the accompanying over-
hyped restaurants catering to their taste for caviar and foie
gras. A few of the rough-edged bars once frequented by
factory workers had remained, however, kept in business
by construction workers and cops from the precinct
nearby.

The Blue Girl sat on the corner of one of these new-
trendy streets. With its black door and dingy neon sign
hanging askew, it didn't look like much from the outside.
But inside the atmosphere was perfect for getting drunk.
The air was stale in the ultra-dark interior. Blasting full

volume from the jukebox in the back, Bruce Springsteen's *Born in the U.S.A.* drowned out any other sound. I stepped through a wall of smoke and headed to the bar. It was not as crowded as I expected. Then I remembered the Yankees were playing the Mets at Shea.

A group of men, each using the American flag as a head tie, were throwing darts at something—I imagined a dartboard, but I couldn't see well enough. There was one empty stool at the bar. I sat down and ordered Jack Daniel's on the rocks. As the barman poured my drink from a half-full Jack Daniel's bottle, I turned to measure the line of men drinking to my left and right.

Smoke burned my eyes. Unable to make out any of the faces, I sat staring at the liquid settling in my glass. The music stopped. A disquieting hush settled on the room, as the men at the bar hung their heads as if they'd been disgraced.

The thump of darts hitting the board became the only sound for a few minutes. A man coughed. Another cursed. Two men teamed up to call the bartender over, in loud, animated voices. One man got up and left.

"Turn on the television," someone shouted.

"Roscoe, I already told you the thing broke," said the barman, a short man with a flushed face and patchy blond hair.

"The fucking Arabs knocked out your TV, Phil?" another man said with a laugh.

"Yeah, it's those fucking Arabs," the man next to me chimed in.

"You all shut up," the bartender said.

"This is still America," a man replied.

"Yeah, you can't tell nobody to shut up in America."

"First Amendment," the man next to me said.

"Where you from, Phil? You American or you an Arab?" Someone at the far end of the bar said with a laugh.

The bartender didn't reply.

"We need to send all those fucking Arabs back to the desert. Let them eat sand," the man said.

"Yeah," three or four men said in chorus.

"We don't need no non-Americans in America."

"Yeah," came the chorus again.

The man next to me looked at me suspiciously. I turned my face away and sipped my drink. The place fell silent.

As if deciding it was dishonorable to get drunk in silence, someone got up to feed the jukebox. The room was filled with music again, and the men lifted their heads and looked at each other and smiled.

The whisky soon found a soft spot in my brain, and I began to feel warm and separate from my surroundings. I finished my first drink, and the bartender refilled my glass. I nodded a thank-you. I didn't want to move again. I felt a happy solitude in this seedy bar, surrounded by men trying to soothe their pain with alcohol. I'd been there before. And right now I felt like giving it another try.

The door opened and a chunky bald man came in. He strutted through the sudsy smoke as if he expected it to dissolve. And if it didn't he looked like the kind of man who'd pull out his gun and blast his way through. He sat at the only vacant stool, two down from mine.

Waiting for him to get settled, I swilled my drink quietly. He ordered vodka and asked the bartender about the TV. The bartender told him it wasn't working and turned away.

The man looked around the room. I turned my face when he glanced my way. He took a sip of his vodka and leaned his neck to one side, hunching over like a bear over a meal.

I paid for my drinks and as slyly as I could, curled my fingers around the black polymer grip of the Smith & Wesson, easing it from my waistband. Alcohol and tension combined to make me feel faint.

With the .45 at my side, I managed to walk up behind the man without him noticing.

"Not a sound, Rudy," I said, my gun pressed to his ribs.

He began to turn around.

"Don't, unless you want your ribs air-conditioned."

"Who the fuck are you?"

"Never mind. You and I are gonna walk outta here like we're going to Communion."

"I ain't Catholic."

"You'll go to hell just the same."

"I ain't going nowhere 'til you tell me who you are."

"Bye, muthafucker. I hope your life insurance is up to date."

He shifted on the stool, unsure of himself now. "Okay."

"Now get up. Real slow." I ground the nozzle into his rib cage.

He stood up and looked around as though he expected somebody to come to his aid. Standing at his side, I urged him forward with a sharp nudge of the gun. He began to walk slowly. Keeping the gun wedged to his ribs, I kept abreast, and we marched out into the night.

Outside on the sidewalk he hesitated, looking up at the sky.

I prodded him with the gun. "Too late for prayer. Keep moving."

"If you're going to shoot me I wanna see your fucking face." He turned around. "I shoulda known it was you."

"Where's your brother?"

"Why don't you go peddle your shit somewhere else? Leave Troy alone."

"I hear he's been asking about me."

"Why would Troy be asking about you?"

I felt something hard and cold dig into the base of my neck.

"I guess I found you, Blades."

That cold, arrogant voice, suspended on my brain for three years, swept over it like a lathe, dissecting my nerves, reducing me to an invalid. I tried to swallow but couldn't. My gut burned as if a grenade had just exploded in it.

Rudy wrenched my gun away and smirked at his brother. He pointed the .45 at me. "Be doing the city a favor if we plug this nigger right here."

"Leave us alone, Rudy," Troy said in an avuncular voice.

Rudy gazed into his brother's eyes, as if he was in the presence of a prophet, his breathing coming in small, uneven gasps. He lowered the gun. "You sure?"

"And you ain't seen nothing."

"Shit, this nigger already dead as far as I'm concerned."

"Good. Give me his gun and go on back inside. I'll join you in a bit."

Rudy handed over my gun to his brother and walked away with a sneer on his face. "See you in hell, nigger."

"Where's your car?" Troy said to me.

"I took the train."

"Don't think I wouldn't shoot you."

"I have no doubt about that. But I want you to look me in the eye this time." I started to turn around.

"Don't," he barked. "Now walk to your fucking car."

I sensed that he walked with a limp. He leaned his heavy frame on me as we walked. He smelled of beer and salami, and his clothes gave off the nauseating odor of burnt barbecue ribs.

He directed me to open the passenger door of the 4x4. Then, pushing me inside, he motioned me into the driver's seat before getting in.

Our eyes met for the first time. His were red and half-closed. His face was stiff as stone, his jaw muscles jutting out on both sides like broken bones. He seemed to have lost a lot of weight and most of his hair; the few strands that remained hung in a disorderly manner on his head.

"You ain't looking too good there, partner."

"Wipe that smirk off your face before I make it permanent," he said, waving both guns at me.

"Sorry I missed you last night."

"Drive."

"Are we going to meet your friends?"

"Just drive."

I started the Jeep and pulled away from the curb. For the next few blocks the lights were solid green. I drove slowly. A police cruiser passed us going in the opposite direction along Canal Street. We hit a red light at Church Street, and I squeezed the brakes, letting the Jeep creep to the stop. Taking my eyes off the road, I stared hard at Pagano, anger roiling in my gut.

"Where're we going?" I said.

"I want you off my conscience, Blades."

"You make me want to puke. You shoot people in the back. And you and your friends pick on poor defenseless immigrants."

"I see being a crackhead runs in your family. What the fuck are you talking about?"

"Last night I rescued one of the girls you kidnapped and assaulted. But I'm sure you know that. I just missed you."

"I was with my brother all last night." His laugh was flat.

"Then I guess I just missed him too."

The light turned green.

"Drive," he ordered.

I eased off the brakes and the 4x4 jerked into motion.

"We got to the Blue Girl around eight and stayed until three A.M. Phil, the barman, would tell you as much if you live long enough to ask him," Pagano said.

"It was very clever of you to target immigrants. They're so afraid of deportation they're hardly gonna go running their mouth to anybody. But you made the mistake of kidnapping the daughter of a woman who worked for me. She came to me. And when I began to ask questions, you shot me in the back."

"You're not on crack. I take that back. You inherited a brain defect from all those mixed genes. How many times you gotta hear it was an accident?"

"We ran that sting dozens of times. All of a sudden you don't recognize me? Bullshit, you lying sonofabitch!"

"Stop the car!" he screamed.

I began to slow down.

"Stop the fucking car! Now! Stop it!" He waved the guns menacingly.

I slammed on the brakes, stopping in the middle of the street. A number of hapless drivers behind me had to swerve sharply to avoid smashing into the back of the Jeep. One woman flashed me the middle finger as she went by.

"If you want to call me racist because I called you a nigger, go right ahead. But I would never shoot a cop. You don't know how hard it has been the last three years trying to live with myself."

"I'm sorry, but I ain't feeling your pain."

He screwed up his face. "I ain't begging you for shit, Blades, okay? I just want you off my conscience. I hate myself for what I did. It was dark in that alley. I was tired. I'd had a few drinks. Shouldn't have done that, but fuck, I did. I just wasn't on that night. I wanted to get home. Get some sleep. I hadn't been monitoring the radio. I didn't hear the description of the perp. I didn't know what he looked like. All I saw was a dark figure running down the alley and I thought, shit, he's getting away. It's gonna be on me if the muthafucker gets away. I didn't want to let you guys down. My gun was in my hand and I just started shooting. I just wanted to stop him."

"If you hadn't heard the description, how'd you know he was black?"

He sighed and lowered the guns. "I just thought he had to be. I'm sorry I shot you, Blades. That's why I was asking about you. I wanted to tell you I'm sorry. I don't expect you to forgive me, but it's on my conscience that I never came to see you in the hospital. That I never said I was sorry. I may not have been a good cop, but I don't know nothing 'bout any of that shit you're talking about."

He got out of the car. Leaning through the window, he tossed my piece onto the seat.

"I hope you die like the fucking cockroach you are," I said.

He walked off down West Broadway. I picked up my gun and got out, intent on following him. I still wanted revenge. I was not ready to give up my anger. Yet I also felt a gnawing frustration that anything done hereafter would be anticlimatic. There was nothing left. Nothing more to be gained from holding onto the rage. Anais had been right. It's easier to hold resentment than to forgive.

I stood on the sidewalk, fighting the urge to cry. Around me, New York, drunk on its own energy and monstrous myth, seemed to change before my eyes. The golden streetlights became crystals of fire and the black buildings, trees in a murky forest. And I was lost.

# 34

MY HOTEL ROOM was well chilled when I returned. I sat on the edge of the bed staring at the cheap water-color prints on the yellow walls. I hated to give up on the notion that Troy Pagano was part of this conspiracy. I wanted him to be dirty as sin. I wanted him to be the devil. But he was just a sad, misguided man.

The cell phone rang. I picked it up off the bed.

"Hello?" I expected it to be my mother.

"Blades?"

"Anais?"

"Yes, it's me. Are you okay?"

"How did you get this number?"

"Your mother. She called. Said you did something crazy. That the police were going to shoot you down."

"Trust my mother to paint a grim picture. I can't talk to you now, Anais," I said.

"Blades, please don't hang up. What the hell is going on? Are you okay?"

"It's nothing. I'm fine."

"The last time you said that to me, the next thing I knew you were holding a gun to my head."

"I don't remember that."

"The more you say that the more it hurts."

"I'm sorry. I can't help if I don't remember."

"It was right after that cop was sentenced. You went out and got drunk, remember that? We got into a big argument when you came home. I told you I was leaving. You went silent. I asked you how you felt. You said you were fine. Then you put a gun to my head. I thought you were going to kill me."

I said nothing. There was a long pause. I heard the phone click as if she'd put it down. She spoke again. "So what is she like?"

"Who?"

"You know who. That woman. The one you're seeing."

"I'm not seeing anybody."

"The woman you're fucking, if you want me to be vulgar."

"Since when did that bother you?"

"Sometimes you can be such a prick."

"She's dead. The police think I killed her."

"Did you?"

I hung up the phone. Seconds later it rang again. I hesitated before picking it up.

"Why did you hang up on me?" Anais shrieked.

I didn't answer.

"I can be on the next flight to New York," she said.

"What for?"

After a hush, she whispered, "I'm sorry. I'm sure you didn't kill her."

"That's not what I asked."

"Blades, sometimes you scare me. You've never told me what you did in Miami when you took off three years ago. And then all those weird dreams you were having."

"What dreams?"

"Oh come on, Blades. The ones you didn't want to discuss with the therapist until I forced you to. The ones about killing your family. Have you had one of those dreams lately?"

I wanted to say no, but I couldn't lie. "The night before she was killed. I dreamed I'd shot Jason accidentally."

"You've got so many things going on in your head, it's hard to feel comfortable with you."

"The only thing in my head is that I can't seem to stop loving you."

She chuckled. "Always with the sweet talk."

"It isn't sweet talk."

"Did you sweet-talk that woman into your bed?"

"I wasn't in love with her, Anais."

"You slept with her!"

"What're you wearing?"

"What?" Her voice punched through the receiver.

"What're you wearing?"

"Don't try to change the subject."

"I just want to know what you're wearing."

"You're trying to change the subject."

"What if I am? Arguing about this isn't going to get us anywhere."

"I can't talk to you anymore right now, Blades."

"Wait. Just tell me what you're wearing."

"It's not going to work, Blades. What I'm wearing is none of your damn business anyway."

"You're afraid." There was dead air for a while. I pressed my advantage. "Why're you afraid to tell me what you're wearing?"

"I'm not afraid. I don't want to."

"Why not?"

"Because I know what you're trying to do."

"I'm not trying to do anything. I wanna picture you, that's all. I'm a man on the run. One sharpshooter away from eternity. All I have right now is an image of you. I just want it to be real."

Her voice softened. "One of your shirts."

"Are you telling me the truth?"

"About what?"

"Wearing my shirt."

"Why would I lie? It doesn't mean anything anyway. So don't get excited. It's just a shirt."

"It means something to me. I don't remember leaving any clothes there."

"It's old. I brought it with me when I came out."

"You little thief."

She giggled softly. "You never wore it."

"What does it look like?"

"White. Long sleeves."

"I hate white shirts."

"I think you wore it once."

My heart was racing. "Is that all you're wearing?"

She laughed out loud, a clear, intoxicating sound. "Blades, I'm not going there with you."

"Going where?"

"You know where you're going. I'm not going to let you lead me into the wilderness."

"I would follow you into the wilderness."

"That's because you're incorrigible. I'm not."

I sensed that she was smiling.

"Answer my question," I said.

"Answer mine first."

"What was your question?"

"Miami. Tell me about Miami."

"What did you hear?"

"That you killed a man."

"Where'd you hear that?"

"You're never gonna tell me, are you?"

There was a pause, and for a moment I thought she would hang up. I wanted her to stay on the line, but I didn't know what to say.

"You're never going to tell me what happened in Miami, are you?" she persisted.

"Forget about Miami. Why can't you leave it alone?"

"One day you're going to have to tell me, Blades."

I wanted to tell her about Miami, but I didn't know where to start. "So, is that all you're wearing?"

"You are persistent, I'll give you that."

"Loving you has taught me that."

"Yes, that's all I'm wearing."

"Just my shirt."

"Just your shirt. Nothing else. But that's all you're gonna get. No phone sex."

I laughed. "Why not?"

"Because I said so."

"Do you miss me?"

"I miss you, Blades. Are you happy now?" she said.

"Very happy. If they shoot me tonight, I'll die happy."

"There'll be no dying tonight. I'll be there tomorrow. Late."

"I might not be alive when you get here."

"That ain't funny."

"Wasn't meant to be. Every cop in the city is looking to boil my noodles."

"Well, your ass better still be as hard as I remember it when I get there. And I don't mean from rigor mortis."

"What happened to your movie?"

"They cast it. Without me. My turn will come."

"Sure it will," I said.

"What's that supposed to mean?"

"I should go."

"Wait. Tell me where you're staying, Blades."

"I can't tell you that."

"Then call me. I'll be at your mother's."

"I love you."

I waited for the click that signaled she was gone. Holding the phone to my chest, I lay there in dizzy bliss. I had almost resigned myself to the idea that Anais would never come back to New York. Trying to get her back from three thousand miles away hadn't worked. If I had known all it would take was for me to become Richard Kimble for a day, I would've done it ages ago.

The metallic jingle of the phone broke my daydreaming.

"Can you meet me in half an hour?" It was T-J.

"Where?"

"Do you know the White Castle on Utica? Near Empire Boulevard?"

I hesitated. It could be a setup. "You have a cell?"

"Yes."

"Where're you?"

"Utica and Church."

"Take a cab."

"Where'm I going?"

"Call me when you get to White Castle."

I ended the call, stuffed the Smith & Wesson in the back of my waist and went to take the elevator.

I GOT INTO the Jeep parked on Willoughby and drove off, turning down Smith and then onto Atlantic Avenue. When I reached Flatbush, the phone rang.

"We're at White Castle," T-J said when I answered.

"What kinda car are you in?"

"A white Lincoln."

"What's the license-plate number?"

"Hold on." After a few seconds T-J said, "T-eight-seven-three-nine-oh-one-C."

"Tell the cabby to drive along Empire Boulevard. Call me when you reach Flatbush."

I hung up.

I sped down Flatbush. My goal was to reach the intersection of Flatbush and Empire Boulevard before they did. Just as I swerved into the Wendy's parking lot at the Flatbush–Empire Boulevard junction to turn around, my phone rang.

"We're here," T-J said when I answered. "Now what?"

"Just wait."

I saw the white Lincoln at the intersection. The light was red. I waited to see if any cars would sit behind the Lincoln after the light turned green. The line of cars behind the Lincoln pulled out at the light change. I waited until the light became red again.

"Get out," I said, into the phone.

"Where're you?"

"Just get out."

She paid her fare and got out. Carrying a small handbag, she was dressed in a black fitted blouse and green pants. I waited until the Lincoln drove away, and I pulled up next to her and opened the passenger door.

"Get in!" I hollered.

She peered into the Jeep for a second, then slid into the passenger seat. I burned rubber as the light turned red again.

"I came alone," she announced.

"I noticed."

I pointed the Jeep down Ocean Avenue.

"Mind if I smoke?" she said.

"Not at all."

"Where're we going?"

"Nowhere. Just driving."

She opened her bag and took out a pack of Slims and a blue Zippo. She lit a cigarette and took a couple of deep puffs, exhaled just as deeply and leaned her arm out the window of the Jeep.

"Stubby didn't order the hit on the agent," she said.

"How do you know that?"

"I just know."

I looked at her through gray smoke. "What else do you just know?"

"Stubby don't believe in killing cops." There was a malicious grin on her face. "Not even ex-cops that he hates. He could've killed you a long time ago."

"I'm glad to hear he's such an honorable man. I'll be sure to tell that to the mothers of the girls whose lives he has trampled."

"I didn't say he was a saint."

"Thanks, but I'd already figured that out."

"He tried to tell The Genius it was a bad idea. That it'd fuck up their business."

"Who's The Genius?"

"That's what Stubby calls him. His real name is Gabriel Aquia. I call him The Monster because he's such a big fucking dude."

I looked at her sharply. "Gabriel Aquia and Stubby are business partners? What kind of business?"

"What do you think?"

"Child porn?"

"Stubby called him The Genius because he knows a lot about computers. The Genius wants to build a real estate empire but didn't have the money to get it started. So he came to Stubby. He told Stubby there was a big demand in Europe for videos with black women, and they went into business. The Genius set up these web sites based in Europe and Latin America so it'd be hard to track their operation back to the States. Their tapes are sold only on the web sites. You can't even buy them in stores."

"You know why that is, don't you?"

She flicked ash out the window. "I swear I didn't know they were using girls so young."

"How do you know all this?"

"Stubby and I are lovers. I'm the only person he really trusts. He tells me everything."

"Except that he kidnaps innocent undocumented immigrant children whose parents would never go to the police. Especially now."

She fell silent. I glanced at her, wondering if she knew about his condition. She looked at me. Our eyes met for a second and she must've noticed the question in mine.

"Yes, I know about his situation," she said. "He blames you."

"Yeah, I'm really sorry about what happened to him in prison."

"No, you're not. You hate him."

"It's none of my business, but I hope you're being careful," I said.

"Thanks for your concern but I don't need it. We both got it. I didn't get it from him, though. It ain't the end of the world. He helped me realize that. You can still live your life. I'm taking all my meds, and I'm doing alright. I can still look forward to tomorrow. I can still dream of seeing Adora in Carnegie Hall."

"Why're you still in the business?"

"What should I be doing? Selling insurance? This is a business. It's my business, you know what I mean? It's all I know."

"I've heard that before. And no matter how many times I hear it, it still sounds like a cop-out to me."

"You don't know nothing."

I made a left turn at Foster Avenue. "How'd you get into this business, anyway?"

"Started when I was fifteen. I wasn't forced. I wasn't coerced. I wasn't tricked. Sex was the only thing that kept me from getting bored. I had a friend who was making stupid money tricking. She hooked me up." She dragged hard on the cigarette, then let the smoke out slowly. "Listen, this whole thing would collapse if Gabriel went to jail. Stubby don't know nothing about running no Internet business."

"You can't save Stubby. He's going to jail. If he doesn't go to jail, I will kill him myself."

She threw the burning cigarette into the street. "You ain't no better than Stubby with all your talk about revenge and killing."

"I'm not the one kidnapping children." I glanced over at her. Her lips were dark and pouty. "You in love with Stubby?"

"Is that what you think?"

"I'm asking."

"I ain't trying to save Stubby. He can take care of himself. I'm telling you this because I got a little girl. I remember when Adora was thirteen. She was so innocent. She's got a chance to be something. There ain't nothing worse than never getting a chance to dream. I ain't in love with him. He takes care of me. But knowing that he's hurting innocent children in his business—nobody can't take this kind of shit off my conscience."

She leaned out the window. We were now heading north on Utica Avenue.

"Did you see who killed the agent?"

She shook her head.

"Did you move into that apartment to spy on Edwards?"

"Yes. Stubby was afraid he might've been onto their operation. But all the fool wanted was money and pussy. He liked to gamble."

"Who was paying him?"

"I guess it must've been The Genius."

"And you didn't see who went into his apartment the day he was killed."

"A tall black man went to see him in the early afternoon. I couldn't make out his face. Then you and the woman. I didn't see anybody else go in or come out."

We were approaching Eastern Parkway. I was glad for the information, but I couldn't bring myself to say thank you. I didn't even know if I believed her. Even if her conscience was speaking to her, it was a little too late for Serena.

I dropped her off at the corner of Utica and St. Johns Place. She got out without saying good-bye. I watched her until she had gone halfway down the block. Then I turned on the radio and drove off.

# 35

"BLADES! WHY THE fuck don't you get a proper phone, man?"

The phone had woken me out of a deep sleep. I'd fallen off in my clothes with all the lights on. It was almost midnight. I'd been asleep for an hour.

"Trevor! Where the hell are you?" I mumbled.

"I'll tell you where I am. I'm hiding out like some goddamn convict."

"Are you okay?"

"Man, don't ask me if I'm okay. How could I be okay? My wife's in DC worrying about me, and I'm here hoping my face doesn't show up next to yours on *America's Most Wanted*. On top of that I'm trying to get hold of you and can't find you. I got your shit, so come and get it."

"Tell me where the hell you are."

"Remember where we had my bachelor party?"

"Word?"

"Same room."

I started to laugh.

"What's so damn funny?" he said.

"You ain't gonna believe where I am," I said.


SOME OF HIS friends had rented a room on the twentieth floor of the very hotel I was in, the Marriott, to throw a party for Trevor the night before he got married. It was ten floors up from where I was. He had an opened Heineken waiting for me by the time I got there. We pounded and he handed me the beer. Still feeling the effects of the alcohol I'd had earlier, my first long sip of beer slid down quick and smooth.

I whistled softly as I looked out the window. He had a great view of the Brooklyn Bridge and Manhattan, whose lights sparkled like falling stars.

"How's Patricia?" I asked.

"She's still upset about the dog."

"Did you tell her I was going to get her another dog?"

"She don't wanna hear that shit, son. You've never had a dog, have you?"

I sat on the bed. "No, I haven't. My brother was allergic."

"I knew it. You're a dog hater."

"I don't hate dogs. They're fine when they're sleeping."

He got up and went into the closet, returning with a gray laptop bag. "I'm risking my life to help a fucking dog hater. Wait until Patricia hears this." Flipping the laptop's cover up, he powered the machine on. "I want you to know my people used every ounce of their resources to crack this shit for me. Because they love me. And I did it for you, who don't like dogs."

Trevor hastily input information at the username and password prompts, and a few seconds later a graphic interface that looked like Windows came up. Trevor then swiveled the computer onto my lap. I scrolled through the files, opening some at random. There were pages and pages of specs and photographs and diagrams of electronic equipment. I couldn't tell exactly what the equipment might've been used for, but some of it appeared to be airport scanning machines. There were also photographs, grid maps and layouts of several airports. And plenty of photos of Middle Eastern–looking men, along with names and profiles. I stopped after awhile.

"Is this all?" I said.

"There some more files hidden away in another sector."

Trevor took the computer off my lap and clicked the mouse a number of times, then gave the computer back to me.

I opened some of those files. They were similar to the ones I'd opened earlier. The next file I opened made me pause. It was a document that looked to have been scanned. It was an FBI report on Congresswoman Richardson, dated 1967. Seemed as though the FBI had watched her closely between 1964 and 1967, the years she'd been active in Stokely Carmichael's organization. It contained her name, address, the name of her child, names of friends, places she visited, transcripts of telephone conversations and one other piece of information that left me speechless: The name of Precious' father.

Now I knew why Gabriel Aquia wanted Edwards dead, why he was paying him off. Edwards was blackmailing the congresswoman. The information in this report—the identity of Precious' father—would destroy Congresswoman Richardson's campaign if it got out. And without her help, Gabriel had little or no shot at getting that contract to rehabilitate the waterfront.

I shut down the computer, finished my beer and got up, setting the bottle on the edge of the television console.

"So you got what you looking for?" Trevor said.

I walked to the door. "You'll soon be able to go home, my friend."

"Where're you going?"

"To rouse a woman out of bed."

Trevor laughed. "And here I was thinking you ain't getting none, Blades."

I smiled. "You keep thinking that." .

**36**

❧ J'OUVERT IN CARIBBEAN patois means "day open," and refers to the early morning parade of *Ole Mas* costumes that signals the beginning of Carnival. The origins of *Ole Mas* lie with the elaborate fetes that the French plantocracy in the Caribbean staged in the period immediately before Lent. The slaves began exaggeratedly mimicking the planters' elaborate dress and courtly manners with whatever was handy, the elegant chiffon and taffeta becoming coarse cloth and rags, and *Ole Mas* was born.

As time passed, *Ole Mas* became symbolic for the lampooning of all that was dishonest and evil in society, characterized by mythological devils, supernatural bats and parodies of corrupt politicians or officials. This parade gave way to the clean, purified costumes of the large Carnival bands later in the day.

I'd forgotten that it was Labor Day morning; the J'Ouvert parade to kick off Carnival festivities would be taking
over the streets of East Flatbush. I reached Rogers and Empire Boulevard around one A.M. There, Hell had over-
flowed onto the street. Crowds lined the sidewalk to watch
costumed J'Ouvert revelers dance to pounding calypso
music played by steel bands on floats and people banging
garbage bin covers and cowbells.

Faces painted, bodies covered in mud, some draped in
national flags of the various Caribbean islands, others
painted in a mad variety of colors, some in sequins and artfully ripped tee-shirts, the dancers passed water and spirits
back and forth as they pranced along Empire Boulevard.

As I waited at the corner of Rogers and Empire for a
band to pass, I called Bressler. It took him awhile to answer
the phone. His hello came from deep inside his nose, as if he
suffered from allergies or had a cold. But I knew it was him.

"Bressler? It's Blades."

"Are you about to end your miserable life, Blades? Because that's the only thing you can say to make me happy."

"The laptop is in my hands as we speak."

"Where are you?"

"Meet me at Congresswoman Richardson's house."

"I'm not meeting you anywhere. Bring the laptop to me."

"Agent Edwards was blackmailing her."

"Why?"

"It's all on the computer. See you in half an hour."

I hung up. The band passed, and police directing traffic
waved me through the intersection. My phone rang. It was
Noah.

"Isn't it past your bedtime, old man?" I said.

He grunted. "I still got a wife, so I'm used to being up
late. You probably forgot what that's like. One of the joys
of marriage."

"Low blow, my friend."

He laughed. "Are you okay, kid?"

"Keeping it real, babe."

"You know a cop named Tim Samuel?"

"Sure. Works homicide in the Seven-Seven. Good man."

"He got any beef with you?"

"No, Tim's one of my peeps. He's helped me out of a few tight spots. Why?"

"Did he know I was holding your guns?"

"It's possible I might've mentioned it."

"I think he's the one boosted your weapons."

"Timmy? No way. You got dropped on your head too many times, cuz."

"He came to see me about a week ago."

"You knew Timmy?"

"Not really. I worked with his father. He was a cop. Anyway, your friend came to me and told me how sick his father was and how he wanted to do something special for his sixty-fifth birthday, which was coming up. He wanted to get all of his friends and people who worked with him over the years together for a big celebration. I told him I'd be glad to come."

Through the creep of traffic I had reached Maple Street, where I made a right. This estuary was less clogged, and I felt the 4x4 buck as I lowered the gas pedal.

"I don't believe it was Timmy," I said.

"Hear me out, kid. He was here for about an hour. We had a few drinks. Muthafucker started blowing smoke up my ass. Kept talking about the great things his father says about me, about my commendations and awards. Made me feel like I was the president. And I was sucking it up shamelessly. I brought them out for him to see."

"What, my guns?"

"My awards from the department. We were having a good time. Then my doorbell rang. A kid off the block came to tell me the maids were towing my car, so I rushed out. When I got there my car was on a flatbed. I went into overdrive on the bitch. I was out there for half an hour before she released my wheels. I realize now it was a setup."

"You left Tim in your house?"

"If you can't leave a cop in your house, who the fuck can you leave? Besides, I didn't think it'd take more than five minutes."

The line sagged with dead air.

"You there, Blades?"

"I'm here, kid."

"You sure this guy don't have a grudge against you?"

"No, cuz. We cool. I still don't think it was Tim."

"Think what you like. I was a cop before you could pee straight. I worked the street without fancy computers to do my job. I had to use my instincts. And I'm telling you this muthafucker is addled. He's dirtier than the Hudson. And I know where he lives. Nobody craps in my house and walks away clean. I'm gonna make him eat his own shit."

"Stay outta this, Noah."

"What's that?"

"I said stay out. I can handle this."

"Don't talk to me like I'm some snot-nosed kid, Blades."

"I'm sorry, Noah, but—"

"Let me tell you something, Blades. Maybe you don't need my help, but don't think for one minute that I can't handle this punk. Don't think this Ph.D. has made me soft. I've still got a network out there, know what I'm saying? I don't have to touch this guy. I know people who'd rip his balls out and eat them while they're still warm. You got two hours. After that, it's my show."

The line went dead.

Tim and I never worked together, but we'd always been cool. Like me, he'd graduated at the head of his class and had never worn a uniform. Tim wanted to study law with the hope of moving to the DA's office. After his parents divorced, his older sister married and moved to California, leaving him to care for a sick father in a nursing home. And so went his dream.

I racked my brain trying to think of a reason Tim would screw me. Couldn't come up with one.

VONDELLE RICHARDSON HAD been chosen as one of the Grand Marshals of the West Indian Carnival Day Parade, which was to get underway in about nine hours. Expecting her to be asleep, I banged hard on her front door.

To my surprise I heard the swish of slippers across the wood floor soon after.

"Who's there?" Her voice was lively, almost inviting, as if she'd been up awhile.

"Blades Overstreet."

"What do you want?"

"We have to talk."

"Do you want me to call the police?"

"Go ahead. And while you're at it call the *Post* and the *Daily News* and the *Times* and tell them you're pulling out of the election because you had a child with one of the most reprehensible killers this country has ever seen."

I heard bolts being unlocked. The door swung open. Wrapped in a burgundy silk robe, Congresswoman Richardson stood before me, her face mottled like curdled milk. After staring me down as if she was trying to julienne my face with her eyes, she stepped aside to let me in. I stood amid plants in the atrium as she closed the door.

"Let's go in here," she said, pointing to an area off to the right.

I followed her to a room behind the staircase. She flicked on the light, and I stood in a jungle of potted trees and beautiful African wood sculptures. The floor was made of shiny red wood.

"I call this the African room," she said, plopping herself down on an olive couch. "I come here to meditate."

"Agent Edwards was blackmailing you, wasn't he?" I said, not interested in her personal rituals at this point.

She crossed her legs and reached for a box of Winstons and a gold-laminated lighter on the end table next to the couch. She lit a cigarette. "I'm not going to ask your permission to smoke."

"It's your house."

"Exactly. And I don't like you barging in here threatening me."

"I don't have time to kiss your feet."

She uncrossed and crossed her legs again, looking around nervously. "What do you want from me?"

"Who killed Agent Edwards?"

"I can't help you."

"Your life is all here on this computer. It's up to you who gets to read it."

She snuffed out the half-smoked cigarette and stood up. "He wanted money."

"Did you pay him?"

She was standing a few inches away from me. She stunk of sweat and a familiar men's cologne. One that I couldn't stand. And there was a tender spot on her neck just above her collarbone. The congresswoman had just finished making love.

"I told him I needed time. But he was killed before I could get the money together."

"I don't believe you."

She opened the box and took out another cigarette, but she didn't light it. She tapped it against her cheek, as if attempting to jar a long-forgotten memory in her head. She squeezed her eyes closed. Then she opened them again, wet her lips, stuck the cigarette in her mouth and flicked the lighter. The tip of the cigarette glowed orange.

"I came here to study in the sixties," she began. "A volatile but exciting time for a young woman from a staid middle-class West Indian family. And Spellman was a

great place to be. I soon got involved in SNCC. You know
what that is?"

"I know my history," I said.

"Then you know that the leader of SNCC was from
Trinidad."

"Stokely Carmichael."

"I'm impressed."

I let her condescending tone slide.

She continued. "My family was very upset when they
heard about my political involvement. They were afraid I
would get arrested and thrown out of the country. Or
lynched by the KKK. They threatened to cut off my money
if I didn't stop. I refused. They stopped paying my tuition,
and I dropped out of school my sophomore year, determined to get a job and register the next semester. I was doing volunteer work for SNCC. I had a sister in New York,
and I came up to visit her to get some money. On my way
back to Atlanta I met a really nice man on the plane. He sat
next to me. At first I resisted talking to him because he was
white. But he said he was from New York, at which I
thought, well, he's not Southern. His name was Gene
Kurtz. We talked the whole trip. He was well-spoken, very
polite and smart. He was slender and handsome and had
this strange fire in his eyes. He talked mostly about his
family and about politics. And he was very sympathetic to
our cause. I was very impressed that he knew so much
about our struggle. He said he was a journalist and was
writing a book on the civil rights struggle and wanted to
stay in touch with me to get my impressions. I guess on
some level I was flattered. We left the airport together, and
though I had to sneak into his hotel through the back door,
I spent the night with him. We kept our relationship secret,
and many times I thought of breaking it off but didn't. He
knew so much about politics. I never thought political discussions could be so arousing. But I always wanted to
make love after one of our discussions. When he found out

I was pregnant, he disappeared. I later found out he was an FBI informant."

"Why didn't you have an abortion?"

She puffed remotely at her cigarette. "I don't know. I came from a Catholic family, and in some twisted way I thought I loved him. My sister in New York offered to raise the child as her own, and nobody would have to know. I moved to New York to stay with her. After Precious was born, the two of them moved to England."

"Why didn't you tell Precious?"

"By the time Precious found out I was really her mother, the real truth about Gene Kurtz was out. He'd been playing everybody for his own sinister plans. Even the FBI. How do you first explain to your daughter your decision to give her up at birth and then tell her that, by the way, your father was a murderer. He'd firebombed a black school, killing dozens of children. It was too late. I should've taken her back when my sister died."

"Gene Kurtz was found dead in Prospect Park. Who killed him?"

"Who cares?"

"Did he try to blackmail you too?"

She spiked her cigarette angrily in an ashtray. "Look, Mr. Overstreet. It's late. I have a long day ahead."

"Did you tell your lover that Agent Edwards was blackmailing you?"

"My lover?"

"Gabe."

"Tell me what you want," she snapped.

"Here's what I want. I want to be able to go home and take a shower in my own bathroom. I want the dog you're sleeping with to pay for what he did."

"Get out of my house."

I grabbed her arm as she walked past. "You must know he had Precious killed. He killed her to protect his interests in you. You're nothing but a piece of property to him."

"Let me go, you animal!" she cried.

I held on, digging my fingers into her arm. With the alcohol swirling in my head, I could feel myself about to lose control. "You're the one with fleas in your crotch!"

"Let her go."

The deep voice had detonated behind me. I turned sharply. He was standing in the doorway a few feet away. Shirtless and wearing gold boxers, his muscular upper body solid as a brass statue, he was pointing a shiny silver pistol directly at the center of my chest.

I released Congresswoman Richardson and took a step toward Gabriel. He held up a thick palm.

"Sit down, Mr. Overstreet," Gabriel said, taking the laptop from my hand.

The congresswoman moved to stand by Gabriel's side, looking at me with a sorrowful expression on her face.

"Why did you have to kill her?"

"It doesn't matter."

I sat on the sofa. "What matters to you, Mr. Aquia?"

He spoke deliberately, in a cocky tone. "I was born in Harlem. My family left a war in Ghana to come here. They struggled to make a better life. I despised Harlem. If there were ten people on my block with a steady job, that was plenty. Little kids talked about what kind of funeral they wanted the way kids in other neighborhoods talked about what kind of clothes they wanted to wear to their prom. I dropped out of school and sold drugs for a little bit. Then I realized I would end up just like all the people I despised on the block. Stoop-dwellers, I called them. People who heard the word *future* and ran in fear. Every morning I walked down my block I saw a Chinese man opening his restaurant, a Lebanese his grocery, an Indian his newsstand, a Korean his green grocery and a black man stashing his drugs in a garbage can. Now tell me, what does that say to children?"

"I'm kinda slow. Educate me."

"Recently I went back and bought a brownstone on that

block. You should see it now. Beautiful. Many of the buildings have been restored with terrazzo floors and beautiful
lights. White people are moving into the neighborhood.
There's an explosion of construction in Harlem. Great for
everybody, right? Wrong. Nobody from Harlem is doing
the rebuilding, and nobody from Harlem is getting hired.
You know who the white developers are hiring instead?
Mexicans."

"It's a free country."

"Free for whom? Black people paid a price for their
freedom. Now they're being left behind. When I finish that
waterfront, this city will see what a difference one determined black man can make. That's what's important to me,
Mr. Overstreet."

"You've certainly made a difference all right. I'd give
you a pass on Gene Kurtz. He should've been killed a long
time ago. But what a difference you've made in the lives of
those children forced to perform in your videos. And in the
congresswoman's life by having her daughter killed. And
definitely in the lives of the family of that murdered FBI
agent."

"That agent was stupid and greedy. We paid him a hundred large. He refused to turn over the report. Demanded
another two hundred and fifty thousand. Because he's a
fucking government employee he thinks he gets a free
ride? Did he think we were going to support his gambling
habit until he decided to retire?"

The doorbell rang.

"Ah, that must be your escorts," Gabriel said. "Would
you let our friends in, babe?"

Face pinched as if she was experiencing a toothache,
Congresswoman Richardson drew her robe around her
hunched shoulders. Her body language suggested a mind
in turmoil. She hesitated.

"Go open the door," Gabriel ordered. "I'm tired of looking at this fake-ass nigger."

I took a step toward her. "How can you live with yourself?"

She stared at me, her eyes shrunken. She lifted her hand to cover her mouth as if to prevent it from acting on its own accord and saying something she would regret.

"Did you go see her in the morgue?" I said, stepping closer. "Did you see what they did to her face? This is the man responsible."

"Shut up!" Gabriel snapped.

"Perhaps you didn't know it before. Perhaps you knew it but couldn't bring yourself to believe it. But you can't ignore it now. He killed your daughter. He doesn't even bother denying it. Does being a congresswoman mean that much to you? To sleep with the man who killed your daughter. If you've never done anything for Precious in your life, take back her soul from under his feet. She deserves that, at least."

I didn't see the blow. The suddenness of it sent me reeling. At first I felt no pain, just a strange desire to vomit. Then Gabriel struck me again with what felt like the butt of the gun, just behind my ear. I blinked and fell to the floor. Then I felt the pain, like a drill excavating my eardrum. I prayed for blackness to come, and it did.

# 37

WHEN I OPENED my eyes again I was struck with awe. I was alive. My head was spinning wildly as if I'd just stepped off a Ferris wheel. I had no sense of my body for a while; when I did it felt as if my inner organs had been tumbled together in a washing machine. I mustered enough strength to control the urge to puke. It took me awhile to focus; the room was dark but weirdly familiar. I was lying on the floor on my right side. My head whirled so terribly I thought I would black out again. I smelled blood. Probably my own. The urge to vomit returned, and this time I couldn't control it. I twisted my head to one side and released the water from the washer. My hands were cuffed in front of me. I bent over and wiped my mouth on my wrist.

Then it came to me. I was in the room where this nightmare had started for me. Back in the room where I discovered Agent Edwards' body. I felt myself trembling, and try as I might, I couldn't stop the shaking. It was fear. The room still had the reek of death. I was beginning to imagine my own. I thought of my wife. Of my mother. And of a song my grandmother used to sing. An old West Indian folk song. I tried to remember the words, but I couldn't.

The door opened outside. Then I heard voices. People had entered the apartment. I rolled onto my back and felt something hard under me. They hadn't searched me before bringing me here. My gun was still stuck in the back of my waist.

Balling myself up into a tight cocoon, I managed to get both my feet through the loop of my arms, so that my handcuffed arms were now behind my back. I grasped the gun with both hands and slid it free.

The sound of boots was getting closer. I struggled to get my hands in front of me again. I was having difficulty with the gun in my hand so I laid it on the floor. I got my feet through and picked up the gun. Just as I got to my knees, the light was turned on, stunning my eyes. I sank back to the ground on my side, curled in a fetal position, the gun wedged between my legs.

I noticed Tim Samuel first. He stood in the doorway holding a gun to my brother's head, a perverse fire in his eyes. Jason looked dazed, out of it. Then Stubby came into view. He stood behind Tim in red cowboy boots, grinning like a freak.

"See, Blades," Tim sneered. "You asked me to find your brother, and I didn't disappoint you. Why did you disappoint me?"

"Jason, are you okay?" I said.

Jason opened his mouth but no words came. His head lolled from side to side. His clothes were dirty, his face pale, his eyes dull.

"What have I ever done to you, Tim?" I said. "All this because I didn't take you to Le Bar with Big Ron?"

"Don't flatter yourself, Blades. This ain't personal. At least not with me. Now, my man Stubby here, he's got a different story."

"I thought we were friends."

Tim snickered. "Take your dick outta your mouth, Blades. The world doesn't revolve around you. You're just a piece of asphalt under my feet as I struggle to get out from under the system. As Malcolm said: by any means necessary."

"Even if it means destroying the lives of innocent children?"

He laughed with scorn. "I know. I'm immoral. Call the welfare board."

"I'm gonna kill you myself."

He stuck out his chest. "How? By shooting me full of guilt?"

"I know Stubby doesn't have a soul any longer, but you . . ."

"Soul? Do you have any idea how much money it takes to keep my father in a fucking home? His police pension ain't even enough to cover the cost of his bedpans. I offered the nursing home some soul, but they replied that that currency dried up when Marvin Gaye died. They're only taking Benjamins these days. Lots of them."

"Nothing you say can justify what you're doing."

He took a few steps toward me, pushing my brother ahead of him. "You're right. I don't need to justify shit to you. I'm the one with the gun."

"You two are nothing but lackeys for Gabriel Aquia. He's the one with the real Benjamins."

Stubby puffed himself up to occupy the space in the doorway. "That's why we gonna fuck your shit up."

"I knew Tim stole my guns and popped Edwards. Which one of you killed Precious?"

"That would be me, with Jimmy's help," Tim said. "I also killed your friend's dog. Now it's your turn."

"Where's Jimmy now?"

"Drinking PCBs somewhere in the Hudson. He sold you out for a lousy five grand."

"Jimmy always backed losers, so I'm not surprised he hooked up with you," I said. "But why did you pick me?"

Tim said, "We had to get rid of that agent, but knew the FBI would never give up hunting his killer. We needed a sucker. Somebody so arrogant and self-absorbed that he'd refuse to surrender to the police. The police hated you and you hated them. It was a perfect plan. I tried to give you your fifteen minutes of fame, Blades. Imagine the headlines: Former Cop Dies in Shoot-Out with FBI. But you blew it. You disappointed me."

"What do you want with my brother? He's nothing to you."

"But he's something to you. You're gonna die, Blades. The question is, do you want to watch your brother die first?"

"Let him go, Timmy. Look at him. He doesn't even know where he is."

"I've decided to do your mother a favor," said Tim. "I'm sure she must be cursing the stork that delivered you two crazy muthafuckers on her door. Which one of you is closer to the edge? You or him?"

"What's your angle, Timmy?"

"You wanna save your brother's life, Blades?"

"I'll do whatever you want."

He glanced at Stubby and they both smirked self-confidently.

"Are you ready to write your suicide confession?" Timmy said.

"After I see my brother walk out that door."

"That ain't the way it's gonna go down, Blades."

"That's my play."

He pushed my brother toward me, his arm around Jason's neck. "Do you recognize this piece, Blades? It's your

Glock. You wanna see your brother die with a bullet in his brain from your gun?"

I blew him a kiss. "Let's stop playing this game, sweetie."

"Who the fuck you calling sweetie?"

"Stop fronting. You know you love me. You're doing this because you can't have me. You don't have to pretend in front of Stubby. He's been in the joint. He knows what it's like to love a man. Don't you, Stubby?"

Tim released Jason and came and stood over me. I looked up at his dark face. At his bright healthy-looking skin. The whiteness of his eyes. The knot of muscle in his jaw. The slope of his cheeks. His eyes glowed with anger.

He aimed the gun at my head. "Your fucking jukebox is out of songs, Blades."

There was a thunderous crash at the door outside, like someone was trying to break it down.

"Open up! FBI!" Bressler's voice boomed from the hall.

Tim swung his head to look at Stubby. Enough time for me to uncoil myself, exposing the gun which I held in both hands. By the time Tim swiveled his head back to me my gun was cocked. I pulled the trigger.

A bullet ripped open his neck. Another one slammed into his chest, lifting him off his feet. He fell back to the ground, taking my brother with him.

Stubby had drawn his gun. He got off a round at me as Bressler and his team broke the door down. The bullet ripped up the floor next to my head. My shot was on the mark, however. I shot him twice in the chest. He stumbled backward and then pitched forward on his face.

Bressler and Slate rushed into the room, followed by officers of the Emergency Unit of the NYPD.

"Drop it!" Bressler ordered.

I was so tensed my fingers were locked around the trigger. I wanted to let the gun fall from my hands, but my finger wouldn't uncurl.

"I'm not gonna say it again," Bressler said.

I grimaced. "I can't."

"Do it!"

I breathed deeply and thought of making love to Anais. Slowly the gun slipped from my hands. I smiled.

My brother was puking all over the floor.

# 38

THERE IS A dull emptiness about New York just before daybreak. A deep buzzing of nothing, when drunks awake and only the hopeless romantic can see beauty in the filth left by last night's revelers. Intoxicated young men peeing on themselves as they search for their last quarter to call their girlfriends, young girls with sore tits from being mauled all night in some dive by out-of-touch perverts, prostitutes crawling into bed with sores between their legs.

But there's also the joy and hope in the eyes of men and women going home from the lobster shift at some hospital where they've just saved the life of a kid who'd overdosed in a club. And the fireman, turning over his watch to the day shift with a deep smile of satisfaction, having put out two potentially deadly fires before the sun came up. Or the cop who's just taken the gun from some alcoholic's hand, preventing him from shooting his wife and himself over something as benign as a misplaced photograph.

After two hours of questioning by the FBI and the police, here I was lumbering through the humming of daybreak up the steps to my apartment, with my brother, who was too stoned to recognize me. And with all that had happened, I was happy. Jason was alive. And somewhere en route from California was my wife who was finally coming home.

NO ONE SEEMED to notice that Congresswoman Richardson did not show up for the parade. It was late in the afternoon. The rain had been falling all day, but the downpour couldn't stop the celebration. I was one among the tens of thousands who stood in the rain, loving its warm bite, as music pulsated around me. Jason stood with me, subdued, eating curried goat. I'd decided that it would be good for his spirit as well as mine to get out in the rain. We wore bright-colored tee-shirts and straw hats purchased from one of the street vendors.

On the sidelines we danced to the music and gazed at the colorfully costumed dancers as they came by in waves: half-dressed teenage girls, their midriffs exposed, tender breasts barely covered, wearing headbands of red and gold feathers and sequins; old women in colored tights, their faces painted with stripes and bars; young men strapped to huge multicolored dragons and snakes on wheels for easy manipulation and women in shorts, large breasts flopping out of skimpy tops, rubbery hips spinning circles, jumping, waving flags. And when Milo reached us with his band, we left our perch on the sidewalk to join him and his group behind a truck festooned with red and black cloth.

Milo handed me a Trinidadian flag.

"What do you think, Blades," he said as we chip-chipped to the music.

"It's great. Better than Mardi Gras."

"Mardi Gras! That ain't Carnival. This is Carnival."

I laughed. "Whatever, Milo."

"Now watch in the newspaper tomorrow what they gonna write. They gonna write about the sexual frenzy of the dancing and shit like that. They do it every year. They don't get it. You gotta jump once to get it. It ain't about sex. It's about the spirit. You get it now, don't you?"

I nodded. I did feel an unburdening that was rare for me. There was such a sense of awe at being in the center of all this color and sound and smiling energy that I felt light. I felt like singing.

# 39

LATER THAT NIGHT the phone rang as I was getting out of the shower. Jason answered it in the living room and brought it to me in the bathroom. I wrapped a towel around myself and took the phone from Jason's hand.

I heard the sound of heavy breathing but nothing more and was about to hang up. Then the person on the other end spoke.

"Blades?" The voice was weak, but I'd know that raspy croak anywhere.

Anger bubbled immediately, so much of it that I couldn't speak.

"Blades?" the creaky voice groaned again

"How're the PCPs this year?" I said.

"Not worth the investment."

There was a long pause. I had so many things to say to

Jimmy. I never thought I'd get to say them, and now that the chance was here I couldn't get anything out.

"I'm really sorry, Blades."

"Think nothing of it, Jimmy. I let my friends fuck me in the ass with hot stakes all the time."

"I didn't know what they were planning. I was broke. I have a five-hundred-dollar-a-day habit. I wasn't thinking."

"You still aren't. You should've remained dead, Jimmy. Because now I'm gonna have to find you and kill you myself."

"It would be the best thing you could do for me, Blades. I wish I'd died when they shot me and threw me into the Hudson. I wished I'd died. But I'm like you, I guess. Blessed with nine lives. The bullet went right through me without damaging any vital organs. When I hit the water I came to. It was night. It was dark. They didn't even realize I was still alive. Just wasn't my time, I guess."

"You've lived your last life, Jimmy."

"Come and take it, Blades. Come on. I'm not going anywhere. You know where to find me in Buffalo. I gave you your life back, now I'll give you mine."

He hung up. I stood there with the phone in my hand. My hands were shaking. I felt like crying.


THE PHONE RANG again a few seconds later. I let it ring for a while, debating whether to answer. I couldn't listen to Jimmy's voice again. In fact I didn't want to talk to anybody but Anais. But it was Noah. I told him I couldn't speak to him, using my having to drive Jason home to New Jersey as an excuse. But Noah was persistent.

"What's the matter, Blades? Why don't you want to talk to me?"

"It ain't you, Noah. I don't wanna talk to anybody right now."

"Did I scare you last night?"

"What're you talking about?"

"Nothing. You took care of your business. That's good."

"I gotta go, Noah."

"Don't run from me, Blades."

"I ain't running. I gotta go."

"Fine. Go on. Hey Blades, can I ask you something?"

"What?"

"I've wanted to ask you this for a while. I travel in some circles that would surprise you, understand what I'm saying. Word gets around. The way you took care of that business last night made me think of a rumor that's been around."

"I don't have time to dance with you, big man."

"I heard you buried an ex-Panther in Miami."

"I don't know what you're talking about, Noah."

"You know where your father is, don't you?"

"I gotta go, Noah."

"Next time you see him, tell him I send my regards."

"Can I go now?"

"I want you to tell him something else."

"What?"

"Tell him I'm sorry."

"You're sorry?"

"Yes, tell him I'm sorry."

"For what?"

"I was his go-between with the FBI. I was the one he gave the information to that put those two Black Panther leaders in jail. I was the Iago whispering in his ear. I took advantage of our friendship. Not that it was hard. It's because of me he's been running for his life ever since."

I paused for a long time. The phone felt like a block of iron in my hand.

Noah's voice was persuasive. "They killed a cop. A friend of mine. I was gonna get them any way I could."

"Why're you telling me this now, Noah?"

"I don't know. Just felt like I had to. Set things straight."

"I hope you sleep better tonight, big man."

"It was the times, Blades."

"It's always the times, Noah. Especially for people like my father who get left in the time machine."

"Was it easy to kill those men, Blades?"

"I didn't think about it then and I don't want to think about it now."

"Why? You afraid you might discover you enjoyed it?"

"I don't like injustice, Noah. I used to think I became a cop to save my brother from drugs. But that really wasn't it. I grew up listening to my parents talk about civil rights and marching against injustice. I guess that stuck in my mind somewhere."

"I'll always love you like a son, Blades."

THE DRIVE TO New Jersey was quiet until we reached the Turnpike. Jason slept his way through the tunnel crossing, waking up on the other side of the river with a strange expression on his face, as if he'd had a bad dream.

"You okay?" I said.

"I'm hungry." He yawned.

I laughed. "After what you ate today you got the nerve to be hungry?"

"We shouldn't have left. I was having a good time," he groused.

"Mom is anxious to see you."

"Jesus, I'm not a baby. I still don't understand why I can't stay with you."

"I already told you. Anais is back. The apartment is too small. We gonna need some privacy for a while."

He frowned. "I still don't get it. I won't get in your way. I'll be out most of the time."

"I don't think New York is a good place for you."

"Why not?"

I glanced at his face fixed in a scowl. "You know why not."

"I don't like living in New Jersey. It's boring."

"Not today, I promise. Mom's got something special planned. We really didn't get to celebrate your birthday, remember?"

He screwed up his face. "I don't want to go home. I don't like living with Mom. She drives me crazy. She's too nosy. And I've had enough of celebrations."

"Don't talk foolishness, Jason."

"I'm not talking foolishness. Why is everything I say foolishness to you?"

"Did I say that?"

"You say it all the time."

"I do not."

"Yes, you do." His voice turned shrill. "I told you all before. No parties. No celebrations. Why don't you listen to me?"

"Look Jase," I said, trying to calm him down. "Mom sounded so relieved when I told her I'd found you that whether you like it or not she's gonna have a little party. You know how she is. I'm sure she's cooking all like now. I bet she's got some catfish seasoned just the way you like it."

He began to bang his fists on the dashboard. "She isn't doing it for me, she's doing it for herself. And what do you mean by you found me? I wasn't lost. Who appointed you my guardian, anyway? You almost got me killed. If you hadn't sent that guy looking for me, I wouldn't have been involved in your crazy shit."

I reached over and patted his forearm. "Just calm down, okay."

He knocked my hand away. "Stop patronizing me."

I swerved into the right lane to pass a slow-moving truck. "Okay, Jason, you want the straight fucking dope?"

He looked at me bug-eyed. "Yeah, give me the straight fucking dope, man. I can handle it. I don't need you to protect me."

"You can handle what? Tell me. What can you handle?"

"I can handle it."

"You can't even piss without hosing your shoes, Jason. I'm tired of saving your ass, okay? I'm tired of it. I'm tired of watching you fuck up all the time. You're not the only one in this family with a problem. We all got problems to deal with. You don't think Melanie's got problems? You don't think I've got problems? You don't think Mom's got problems? The question is, Jason: When're you gonna grow up and do something about your fucking problem before you kill yourself and our mother along with you?"

He began to laugh. "If I die, that would take care of my problem, wouldn't it?"

"Is that what you want, Jason? You want to die?"

He was still laughing. "If I die and Mom dies, she wouldn't have any more problems either, would she?"

I looked at him, and for a second I hated him. I mashed my foot on the gas and the Jeep leapt forward. With both hands I gripped the steering wheel hard, my foot grinding the accelerator to the floor in an attempt to turn it to pulp. The speedometer shot past seventy-five. It hit eighty and kept going. Ninety. One hundred. I looked at Jason. His eyes were fixed ahead, wide with fear. I was now doing a hundred and ten, zipping by cars as if they had stopped. One hundred and fifteen.

"Slow down, Blades," Jason screamed.

"You wanna die, Jason? Then we die together."

"You're crazy! Slow down! Stop! You're gonna crash!"

"What difference does it make how you die? An over-dose or a car crash. It's all the same. You're dead."

"Slow down, Blades. Please!"

"I thought you wanted to die."

"Please, Blades. Slow down. I don't wanna die."

I lifted my foot off the gas and touched the brakes softly. The Jeep began to slow down, easing to an even cruising speed of sixty-five. Jason was hunched over in his seat, his body shaking. I thought he was crying, but then he straightened up and I realized it was the shiver of relief. I drove for another mile in silence.

"Are you okay?" I said.

His face was bloodless. "I'm okay."

"You sure?"

"You're crazy."

"I'm sorry."

"It's okay."

"It's okay?" I laughed. "You're stealing my lines."

He tried to smile. "Everything is so easy for you, Blades. The way you handled those men last night. You were so cool."

"Killing people isn't cool."

"I heard you tell somebody on the phone you're going to kill him."

"That's not cool."

"You really gonna kill him?"

"The killing is over, Jason. I just wanna see my wife."

"You sounded like you wanted to kill him."

I paused. "Maybe I did then."

"You don't let shit get to you."

"That's not true."

"That's how it looks."

I took a deep breath and looked out the window. A lump of pity knotted in my throat. "You know what gets to me, Jason? You. I don't even know if I like myself anymore, but the person I am today is because of you. You were the first person not to take notice of the other in me. And to me that made you special."

"I was just happy to have a brother, dude."

"Did you like my father?"

He looked at me, massaging his chin. "He was alright."

"Would you've liked him better if he was white?"

He smiled, as if he was not at all surprised by my question. "I don't know. Maybe. I know Melanie didn't like him, but he was an alright guy." He paused. "I mean, I liked him. He was alright. He knew a lot about baseball. And he always came to see me play. That was cool. Do you know where he is?"

I paused. No one in my family knew that I'd found my father. Not even my mother. "Yes, I know where he is."

"Does Mom know?"

"I didn't tell her."

We fell silent. My eyes shifted from the road to his a few times. We both knew what was going through the other's mind.

"Are you going to tell her?"

"I don't know."

"If you don't want her to know, your secret is safe with me," he said. "I don't know the last time I talked to my father. I missed him a lot when he left. And I was angry. At your father, too, for a while. And at Mom. I really wanted to go live with my father. But he didn't want me."

A row of New Jersey state troopers zipped past, sirens and lights going off. Jason reached out and touched my arm. "I don't want to go back to one of those rehab clinics, Blades."

"It's the only way for you to get better."

"Suppose I can't get better?"

"You can get better."

"I don't want to go back."

"I'm sorry, Jason, but you can't fuck up anymore. You gotta get better."

"I'll only go if you promise to come and look for me."

"I promise."

"Will you teach me how to shoot?"

"No."

The sun sank behind a clot of trees, leaving a vibrant yellow stain on the gray sky. I rolled down my window. The evening air was dry and crisp. I wet my lips. Jason reached over and switched the radio to a rock station. I thought of Anais and smiled.

## 40

TWO NIGHTS LATER I cooked a simple dinner of grilled Chilean sea bass and roasted Yukon gold potatoes for Anais. She had brought several bottles of Rutherford Hill Merlot and Chardonnay Reserve from California, and we ate picnic-style on the rug in the living room.

After dinner we relaxed on the sofa, sipping wine and listening to Mingus' masterpiece, *Fables of Foibus*. We finished two bottles of chardonnay as I filled her in on the story.

Congresswoman Richardson had finally discovered her conscience and sang to Bressler when he arrived looking for me. She withdrew from the race the next day. The Feds got their computer back. Gabriel Aquia was charged with murder, kidnapping, child pornography and a number of other felonies. He tried to cut a deal by supplying investigators with the names of several police and Immigration officers on his payroll and a list of his *special* clients. The police raided his warehouse and found boxes of digital masters of movies with such titles as *Under 13, Underage Blacks, Too Young To Tell*, and so on, ready to be sent to Europe and Latin America, where CDs and tapes were made for reshipment. These tapes and CDs were sold to these special clients at hefty prices.

I didn't tell her Jimmy Lucas was still alive.

"I always thought Jimmy Lucas was a little creepy," Anais said afterward. "He and that stupid collection of Buffalo Bills sweatshirts."

She was lying in my arms, her back slack against my chest. I felt light, as if the carnival of a few days before had not yet ceased in my body. I lapped at her neck.

The phone rang. I went to answer it in the bedroom. Frankie, my lawyer, was on the other end.

"Guess what, Blades," he boomed.

"You're going to announce that you're running for mayor."

He laughed. I had to move the receiver away from my ear temporarily. His volcanic eruption was deafening. When I resumed listening, he said, "They're offering two-point-five million to settle."

"Is that what you expected?"

"We could probably hold out for more."

"Settle it."

"You sure?"

"I'm sure."

"We'll have the papers in a couple of weeks."

"Fine."

"Are you okay, Blades? I know the last few days have been rough. You want me to arrange for you to talk to somebody?"

"I was talking to somebody when you called."

"I meant a professional."

"I don't need anybody else."

"You sure?"

"Good night, Frankie."

I hung up and went back to the living room, where Anais was opening another bottle of wine. I reclined on the couch.

"That was Frankie Rose," I said.

She gave me a glass of wine and snuggled into my arms again, assuming the same position as before.

I stroked her neck. "They've put two-point-five mil on the table. I told him to take it."

She purred. "Is it over now, Blades?"

"No."

"What more do you need?"

"You. Is there anyone waiting for you to come back to L.A.?" I said.

"My agent."

"You know what I mean."

"No lovers, if that's what you mean."

"That's what I mean."

"I know what you're thinking, Blades."

"You were always good at reading my mind."

"And I don't like what it's telling me now."

"What? What's not to like?"

"I can't promise you I'll stay."

"Why not? I love you, Anais."

"You're not playing fair."

"Where does playing fair get me?"

"Blades, let's not rush things. We need to talk about counseling."

"I've done that already."

"I don't want to be afraid of you, Blades."

"It's over. I promise. My mind is free. I haven't felt like this since the first time I saw you naked."

Trying to stifle a laugh, she turned around and kissed me. "You're too much."

I tongued her ear. "Too much for you?"

She squirmed and giggled. "Let's just get through tonight first. You're here. I'm here. You're safe, thank God. We're together. Let's see how that goes. See if we can make it through one night. It's too early for tomorrow. And too late for yesterday."

"So what do you want to do?"

"What do you want to do?"

"I asked first."

She sucked my thumb in her mouth. "You know what I want to do."

"What if I want to hear you say it?"

"Make love to me, Blades."

I stood up and reached down to gather her in my arms to take her to the bedroom. She pushed me away, settling back onto the floor, her legs spread.

"Right here on the floor. I'm not making love to you in that bed," she said. "You have to change it."

I looked at her, mystified.

She screwed up her eyes. "You made love to her in that bed, Blades."

"That's a new bed."

"I don't care. Get a newer one. Do you expect to make love to me in that bed?"

I sat back down on the rug with a sigh. "Anything you say, dear."

"I will deal with your patronizing tone later." She leaned over and kissed me.

I buried my head in the cave of her thighs as the phone rang. I refused to answer it.

# 1

THAT SUNDAY IN church I cried thankful tears of happiness for the eight-year old daughter I didn't know I had until nine months ago. But I cried most of all for my friend Noah Plantier.

Five days earlier eight of us had gathered at Maiba, a South African restaurant in Brooklyn, to celebrate Noah's sixtieth birthday. His wife, Donna, had brewed a cocktail of surprises for her husband of thirty-eight years beginning with hiring a limo to take seven of us to the Brooklyn Center for Performing Arts for a performance of The National Song and Dance Company of Mozambique, a company she and Noah had seen in its homeland while on their African junket ten years ago.

Stuffed into the limo along with Noah, his wife, and myself were four other friends, all members of Noah's Fellowship of Harlem Playwrights Workshop. I'd joined the workshop a few months after resigning the NYPD full of anger. I did not really expect to become a writer. In fact, I had no clear interest in writing. But it was a choice between that or continuing therapy.

Noah insisted that everybody had a story to tell, even me and pushed me to write. I'm still searching for my story and am yet to finish any of the plays I've started, but I enjoyed the workshop enough to stick with it, even taking a few college courses with Noah, a theater professor at City College. And I have not been back to therapy, so it must be working.

The performance of the National Song and Dance Company of Mozambique was electrifying. I was incredibly moved by the dramatic *In Mozambique, the Sun has Risen*, done with traditional dances, choral and instrumental music, accompanied by poetry and story-telling. I'd never seen anything like it before. It stoked my imagination as well as my spirit enough to have me humming some of the songs in the lobby at intermission where I joked to Noah that perhaps it was time for me to make my pilgrimage to Africa.

After the show we loaded into the burgundy Mercedes limo and cruised up Flatbush Avenue, jabbering like teenagers at the top of our voices, cutting one another off in our eagerness to express our views about the show, making more noise than elephants in a stampede. We'd all been dazzled to the point where we would've followed the company to the next city just to see them perform again.

Donna had made reservations at Maiba located on the ground floor of a brownstone in Fort Greene. We were welcomed at the entrance by a tall man, handsomely dressed in traditional African clothing that shimmered under the pale light. Two large rectangular tables had already been set side by side for our party. The interior was warm and cozy and the mutedly lit white walls were exquisitely decorated with African art. Exotic-looking cooking pots and pans dangled haphazardly from the center of the ceiling, and a collection of colored glass jars and conch shells decked the various ledges. Juju music echoed from ceiling-hung speakers and before long we all were humming, smiling and tapping our feet like school children. Spiced aromas swept through the room from the kitchen to our right, a hint of things to come.

Sweet music. Fine food. Great art. All present in this small establishment. Could there be three more fitting symbols of man's genius?

Still glowing from the high-voltage dance performance our spirits surged to new highs when Donna unearthed a thirty-year bottle of Pouilly Fuisse she'd been hiding in her bag. I joked to her that the bottle of wine must've cost as much as their new Harlem brownstone.

That's when Noah's son, Ronan, walked in. Noah's eyes ripened with surprise; you could've plucked them out of his head and he wouldn't have noticed them gone.

Something had happened to cause a rift between them; Noah would not discuss with me, and for a long time, he and Ronan had not spoken to each other. Ronan was now something of a celebrity in the Black community. A year ago he'd been elected to the city council and his first bill sponsored was one calling for reparations from the government for the atrocities of slavery. As expected this bill caused much furor in the media, and it did not go unnoticed in black America. Soon Ronan was all over the tube, on talk shows, on local news shows; he was quoted in newspapers, he was sought after to speak at local black churches. I knew Noah followed Ronan's achievements and nothing would've pleased him more than to be on speaking terms with Ronan again.

For a few moments he just stared at Ronan as if witnessing the second coming of Christ; then he looked at Donna whose eyes were flushed with glee. She was clearly enjoying Noah's shock. Slowly Noah rose from his chair and walked over to his son whose bony frame was sheathed in an expensive-looking brown wool suit.

There was a mysterious twinkle to Ronan's earthblack eyes which alerted you that he knew something the rest of the world didn't; that behind the mask of his gentle smile and his smooth brown face with its strong jaw, behind the flash of light escaping the gap in his front teeth and the slight rocking of his hips when he walked like the sway of a calypso song betraying his Caribbean roots (his mother was born in Guyana), that behind all that was a mind which had visited the ancients, dueled with monsters and seduced princesses, a mind that was as strong as the slaves who made it across the Middle Passage, a mind that understood how civilization jumped off the blackness of his skin.

And based on his credentials there would be no reason to doubt that. Having earned a master's degree from Harvard by age twenty-two, he went on to graduate with an M.B.A. in finance and marketing from Princeton, later making a fortune on Wall Street before jumping to politics.

After exchanging hugs father and son moved to the bar where they conversed for some time, heads bowed together like monks in prayer. We couldn't hear what they were saying to each other but in a short while there were enough smiles and laughter and hugs exchanged between them to cure all the hatred and misunderstanding in the Middle East. Finally, they joined the table, sitting next to each other at Donna's right.

If you ever go to Maiba I would recommend the blackened salmon flavored with onions, tomatoes and fresh greens. Along with that we also ordered curried shrimp, barbecued chicken, plantains, and brown rice, which came on large silver platters.

As we ate Ronan explained how he defeated Baron Spencer for the seat in the 65th District. Running on a platform that he would make black neighborhoods strong again Ronan used his experience in market research to target communities which had historically produced poor turnout in elections and spent money and time conducting town meetings using Powerpoint slides to illustrate how he would turn their neighborhoods around. Their increased turnout proved decisive in helping him unseat the one term Democrat.

Throughout the meal Noah beamed as if he'd been handed the winning ticket in the lottery. His fleshy round eyes flushed with pride and he kept running his hands over his son's head as if Ronan was ten years old and about to go into his first basketball game at the local Y.

Having pulled off the impossible by getting Ronan to attend his father's birthday dinner party, Donna sat back with a broad smile watching things unfold, her peanut-brown face plump with satisfaction. I'd known Donna for almost as long as I knew Noah. I knew her when her hair was tar black; it was now threaded with an abundance of silver strands, which she vowed never to conceal. I knew her when she was model-thin; she now had more meat on her bones than a buffalo. But she was no less beautiful and her smile was still bright enough to warm a dozen winter days.

I leaned over to Donna. "I've never seen Noah so pleased."

"Not in the last ten years," she replied.

"What did you say to get Ronan to come?"

"That's between Ronan and me."

"Mother's secret, huh?" I said.

She laughed and swept her right hand to partially cover mine. "I've spent twenty years running my own business. I didn't have time to doubt myself. If I did I would still be a nurse's aid. They're both stubborn men. Heck, Ronan is Noah, twenty-five years younger. I knew what I had to do to get them together and I did it."

We had finished our meal and the waiter had begun to clear away the dirty utensils from our table. Noah looked over to me and winked. He was eager to see the dessert menu. You see, Noah had a sweet tooth.

*Pop! Pop! Pop-pop-pop!*

I knew the sound of gunfire like I knew my face. Without looking around to see who was shooting or where the hell it was coming from, I dove for the floor dragging Donna with me. She tumbled on top of me, her black eyes spiked with fear, opened as wide as a subway tunnel. The room had erupted in shrieks and shrill voices, the ricochet of plates breaking and the frightening sound of scampering feet.

I flipped over onto my stomach, one hand clamped firmly on Donna's head to keep it down, my eyes raking the room for the shooter. A figure in a long black coat was fleeing through the door. Everyone else was on the floor. I assessed the room quickly. Broken plates, cutlery, broken glass and twisted bodies were everywhere. Tables had been overturned as if flung about in a storm.

Everyone from our table was pasted stomach down on the floor or cowering cocoon-like behind chairs or tables.

Except Ronan. He was still sitting in his chair, his legs just a few feet from my face. Yellow flecks of couscous had spilled on the shiny surface of his pants. There were specks of brown sauce on his tan shoes. I grabbed his trousers and yanked. He did not move. I yanked again, as hard as I could. Then I felt something dripping down on my fingers. I looked at them. It was blood and bits of brain. First I froze; then I jumped to my knees. Blood oozed from the back of Ronan's head where a large caliber bullet had exited, leaving a hole you could put a fist through.

# 2

BETWEEN NOAH AND myself, we had over twenty years of law enforcement experience, most of it spent patrolling New York's tough streets yet and at this most crucial time that training had not been enough to protect our loved ones. Neither of us had sensed the danger. Neither of us saw the shooter.

At the sound of the first shot we both dove for cover and by the time we'd retrieved our experience and training from under the table the stealthy shooter had dissolved into New York's abyss, leaving behind a young man with one eye and part of his brain scrambled on the restaurant wall.

It all happened so fast. Not one person in the restaurant or anyone on the street got a good look at the shooter. Some swore he was over six feet. Others claimed he wasn't very tall, but slender. Some were certain he wore a red hooded sweatshirt. Others saw a black mask. The only thing anybody could agree on was that none of them got a glimpse of his face.

Donna had fainted and was being attended by EMS who wanted to take her to the hospital. Torn between going to the hospital with his wife and keeping vigil over his dead son's body until the coroner arrived, Noah stood staring at me, his shirt embroidered with Ronan's blood, his face sagged, eyes vague as fog, his mouth opening and closing like a thirsty fish beached on the sand.

"You gotta go with Donna," I whispered. "I'll stay here."

He nodded silently, fingering his thinning gray hair, but did not move. I pushed him into the ambulance which drove off with a wail of sirens and whirring lights.

I returned to the restaurant where detectives were still questioning witnesses—those who weren't too scared to speak or hadn't skipped away into the darkness the first chance they got. In this neighborhood gang-related killings were common and to some of the witnesses who knew the terrain this killing would fit that profile.

The police had arrived quickly; the restaurant sat on the doorsteps of the 88th. The lead investigator, Detective Riley was a moose of a man, standing about six-four with a square head and nose and forehead scaled so sharp you could downhill slalom off his face. He questioned me in a carefully measured voice, as if he was reading from a teleprompter, recording everything on a miniature electronic recorder.

When he was finished he put the device in the pocket of his brown wool coat and ran his fingers through his white-streaked hair. "We're gonna find the fucker who did this."

Then he gave me his card.

Accepting the card I looked at him, but couldn't think of anything to say.

I LIFTED THE black cloth covering Ronan's body. Blood and mucous had congealed in the eye socket, which had been blown out by the slug, the other eye was frozen open.

The thing that got to you about a dead person were the eyes. You can't begin to understand death until you gaze on the emptiness in the eyes of a dead person. That look was something that permeated your soul. You can never forget it.

This was not the first time I'd looked at a dead body. Each time I witnessed a death I'd felt dirtied by the experience, especially if I was the one who'd done the killing. But even in the aftermath of a killing when my sleep rumbled with bad dreams, I knew that the sedative of time would one day restore my good humor. This one would be different. As I stared at Ronan's body quietly growing rigid under the pink light reflecting off the near wall, which made garish purple shadows on his cold face, I felt as if someone had pinned me to a tree by the roots of my hair. I would not quickly or easily recover from this experience. And I knew the healing would only begin when I found Ronan's killer.

THREE HOURS LATER, after the meat wagon rolled off with Ronan's body, I called Brooklyn Hospital and was told that Noah and Donna had left there an hour earlier. No one was answering the phone at their home and I left a message for him to call me. I thought of driving over there but I didn't have my car. I asked for and got a ride home with a cop from the 88th.

It was a short ride to my house on Maple Street and the only conversation that passed between us was the kind of small talk that fell between cracks of your consciousness as you waited for the world to get up to speed with your corrosive pain.

I kept thinking of Donna. Never would I forget the look of shock and horror on her face when she got to her knees on the floor and saw blood gushing from the back of her son's head. She let out one long sustained scream that cut through me like broken glass. Then her voice died completely as she clutched at Ronan's body repeatedly, as if her fingers had lost their sensitivity or as if she was touching fire. Then his body fell out of the chair into her arms.

It had taken Noah and me fifteen minutes to pry Ronan's head from her fingers.

Standing in the street opposite my house I watched the detective's Impala drive off. My body was sore, as if someone had slit my veins and let all of my body fluids drain away. Even the ripple and pulse of the New York night could not reenergize me. Cars filled with shadows buzzed past. But everything seemed to have shrunk away. I stepped out of the street and walked as if blindfolded to my door.

\* \* \*

**A YEAR AGO** I settled a civil right's violations suit with the NYPD for $2.5 million. Some of that money was used to buy this house on Maple Street from a disgraced Congresswoman. That settlement also allowed me to invest in *Voodoo*, a night-club in downtown Brooklyn featuring reggae and soca acts from the Caribbean, with an English-born radio personality who also dabbled in concert promotion. My other business, a music store on Nostrand Avenue, which I owned with a former calypsonian from Trinidad, was still holding its own, though it was growing increasingly difficult to compete with pirates who were not afraid to set up their street bazaars on the sidewalk outside the store to hawk their stolen CDs and DVDs.

The love of my life was not expected back before next week. I had asked River Paris, the woman who managed *Voodoo*, to stay with my eight-year old daughter, Chesney, while I was out.

I'd met River six months earlier at my club on Lawrence Street. She was lusty-looking and full at the hip with a sharp tongue. Just the kind of person my partner and I were looking for. She'd come to us to drop off a demo tape, hoping to book a dancehall artist she was managing into the club. In a black silk mock-turtleneck shirt and with her python-thick thighs threatening to bust out of their black leather cages, she looked like she'd just stepped out of an *Essence* fashion show. My partner in the club, Negus Andrews, was smitten right away. I was prepared to be more cautious. The three of us spent the night together at the club drinking and swapping childhood stories.

She'd recently arrived in New York from Miami where she'd managed a club not unlike ours. We couldn't believe out luck. Later as we stood outside her car parked on Jay Street, we offered her the job. She accepted on the spot.

River was sitting in my living room watching a movie with the lights dimmed when I walked in. It was minutes past two in the morning. I had called her from the restaurant to let her know I would be home later that planned, but I did not tell her why.

She got up from the sofa and came toward me. "Jesus, you look like you just saw your best friend gassed."

I screwed up my face and said nothing. She didn't know how close she had come to the truth. She held a glass in her hand and offered it to me. "Scotch."

I took the glass and drained it.

"Damn!" She leaned forward searching my face in the soft light, a stony smile of concern fixed on her face.

"Get me the bottle," I mumbled.

She turned away, taking the glass with her. I stood for a moment lost in my own house, remembering the first time I'd entered this house a year ago to speak to the Congresswoman about her daughter who'd been killed in my apartment. It was a beautiful house and I fell in love with it then. When it went on the market a few months later I jumped on it.

River returned with the bottle of Black Label and two glasses. I snatched the bottle from her hand and sank the spout into my mouth. She leaned against the balustrade watching me intently as I gulped half the scotch in the bottle.

"Can I have some now?" she said gently. Like a thirsty woman scouring the desert for water her eyes swept across my face searching for an explanation to my odd behavior.

"Sorry." I wiped the mouth and handed her the bottle.

"What happened?" She put one glass on the end table, then poured two fingers into her glass and passed the bottle back to me.

Shock had finally conquered my mind and I stared at her silently. My brain felt like it was exploding in my head; my body so stiff I thought it was encased in brass. I heard her question, but my brain was having a hard time comprehending simple words. Everything in this room including her, were part of a cyclorama of colorless images. The cushion of experience I often used to suppress my inner feelings had been stripped away. I was on the cusp of tears.

She held my gaze in her spotless brown eyes and after a moment she said, "Chesney wanted to stay up for you."

"I'm glad she didn't."

"You don't want to talk about it, huh?"

I shook my head.

There was a long pause, like a wasted promise. "Well, I'm leaving." She hesitated. "Unless you want me to stay."

I shook my head again.

She walked back into the living room and picked up her bag from over the arm of the sofa and then sauntered to the closet to get her coat. I watched as she covered herself in black leather. She turned to face me, her dark face tight.

"Thanks for staying with Chez."

She meandered to the door and stopped. "Let me stay with you. We don't have to talk if you don't want to. I've never seen you look like this."

"I need to sleep."

She unlocked the door and went upright into the night.

Upstairs, I walked down the hall and into my daughter's bedroom. She was curled up under the Mickey Mouse comforter, her favorite toy—a fluffy white teddy bear—nestled against her face. As I kissed her softly on the cheek Donna's pain-scalded face flashed before me. My stomach knotted instantly. For a long time I stood looking at my daughter, observing the tiny twitching of her body as it danced in sleep. Then, not knowing why, I curled up on top of the comforter next to her.

CHESNEY'S ARRIVAL IN my life was, to put it mildly, a shock. I'd met her mother, Juliet, nine years ago while vacationing in Barbados. My love affair with the island of Barbados began long before that visit, even before my first visit at the age of ten with my father. My paternal grandmother was born there and after living in Panama for a number of years she moved to New York in 1922. My early years growing up in Brooklyn revolved around the elaborate family dinners she created in her Crown Heights home on Sundays where I was introduced to Calypso music, curried chicken, sorrel, conkies and spicy baked pork and a variety of crimpy old men and women who instilled in me a love for stories with their incredulous tales of myth and magic, all told with a casualness that only certified my awe.

After I got out of the Marines I went down to Barbados to decompress and to relax before deciding on my next move. I loved walking along its tiny roads at daybreak as the sun burned off the night's dew. My days were spent splashing about in the mystical blue sea or eyeing clutters of silver fish swim in unison like chil-

dren holding hands. At night I drank beer, ate grilled fish, and
watched the locals interact with each other with a leisure and
comfort, as if they were all from one family. Sometimes as I lay
in bed listening to the sea pound its chest against rocks under my
window, I'd remember the stories of heroic fishermen told to me
when I was young by my grandmother and her cohorts.

Now I visit the island every chance I get. Recently my father
relocated there to escape ghosts from his past. Since he started
living there he has unearthed legions of relatives which has
made visiting the island even more delightful.

On one of my visits I stayed at a hotel on the South Coast
where I took a few scuba diving lessons. The instructor was a
striking woman with a compact athletic body and a laugh that
bubbled and crested like lava flowing from a mountain. Juliet
Rouse was her name. We began an affair after my third lesson,
capped off by an underwater lovemaking session in scuba gear the
night before I left.

I promised to call as soon as I got back to New York. I don't
remember why, but I never did call or write to Juliet. In fact,
there was no contact between us after that affair. The next time
I visited Barbados was on my honeymoon. I had no idea that
Juliet had had my daughter until eight months ago when I got a
call from Chesney's uncle, Gregory.

Juliet had gotten into an accident while on a shopping trip to
Venezuela. The car she was traveling in flipped a number of
times on a highway and Juliet was killed. Though Juliet had
never contacted me, she'd put my name on Chesney's birth certificate—apparently you can do that in Barbados without the father's permission. Finding me was easy, Gregory said. My
phone number was served up by the Internet white pages. I
agreed to meet him at a restaurant in the city.

Of course I asked why had Juliet not gotten in touch with
me. Gregory, stiff-faced, with a snobbish turn of his upper lip,
laughed and said, "You obviously didn't know my sister." Juliet,
he said, took her idea of independence to the brink of obses-
sion. That, along with a ripe vindictive streak, not only propelled his sister to success in business, it also allowed her to get
satisfaction by keeping Chesney's birth a secret from me as
punishment for not calling her when I returned to New York.

Still skeptical, I asked him if he had a picture.

"I can do better than that," he replied. "Chesney is here in New York."

Anais had been away doing a play in Houston and was due back in New York the next night before heading out to Los Angeles to test for a John Singleton movie. That night I picked up the phone to call her and changed my mind about three times before deciding to wait until she came home.

Anais' flight parked at the gate shortly after midnight. The reasons why I fell in love and married Anais are many, but when I saw her walking toward me in the damp arrivals hall I was never happier to see her and proud that she had chosen me to be her husband. She was simply a remarkably beautiful woman. Always rain clear, her black eyes never lost that elusive hint of a smile and her long strides, loaded with confidence and sensuality, made me think of a loafing show horse. Even before we embraced Anais' uncanny ability to sense disorder in my mind had sniffed out that something was amiss.

"What's the matter?" she said, after kissing me.

I picked up her bags. "Let's get to the car. It's a long walk to the lot."

She gripped my elbow. "There's something bothering you. Let's have it."

"We'll talk about it when we get home."

It was summer in New York. The air was thick and the night bled the odor of smoke as we left LaGuardia. The sky off to our right was carroty-streaked, and black smoke spiraled above the low buildings. The old Volvo whined like a starving puppy when I tried to coax more speed out of it on the Brooklyn Queens Expressway.

"Why didn't you drive my car?" Anais said.

For her birthday I'd bought Anais a brand new BMW-X5, but I'd owned the Volvo for eight years. It was still the best car I ever drove, the soft leather and incredible sound system of her SUV notwithstanding.

I flicked the wipers on as raindrops splattered on the windshield like chunks of overripe grapes.

Anais unbuckled her seatbelt and turned to face me. "What's bothering you? I can't wait until we get home."

"Get your seatbelt back on," I said, without taking my eyes off the road.

"Talk to me, Blades."

"Just put your seatbelt back on, okay? Jesus! Why do you always have to be so damn dramatic about everything?"

"Because you're always so damn mysterious about everything."

"I think I might have a daughter," I blurted.

"What?"

"She's coming to the house tomorrow."

"Hold up. Back up a minute. Did I hear you say you think you might have a daughter?"

"Yes."

"How do you *think* you might have a daughter? Isn't that something you either have or you don't have?"

"Her name's Chesney. She's eight years old. And it's possible she could be my daughter. I had a relationship with her mother in Barbados. Before you and I met."

For a second I took my eyes off the road to look at Anais who just stared at me, her mouth quivering and I knew she was trying to keep her temper under control. I knew it was a battle she would lose which was why I had wanted to wait until we got home before I hammered her with this news.

Moments later I felt her purse slam against my head, the sudden blow causing me to swerve dangerously close to the median. Anais screamed for me to stop the car, but I kept driving. She struck me again with her bag and grabbed the steering wheel. The car swerved into the next lane. I slammed on the brakes and the car screeched to a stop on the shoulder.

"I can't believe you didn't know about this," Anais screamed.

"I swear."

"She's not coming to my house."

"Excuse me. Our house."

"No goddamn way, Blades."

"She could be my daughter."

"Oh, and you can't wait to see her."

"Is that what you think?"

"It's in your voice, Blades. You want her to be your daughter.

And here I was thinking all this time that you didn't want children."

I looked away, my eyes trailing the low ghostlike buildings of Queens.

"We could've had our own child by now, Blades."

"Come on, Anais. You don't have time for children. You're always away. You're always busy. You made it clear. Acting was more important to you."

She threw her purse at the windshield and fell back against the seat with a whale-like bark and I thought she would start crying but after that she was quiet.

We fought all the way home. She threatened to leave me but I was determined to see Chesney no matter what. Finally, Anais agreed to end our feud if I agreed to have a blood test done as soon as possible. To me, it was a small price to pay for peace.

CHESNEY CAME INTO my life on an unseasonably cool July day, the temperature never rising above sixty-five degrees. Arriving with her uncle early in the morning as the sun climbed high in a washed-out blue sky, she wore jeans and a thin black vinyl jacket, her thick black hair caught under a red baseball cap. The corner of her mouth was smudged from the chocolate muffin she was eating.

I took one look at her and knew a paternity test was unnecessary. From her dark placid eyes, to the layered lips and the high slope of her cheekbones, there was no doubt that Chesney was my child.

Two weeks later, after I'd convinced Anais that it was the best thing for my daughter, I contacted my lawyer to begin paperwork for citizenship and Chesney moved in with us after her uncle returned to Barbados.